THE HOSTAGE

THE HOSTAGE

A. F. CARTER

THE MYSTERIOUS PRESS
NEW YORK

THE HOSTAGE

Mysterious Press
An Imprint of Penzler Publishers
58 Warren Street
New York, N.Y. 10007

First Mysterious Press paperback edition: 2023

Interior design by Maria Fernandez

Library of Congress Control Number: 2022906583

ISBN: 978-1-61316-469-3
eBook ISBN: 978-1-61316-348-1

10 9 8 7 6 5 4 3 2 1

Printed in the United States of America
Distributed by W. W. Norton & Company

CHAPTER ONE

ELIZABETH

I'm fifteen years old, being kidnapped, and I know how this usually ends. But I don't do fear, a failing, according to Father, one of many. I'm lying on some cushions, the cushions on a rug that covers the floor of the trunk. It's pitch-black except for an occasional red glow when my abductor hits the brakes. There must be taillights, though, because it's after three o'clock in the morning.

Or maybe not. It was after three o'clock when I was taken, but I can't know how long I've been unconscious. I hate that. I hate not being in control, like right this minute when I throw up again.

Ordinarily, I'm polite, if somewhat cold, and noticeably fastidious. (Prissy, according to Father.) Now I clean my mouth on a corner of the mattress. I'm not about to use my blouse, the only alternative.

The car hits a bump and I slide into the back of the trunk. Butt-first, luckily, because what I hit doesn't give. At all. The pain draws me fully awake and I arrive at a firm resolution because it's the only one out there. I'm the captain of this ship, I tell myself. It's up to me to keep it afloat. I will not succumb, to my captors or despair. As I've already said, I know how this usually ends.

Am I being overly dramatic? Well, that's me, Elizabeth Bradford, that's who I am. Arrogant, too, a product of nature and nurture both. Even my friends dislike me, which doesn't make sense but there it is.

I don't have to ask myself why I've been abducted. My parents and I have only just moved to Baxter, and if we're not the super-rich Bradfords, we're surely the very rich. Father's brother, Henry, is majority shareholder of the Bradford Group. Henry is currently occupied with a half-built pipeline under review by the Department of Transportation. That's why he dispatched Father to bid on the construction of a Nissan factory scheduled to break ground in six months, on the factory and the demolition of the abandoned homes and factories now on the property.

Mom insists that luck plays a major part in life, that each life is filled with unforeseen events that shape its course. I think she means to chide me about my need for control, to humble me, but I've mostly ignored her. Not anymore, not with me riding in the trunk of a car, bouncing from side to side, helpless, my fate almost entirely in the hands of my kidnappers and my parents.

It's going to cost the family a pretty penny to get me back, assuming they do get me back. It's quite possible, perhaps even likely, that Father and Mom will spend the next ten years in a fruitless search for my body after paying the ransom. That's why, of course, I can't remain passive, an obedient victim living on hope.

I begin a search of the trunk, looking not only for a weapon but for anything that might help me to escape, groping in complete darkness. I can't even see my hand as I slide it over the flat cushions beneath me. I'm hoping for a spring, a stiff wire that might be used as a weapon, but the cushions are all foam. Still, my search reveals a loose seam on one side of the largest cushion, a seam that comes away in a long strip that I stuff into my jacket's inner pocket. Maybe I can use it to strangle my kidnapper. Like in all those gangster movies.

I'm not strong or courageous enough to pull that off, but ripping the fabric away from the cushion seems like a victory. Small bordering on insignificant, but a victory nonetheless.

For just a moment, I stop to listen as a car passes from the opposite direction, the first one I've noticed. So we're not on an interstate or any well-traveled road. Farm country? When Father announced that we were Baxter bound (and that we'd be living in this black hole of a city for six months at the least), I checked out the region on Google Maps and discovered the city was surrounded by farms. Wheat, corn, soybeans, pigs, and cattle.

I wonder, for only a moment: Will they put me in with the pigs?

I'm getting banged around, but I continue my search, discovering that I can extend my hand a good foot beneath the partition separating the trunk and the car's interior. Again, as when I explored the mattress, I imagine finding a weapon beneath the seat, a loaded gun. Stupid, of course, and not just because it's so unlikely. I've never fired a gun and I'm as likely to shoot myself as my kidnapper. In any event, I discover only a handful of lint.

I continue to search, doggedly. I'm nothing if not stubborn and I pride myself on being thorough, on completing whatever task I've set for myself. I'm not expecting success—surely my abductor thoroughly examined what amounts to a prison cell—but then my hand touches a length of banded electrical wires that spring from a gap in the side panel. I'm confused for a short moment, until I finally grasp the obvious. The set of thin wires I hold must power a taillight. There's no other possibility.

My first impulse is to just yank on the wiring and let the chips fall where they may. Then I flash on a trunk filled with live wires, sparks flying in every direction. Well, that would frustrate my kidnapper, me electrocuted on the floor of the trunk. Father would never pay a ransom without being sure I was alive.

I recall a demand issued last week by an acquaintance: "Shit or get off the pot." I don't care for profanity, not usually, but the words strike home as I hold onto the wire like it's the only thing keeping my head above water.

Focus. I tap my forehead. You didn't skip two grades because you're a dummy. And you're not a fifteen-year-old senior at Phillips Exeter because you can't analyze. So what will it be? Stay where you are, do nothing, let your future take care of itself, assuming you have one? Or rip the wires out and hope the short circuit brings the car to a stop without electrocuting you in the process? I close my eyes, breathing now in short, sharp bursts as I pronounce myself unafraid. But my hands won't stop shaking and I can't make them move. Then something inside gives way and I yank as hard as I can, falling back onto my head as the entire light pulls free and I find myself staring at a small lightbulb dangling from the end of the wire.

A lit bulb.

I'm dazzled initially and I can't stop myself from gazing at the light though it leaves me as blind as I was in the darkness. I'm feeling like I was present at the moment when God said, "Let there be light." The notion is pleasing, even grand, but then a stray thought banishes this pitiful reverie.

Hey, fool, it's the light going out that should worry you. Like the one that keeps your heart beating, your lungs filled, your body working.

I have a little ghoul of a brother named Sherman who revels in the goriest crime videos he can locate online. "Kill the head," he told me over lunch one Saturday, "and the body dies." He'd snapped his fingers. "Just like that. The brain stops and the body stops with it. That's why snipers and assassins try for head shots."

I turn away for a moment, until my pupils adjust, then begin a second systematic search, this one illuminated. It doesn't take very long until I find what I should have been searching for all along. Right where I should have been looking for it. A yellow plastic handle extends from the trunk latch. I don't have to guess what it's for because its purpose is cut into the plastic.

TRUNK RELEASE.

For a time, eyes closed, I listen to the hiss of the tires, much louder inside the trunk than inside a car. They sound like the band saws on a construction site Father demanded I visit. Father's hoping I'll eventually replace my childless uncle, that I'll become the overseer, guardian of the family's interests. Lord knows he can't rely on my psycho brother.

I don't pop the trunk and jump out, my first impulse. I'm not that desperate, not yet. Even supposing I don't break my neck when I hit the roadway, my kidnappers are sure to see the trunk fly open. As I am sure to be in no condition to outrun them.

I'm interrupted by a vehicle passing from the opposite direction. It doesn't appear to slow and yet there's something happening because I hear voices from inside the car for the first time. A woman's voice, accented, then a man's.

"Please to stay cool, Quentin. Nothing to fear. Remember what we have said."

"I hear you, okay?"

"I hear you also. I hear panic. We are two weary travelers. Remember the story. Live it."

I see flashes of color, blue and red, through the open hole behind the dark taillight, and I hear a single elongated whoop, followed by silence as my abductors' car first slows, then stops. Outside, the wheels of what must be a police car grind against the pavement before coming to a halt behind us. Then a door opens and footsteps approach, finally a stern voice, the voice of authority.

"Good evening, sir. May I please see your license and registration?"

"They're in my wallet."

"Get them."

I seize the handle, cradling the base against my palm, curling my fingers around the inner edge, the cable tucked between my fore and middle fingers. I'm rehearsing my exit, imagining the trunk popping up, me leaping to the pavement, me running away as fast as I can while the cop deals with my kidnappers. I assume they're armed because I don't recall what happened to Chip, the boy I was making out with before I was taken. But I can't imagine football-hero Chip being cowed by anything less than a gun. Myself, I remember only a cloth slapped against my face from behind and an odor that still has me nauseated.

"Have you been drinking tonight, sir?"

"No, officer."

"Nothing?"

"Nothing."

"Where are you coming from at four-twenty in the morning?"

The response seems a bit too fast, even to me. "From my mom's. She's been sick, so me and my fiancée were lookin' after her until my sister came by. We're on our way home."

I hear footsteps on the pavement, coming toward the back, then a pause. I'm telling myself to go now, but I can't seem to move. Like when I first held the taillight wires. I tell myself to pull, pull, pull, but it feels like I'm trying to move an immovable weight.

"Sir, I'm going to have to ask you to step out of the car."

"But . . ."

"Please step out, sir."

Doors open on either side of the car, the little pop of the releasing locks releasing me as well. I imagine the trunk lid popping up, vaulting over the lip at the back, landing on my feet running. But it doesn't happen that way, not even close. The trunk does open, but I jump too soon, cracking my head against the opening lid, rolling forward to hit the pavement shoulder first. Then the gunfire, two shots so loud they might be lightning strikes. I've failed, I know I've failed, and I don't want to open my eyes, not ever again, but I can't stop myself. My eyelids separate by themselves and I'm looking into a pair of empty blue eyes a foot away. Dead eyes, cop eyes. The blood oozing from a deep wound on the side of his neck reaches out for me. His spirit is already gone.

Though I can't see her, the woman's voice, as cold as it is confident, echoes in my brain. "Do not hurt the girl, Quentin. We need her whole."

CHAPTER TWO

ELIZABETH

A bucket! A fucking *bucket*!

I'm not given to epithets. Too easy, too familiar, too Generation Z. That's Z, right? For Zed, the last letter in the alphabet, evolution stops here?

So I try to avoid the conventions of my peers, the prep school obligations that demand we mimic a class of people we'll never know.

But a fucking *bucket*?

I expected to be beaten (at the least) when we finally came to a stop somewhere between thirty minutes and an hour later. And I'd deserve it too. I didn't kill that cop, didn't pull the trigger, but his face, the empty eyes, the narrow gray mustache, the slack jaw? I couldn't escape that face, didn't want to, not until the car rolled to a stop, until the light in the trunk went out, until the trunk popped open and I found myself staring up at a woman. Not old, not even middle-aged, her eyes were dark, as dark as her hair and without emotion. They inspected me as you'd inspect a recent purchase that had just been delivered. Is this what I ordered?

A much younger man stood behind her, tall, blond, and heavily built. His blue eyes betrayed shock and a measure of fear, the look of a boy in over his head. He wasn't in charge and he didn't fire the gun that killed the cop. I made the judgment instantly and without effort, a survival instinct finally emerging. But I couldn't make myself believe that my kidnappers would show mercy, that killing didn't come naturally to them.

"Please get out." Her tone was suitably controlled, her words heavily accented, her expression unchanged. I took the hand she offered, as frightened as I was defiant only a short time before. Just as well because my legs refused to hold me when I stepped out and I sank to my knees.

"Up."

Her tone was peremptory, do it or else, and I did it, staggering for a moment before I caught my balance. I expected to find blood when I brought my hand to my scalp, but found only a lump too sore to be touched.

"If you will do as I say, you will soon go home. If you do not, we will hurt you in ways your family cannot see when you are telling them to pay ransom. Now, come with me."

I was already in pain, but I told myself to think. The dead cop would not come back to life (and I didn't shoot him), but if I made a mistake, I'd find myself as dead as he was.

Pull it together, pull it together, pull it together.

We stood behind a small house surrounded by forest and I knew right away from my Google map searches that we were in Ulysses Grant State Park, the only forested area within a hundred miles of Baxter. I also knew there was a lake in the small park, though it wasn't in sight, and horse trails that wandered through the woods.

"What are you thinking? How you can escape? Where you can go?"

I wasn't ready for the questions, but they settled me nonetheless. These two people, I told myself, don't know anything about me outside of the fact that I have rich parents. Let's keep it that way. I lowered my eyes and said, "I'm thinking about the . . . the policeman. I feel like it's my fault that . . ."

"You are wrong. Is my fault, me alone. You were not supposed to wake up when you did. I am taking full responsibility. You did nothing."

Shortly before my eighth birthday, Father told me that I required a pet. "Caring for a pet," he insisted over my protests, "will teach you something about obligation. This is a lesson you desperately need." He'd leaned in closer, his voice dropping to a whisper. "Because that's what your life will be about, my daughter. Obligation in all its many forms."

Father isn't big on democracy, the rule of the people. We live in a republic, he insists, not a democracy. Bottom line? I would receive the pet, like it or not, and be expected to care for it, the only consolation that I could select the species.

I chose a lizard.

Father cannot accept direct confrontation from anyone besides his brother, who regularly calls him to the carpet. Yet, oddly, he appreciates being outmaneuvered by his daughter. By choosing a lizard, an animal that required no emotional investment and very little care, I'd avoided the most onerous aspects of Father's imposed obligations.

Two weeks later, I received a gold dust gecko, a terrarium, and a packet of gecko food. I think I began to dislike my never-named gecko when I read a little pamphlet on gecko diet: mashed fruit mixed with ground insects, supplemented by the occasional live cricket.

I found the lizard beautiful. I'm willing to admit that much. Its near-luminescent scales were lime green and dusted with gold specks; it's legs and feet were blue-gray, as was its nose and brow. Splotches of red began at mid-back and ran to the tip of its pointed tail, while its body was smooth and sleek, a little rocket that moved in quick, sharp jerks.

As long as I thought of my lizard as some sort of exotic jewel, I remained willing to possess it. But then one day, for reasons unknown, I decided to closely examine the creature for the first time. (Perhaps I'd smoked one joint too many.) As it happened, there was little to examine. The reptile's face betrayed nothing, even when I positioned my own face a few inches away. I wanted a look inside. I wanted to know what makes a reptile tick, but its black eyes were totally dead. They were the indifferent eyes of a light-detecting machine. Looking into them, I found only my reflection.

A few days later, I gave my gecko to the little ghoul I call a brother. And love dearly.

◆

The woman, my kidnapper, had eyes that reminded me of that gecko as I stood beside her, my arms folded across my chest, the cool air raising goose bumps on my forearms and the back of my neck. The contrast between her soothing voice and those dead eyes shook me. This woman had just killed a man, but she appeared as unmoved as my gecko after consuming a cricket.

The judgment calmed me still further, and my tone, when I spoke, was convincingly submissive: "Please don't hurt me anymore."

"Anymore?"

I touched my scalp and winced, then repeated, "Please."

Just what she wanted to hear. I knew that even as the words left my mouth. Whoever this woman saw, it was not me.

Without a word, she took me by the arm and led me toward the small house. The man with us, Quentin, opened the front door with a key, then stood off to the side. The woman urged me forward and we stepped inside, at which point I expected someone to flick on the lights. Instead, the woman used a tiny flashlight with a narrow beam to guide us across a large room to a second door. When she opened it, I found myself looking at a set of wooden stairs descending into a basement.

I had no choice and I knew it. That didn't prevent me from imagining rats dashing across a dirt floor, spider webs clinging to crumbling brick walls, millipedes wriggling between soiled sheets. But the flashlight's beam instead revealed a small, tidy room with a wooden floor, a table, and a sturdy chair made of wood. A lantern rested on the table and the woman walked directly to it after closing the door behind her. She pressed a switch on the side and the lantern produced a light so intense I involuntarily closed my eyes.

"You see," the woman said, "home sweet home."

My eyes, when I opened them, were instantly drawn to the junk food on the table, to the chips, the popcorn, and the beef jerky. I wouldn't starve to death. I'd merely be poisoned. Looking to me like soldiers at attention, bottles of water lined the table's far edge, while a large box of AA batteries and a neat stack of eight paperback novels rested close to a pile of blank pages. The pages were topped by colored pencils tied with a rubber band, ready for playtime.

"What happens next?" I ask.

"You relax here. Later, you will communicate with your parents. Please to understand. I have no reason to hurt you if you cooperate. This we do here is about money, yes? We get money and you go back to parents."

Yeah? Now that I've seen her face? Her face and the face of her silent partner who currently blocked the door, arms folded across his chest. The man was trying his best to play the tough guy, the muscle, but he'd watched too many gangster films. He was the proverbial weak link, appearing for all his bulk more boy than man.

"What's your name?" My goal was to establish some measure of independence, but I made the mistake of looking into those insect eyes and I stumbled through the last word.

"Call me Tashya. And for now, good-bye."

"Wait, can I ask . . ." I don't finish the sentence, my goal only to appear submissive, I won't be any trouble, don't harm me.

"For this time, no questions. Later, we speak."

Then she was gone, the door closing behind her with a thud solid enough to convince me that I'd never break it down.

It could be worse. According my brother, kidnap victims have been confined to coffins that later held their bodies. Here the room was warm and there was food and water, and it appeared a bit of time as well. The lantern was extremely bright and I could see into every corner of the room as I made a slow, deliberate survey. First, sheets and a blanket covering a mattress. Then the windows, or what used to be windows. I found three, set high up on the wall, perhaps eight or ten inches from the ceiling. The windows were protected by plywood panels that appeared to be new. The walls were sheetrock and nailed into studs, with no effort having been made to conceal the nailheads. Sheetrock is nothing more than compressed gypsum sandwiched between layers of thick paper. If I managed to gouge my way through an individual panel, what would I discover on the far side? Dirt or a cinderblock foundation?

I spent the next few minutes crisscrossing the room, looking for anything I could employ, either to escape or as a weapon. I wasn't expecting much—the floor was spotless—but I found a loose nail in one of the drywall panels. I worked at it for a minute, the nailhead digging into my fingertips, until it came free. Slightly blunted at the point, the three-inch nail was still sharp enough to cut through the paper covering the sheetrock panels, or chip at the mortar between the bricks.

A thought leaped into my pitifully obsessed brain, cutting through the tunnel vision that had seized me ever since awakening in the trunk of that car. Tashya's not stupid, and not foolish enough to discount the serious nature of her crime. If caught, she will surely pass the rest of her life in a cage.

Leave me on my own? That would be really stupid.

I made a friend (one who doesn't dislike me, as difficult to swallow as that may seem) last summer at the Bradford Group worksite. His name is Paolo Yoma, Director of Site Security for the firm. According to Paolo, surveillance and security are now inextricably joined, a Gordian knot that only a fool would sever.

I repeated to myself: Tashya's not stupid.

Time to think things out. I sat in the wooden chair at the table, opened a bag of BBQ-flavored potato chips, unscrewed the cap on a bottle of water. As I brought the bottle to my mouth, another thought I might have thought long before jumped into my brain, mocking me.

Of course, there's bottled water in the room. Bottled water's an absolute necessity because there's no *running* water. No running water, no sink, no toilet. No, what there is, tucked beneath the table, is a bucket.

A fucking *bucket*!

CHAPTER THREE

DELIA

Mostly, when you crash through the door, dope addicts are on the nod or sick from cold-turkey withdrawal. They're rational too. Rational enough to get their asses on the floor. Rational enough to recognize overwhelming force when it's pointing a gun in their direction. Not the tweakers, though. Methamphetamine highs begin gently enough. Slammers become instantly social, talking ceaselessly, compulsively. Give them coloring books and crayons and they can amuse themselves for hours on end. Or at least until they start to come down.

I've interrogated dozens of meth addicts. The high, they tell me, is utterly euphoric. The comedown is a nightmare you'll do anything to avoid. Like injecting another dose into your arm, then another and another and another. You don't sleep, not with your heart rate above 150 beats a minute. Not with every neuron flashing on and off like the lights on a berserk Christmas tree. No, you stay awake for days, becoming more and more paranoid as the hours pass. And your reaction when I finally show up is driven by what amounts to a full-blown psychosis.

My name is Delia Mariola. As Captain, I'm the highest-ranking officer on the Baxter Police Department. I was supposed to be Chief of Police. The job was offered two months ago. But then Chief Black learned that he could boost his pension by 40% if he hung on for another eight months. So sorry.

My mission, on the other hand, hasn't changed. I'm supposed to make Baxter safe for the Nissan Car Company. That means cleaning up a drug problem so deeply entrenched it might be included on the city's seal. Maybe a syringe flanked by cornstalks. I should have been disappointed—my son, Danny, thinks I was cheated—but there was a positive angle I couldn't ignore. As Chief, my duties would be strictly administrative. That means a desk and a chair and a gradually spreading butt. Not the biggest thrill for a cop who loves the action.

Call it a reprieve, but I'm leading today's raid on an isolated house where methamphetamine is both sold and cooked. My little army is made up of nine cops, including myself and my second-in-command, Lieutenant Vern Taney. There's no SWAT Team. That's because the City of Baxter doesn't have one, not yet. Nor are my soldiers, with three exceptions, especially competent. But they're all I have for now. Later on, when federal and state funds pour into the Baxter Enterprise Zone, salaries will rise high enough to attract better recruits.

Decent equipment will follow too. Just now, we've donned Grade IIA vests, able to stop handgun rounds, but not bullets fired from rifles. Not even from low-powered hunting rifles in a part of the country where fathers have been teaching their sons to hunt for ten generations. Where killing your first deer is a rite of passage.

"Cade?"

"Yes, Captain?"

"Time to go."

Cade Barrow's a good-looking kid with spiky hair, clear brown eyes, and a ready smile. He's only ten weeks out of the Marines, a sniper, or so he claims. I put him to the test at an outdoor firing range in Maryville County last week. Cade fired off fifty rounds from a scoped Remington at distances ranging from a hundred to four hundred yards. Every round came within six inches of dead center. Most were a lot closer.

I've already covered Cade's assignment in detail. The meth house is located on the eastern edge of the Yards, Baxter's industrial neighborhood and the future site of the Nissan plant. Once thriving, the area's now a wasteland of trailer parks and deserted factories. Those factories and the cover they provide are the only good thing about the Yards.

Cade follows me into the parking lot. It's 5 A.M. and overcast. If there's a moon up there, I can't see it. "I'm telling you again," I tell him again, "there are volatile chemicals inside the house. Volatile chemicals and at least one child. Don't pull that trigger unless you're ordered to do so by me or Vern."

"Got it, Captain. I'll buzz you when I'm in place."

◆

Back inside, I repeat the message. Our job, all of us, is to maintain a perimeter while I convince the occupants to surrender peacefully. Cooking meth involves the use of flammable chemicals that can be explosive under the right conditions.

"Starter fluid, paint thinner, sulfuric acid, drain cleaners, camping fuel, and pseudoephedrine. You can find any of that and more. And we can't eliminate the possibility that John Dwyer has a batch on the stove right this minute. Dwyer's long divorced, but he has a child. Others in his crew have children as well. Given the hours tweakers keep, there's no telling who'll be in the house. We need to avoid a firefight if at all possible."

My eyes move from one man to another as I go along. Vern Taney, first, my partner over the last two years. Vern's a local who knows just about everybody in Baxter. I've trusted him with my life on several occasions and I'm still breathing. Jerome Meeks stands next to Vern. New to the job, Meeks has proven himself competent. But he's never participated in a raid and his nervousness reveals itself in a swipe of his tongue across his lips.

It goes downhill from there, all the way to John Meacham, the Dink. The Dink's got big-time protection. His sister heads the City Council. He's also suspected, by me and Vern, of providing information to a now-defunct mob crew. In fact, we're all but certain, though we lack the proof needed to charge him. Or even fire him.

◆

Adrenaline surging, I whisper a little prayer as I lead my raiding party into the parking lot. One day I'll have an armored rescue vehicle and the ability to approach a target without getting my brains blown out. As it is, I have to settle for a pair of unmodified SUVs. Not bulletproof, not even bullet resistant.

I've been cultivating informants since I joined the force. In addition to Dwyer's house, I've located another ten drug locations. I want to hit them one after another, day after day, no letup. I'm not deluded. I don't believe I can keep Baxter drug-free, not with all that new money pouring in. But I'm hoping to force the dealers into the counties surrounding the city. Let the sheriffs handle the dealers. Let Baxter handle the addicts.

I'm wearing a radio on the left sleeve of my uniform blouse, like everyone else. Cade Barrow's voice, accompanied by a loud hiss, suddenly pours from its small speaker. His form of address is familiar because we're not using codes. There's not enough of us for that, and my crew isn't well-enough trained.

"Captain?"

"Cade."

"I'm in place. No problems. But there are lights on in the house. In every room I can see. And people moving behind the curtains."

"Check, Cade. We're on the way."

The tension inside my SUV can't be ignored. It sizzles, a second atmosphere that fills every empty space. I can deal with it because I've been here before. Vern too. The others have little experience and I'm beginning to think I should have waited a few months. I should have trained a legitimate SWAT Team. Too late now.

The Yards, three square miles of industrially zoned real estate on the southeastern corner of the city, is almost deserted this early in the morning. Some of the trailer parks and rental houses have already closed and the rest are emptying rapidly. Baxter Meat Packing still operates, but except for a small cadre of security guards, it won't resume operations until Monday morning. We're cruising on Baxter Boulevard's southern edge where it skirts the Yards and I can hear cattle bellowing in the distance. Greeting the new day? Or bemoaning their fate? They'll be dead, every one, before noon on Monday. A steak in someone's refrigerator within a week.

As we turn left onto Gauss Road, our driver, Henry Fornier, shuts off the lights. The lights of the following vehicle blink out a few seconds later. That leaves the gloom to settle about us, the cool, wet air seeming to rush into the car. Sitting beside Henry, I can see only a few yards ahead and by necessity we crawl down a road that's more pothole than asphalt. It would be easy to sink into the tension, but I'm not willing to lose myself in darkness. Instead, I bleed the tension away by taking a final review of our strategy.

Not being entirely suicidal, we won't drive straight up to John Dwyer's little house. We're not going to sneak up on the target either. Not with every window lit and people moving behind the curtains. Not with a pair of informants insisting that Dwyer has an arsenal in his house that includes several assault rifles. A close-in firefight isn't to anyone's advantage. Explosions kill cops as readily as crooks.

Dwyer's Booth Lane home is on the eastern edge of both the Yards and the city. My team will approach on Crowley Street to the west. That will put the Grange Leather factory between us and Dwyer. I'm told that Grange Leather once employed hundreds of Baxterites. No more. Every window is broken, including the one in the room where Cade waits, his rifle supported by busted-out bricks piled on a metal table. I can picture the room and its pile of abandoned machinery easily enough. Cade and I were there two days ago, looking for a sniper's nest with a view that included Dwyer's front windows.

Once parked, we'll approach on foot along the factory's northern edge, shielded from view. That will leave us sixty yards from our target. A short wait until Vern's unit takes a position behind a mountain of illegally dumped debris at the rear of the house will follow. This corner of the Yards has been a dump site ever since Grange Leather closed its doors and the piles are high and dense enough to provide adequate cover. Vern's unit will only come into play if someone inside the Dwyer home decides to run for it.

As we approach the Grange factory, I make a little speech that's more or less obligatory. "Listen up, men." And they're all men. The only female's in Vern's unit. "If we can't approach the house unseen, I'm gonna talk them out or wait them out. Remember, there's at least one child in that house, and maybe a lot more. We don't want to be labeled reckless butchers right out of the box. We have a lot more work ahead of us. Let's stay professional. Minimize risk, maximize results."

Nobody responds as we climb out of the SUV, as we walk to the back and unload four M16 assault rifles and a bulletproof shield. The shield's made of carbon fiber and weighs under twenty pounds. It's designed to protect an average-sized man from above his head to mid-shin. I don't expect to use the shield. I brought it along because it's the only high-tech item in the Baxter PD's arsenal. Style points count too.

CHAPTER FOUR

DELIA

Grange Leather's main building is surrounded by a chain-link fence that's been pulled apart in a dozen places. Access is simple and we pick our way, led by a narrow-beam flashlight, through a surreal forest of brush and rusted machinery. A pile of hides well on their way to petrification, stainless steel counters lying on their backs, eight feet of an inch-thick rusted chain with a winch on one end. The sky above is a black, featureless sheet, even with dawn thirty minutes away.

We stay close to the sooty bricks on the side of the factory until we come within sight of John Dwyer's very small, clapboard-sided house. I stop here momentarily and point to a long tank lying on its side to our left. There are tires piled in front and behind the tank. They're high enough to offer sufficient cover, low enough to provide a clear view of the house.

"We've been over this, but I'm going to repeat myself. We do not know who or what is in that house. You're to stand down until I order you to open fire. Now, take cover."

We move silently from the side of the factory to positions along the tank. The windows on the front and northern side of the house are lit, as Chad foretold. But nothing moves behind them and no shots ring out. Have we preserved the element of surprise? The house is sixty yards away, as close as we can get without crossing open ground.

I pull out my phone, punch in a number supplied by an informant and set it to speaker. I have my own number blocked. The phone rings out and I try again. This time someone picks up.

"Dwyer."

"Mr. Dwyer, this is Captain Mariola of the Baxter PD. I have an arrest warrant for you and a search warrant for your home. I want you and anyone else in the house to come out with your hands on your heads. You're surrounded. You can't escape. Look out the window."

I stand up at that point, the shield before me. As a show of force, it's pitiful, but I'm willing to look bad if it'll avoid bloodshed. Then I hear Dwyer scream, "The cops are outside."

Dwyer drops his phone and it lands on something hard, giving off a solid thump. In the background, I hear panicked voices, easily five or six people. They know how painful coming off a meth high can be. Even if you chase the high with a few oxycodone tablets. But in jail? Cold turkey?

There's only the waiting now. For sanity to take hold? A figure appears in the window on the south-front of the house.

A man, torso and head. A second later, he disappears and I hear the phone scraping along some hard surface. Then a woman's voice.

"Hello, hello . . ."

"This is Captain Mariola. Please take a second. Please listen."

"What?"

"Nobody's been hurt. Nobody's been arrested. We have a warrant to search the house. No need to make it worse for yourselves. Hear me? No need."

"Please don't shoot. Please. . . ."

"Hey, cop." Dwyer's voice replaces the woman's. "We got a kid in here. Awright? You come through the door, anything could fuckin' happen."

"Sure, okay. But no one's coming through the door. You're coming out instead. Please think it through. If you use the child as a hostage, you're committing a far worse crime than drug possession."

"Fuck you, pig. I'm not goin' back to prison. You want me, you're gonna have to take me, hear?"

"Just slow down, John. Just slow down. You're inside and we're out here. You've got time. Don't do anything . . ."

Shots ring out from behind the house. The sharp crack of pistols, followed by a barrage of rifle fire. I can't see anything, but I have to assume there's been an attempt to escape through the back where Vern and his unit are stationed.

The firefight is over almost before it begins and I'm back to hoping again. Maybe there's nobody left inside, maybe they've surrendered, maybe the child is safe. But it's not happening. I hear Dwyer first: "Fuck you, fuck you, fuck you." Then he's in the window, holding a rifle in his hand and I'm diving for cover. Bullets thump into the tires, crash into the tank, a fusillade that continues on, round after round, for a good ten seconds. I stay on the phone throughout, demanding calm, that no one return fire. My crew listens for once, probably because nobody's all that eager to stick his head up.

"Cade?" For some reason, just as Dwyer releases another barrage, I'm whispering.

"Here, Captain."

"What's your situation?"

"I've acquired. Ready to go."

"Hold off, Cade, but stay ready."

"Roger that."

Dwyer's missing badly by this time and I slowly raise my head and look around. What I find sets my heart racing again. Flames licking though an open window on one side of the house. Is the child inside? Does it matter? I'm a cop. I have to do something and do it right away.

"Take the shot, Cade. Now."

I see the bullet slam into Dwyer's chest before I hear the report of Cade's rifle, the bullet traveling much faster than the speed of sound. Then I'm on my feet, running toward the house, tossing my rifle away, pulling my sidearm. My legs are moving faster than they've ever moved, yet it takes forever to reach the door. I don't even try the handle. I fire two shots into the lock instead and the door flies open. The fire's on my left, well established and moving along the kitchen cabinets. Several plastic containers, the kind meant to hold gas or kerosene, are on the counter, waiting for the flames. To my right, a little girl, a toddler, stands in a crib, hands clamped to the railing. Her wail, barely audible, speaks to an abandonment and despair that runs so deep it rips into my heart. I cross the room in two steps and snatch her up. Her legs curl around my chest, her hands circle my neck, then I'm running for both our lives, tearing across the field to finally shelter behind the Grange Leather warehouse.

We're safe, but the child's grip tightens as I drop to a knee. I'm all she has and she continues to cry. Not the demanding cry of a child in need, but the helpless, hopeless lament of the truly forsaken. From behind, I hear an enormous whoosh, the released breath of a dragon. When I peek around the corner, a geyser of yellow flame rises twenty feet above the house. There are no more gunshots now. The battle is over.

Two dead, one seriously wounded, none ours. While I was on the phone with Dwyer, seven individuals—all except Dwyer and his daughter—ran out through the back door. Vern and his crew confronted the group. Four hit the ground, arms spread. Three decided to fight it out. Their handguns were no match for the squad's rifles and the gunfight was over in less than fifteen seconds.

"We're gonna have to let them go," I tell Vern. "The four who surrendered." I'm still holding the child. She's fallen asleep in my arms, but her grip has yet to fully relax.

Vern doesn't argue. Our prisoners aren't carrying meth and the building has now been incinerated, along with any evidence still inside. That leaves our wounded gunman the only one left to punish. The bullet that brought him down passed through his kneecap and his lower leg was hanging by a thread when the ambulance took him away. He was only alive because of a makeshift tourniquet applied by Patrolwoman Maya Kinsley, formerly a paramedic. Most likely, the loss of his leg will be followed by twenty years in prison for the attempted murder of a police officer.

"You okay, Delia? You look as if you're in shock."

"I keep thinking . . . I mean what if I didn't go into the house? What if nobody went in? She was standing in her crib, Vern, so little. . . . She would've burned up. All alone."

Vern nods and I know I've said enough. The kids are the worst, always the worst. There's no point in dwelling on them or their fate. For cops, or for this cop, the kids are the abyss we're not supposed to look into.

Five minutes later, a woman approaches. She's wearing a maroon suit, jacket and skirt, over a pink blouse. Her name is Zoe Parillo and she's come to fetch the child. A handsome woman in her forties, Zoe's face reveals nothing. I read her composure as indifference the first time we interacted. I know better now. The woman mixes competence with confidence, along with a determination to endure what has, at times, to be unendurable. Zoe works for Baxter's Department of Social Services and passes most of her working days responding to allegations of child abuse. She's the Department's specialist.

"What are you going to do with her?" I can't help myself. I don't want to give the child up. Not without even knowing her name.

"I'm going to take her to the hospital and have her evaluated. If she's not injured—and I don't think she is—I intend to bring her home pending a psychological assessment."

"To your home? Or the group home?" Baxter has only one group foster home. A training academy for criminals, the place is notorious. "You're going to become her foster parent?"

I want Zoe to nod, but she only smiles. "It's too early for any decisions. She might have relatives eager to raise her. Sober relatives. But I'm going to take her into my home until we get our bearings."

That's as far as we get before my radio crackles into life. It's Chief Black, sounding worried, as always. "I want you to call me, Delia. On your phone, in private."

"But . . ."

"Like now, Delia. Right now."

I have only one response and I take it. "Yes, sir."

CHAPTER FIVE

DELIA

"A kidnapping, a fifteen-year-old girl," Chief Black tells me. "Elizabeth Bradford."

"Who?"

"Elizabeth Bradford? The Bradford Group? Christopher Bradford's daughter? There's a ransom note."

That does it. Headed by Christopher Bradford, the Bradford Group is in the city to bid on the Nissan plant's construction, as well as the demolition of all existing structures in the Yards. I recall a profile of the family in the *Baxter Bugle*'s Sunday edition. Every other word in the story made some reference to the family's immense wealth. At the time, I wondered exactly what were they doing in our impoverished little city. Why hadn't they sent a few of their minions to handle the estimate? Then I'd forgotten all about them, closing down methamphetamine cooking sites requiring my full attention.

"We've got three bodies to deal with, Chief, one of them severely burned, and a homeless toddler."

"I'm sending my car. When it arrives, get inside."

The Chief's official car, a gray Buick, rolls up ten minutes later. Davey Cray's behind the wheel. Cray's pushing sixty, well beyond policing age. He only has a job because he's there for the boss 24/7, a personal chauffeur.

Settled inside the Buick, I check myself out in the rearview mirror. A pair of smudges runs across my forehead, my short hair is still a mess, both knees are dirt stained, and my fingers won't stop trembling. Worse yet, my adrenals are empty and I'm having a hard time putting two thoughts together.

Not Davey. The peak of his hat has been polished to a high gloss that nicely matches his shoes. His uniform trousers display creases sharp enough to slice bread.

"Tough go?" he asks.

Not as bad as it would be if we'd lost the child. That's what I'm thinking, but I'm far from ready to review the impulse that drove me into that burning house.

"We won," I tell him. "Now, what do you say to a quick head's up on the kidnapping? What am I walkin' into?"

"There's not much to tell." Davey turns slightly to look at me.

"Why's that?"

"Because the Chief's not talkin' to me, which he usually does. In fact, mostly I can't shut him up when he gets goin'. I'm thinkin' he can't decide how he wants to play it. On the one hand, you publicize a kidnapping and it can go real bad for the victim. On the other hand, if you bottle it up and word gets out, you're fucked with the public. There's the family too. I have no idea what position they're takin'. Plus, they're not the kinda family you can dismiss. Plus, you can't forget the FBI."

Kidnapping is a federal crime and the Bradford family has a reputation for funding politicians in Washington, at least according to a piece in the *Baxter Bugle.* But there's an additional issue. The Chief said there was a ransom note. Did it warn against calling the police? We've already been called, obviously, but there's no good reason to let everyone in Baxter know that.

The sun's up now, barely visible through a layer of gray cloud that seems close enough to touch. This early on a Sunday morning, Baxter's streets are deserted and we're making good time. I only have a few minutes before we reach the Mt. Jackson house rented by the Bradfords. I take that time to call Lillian Taney. My son, Danny, is at the Taney's, hanging out with Mike, their son and his best buddy.

Lillian's voice trembles when she answers with a single word: "Delia?" She's spoken to me about the fear shared by every cop wife. Especially when that call is made by a superior.

"All good, Lillian. Nobody hurt but the bad guys." I'm trying to keep it light, only my hands are still trembling. Maybe my voice trembles a bit too.

"What happened?"

"Look, Lillian, something came up, something I have to deal with. Vern's in charge of the investigation now. That's probably why he hasn't called you. But there's nothing to worry about. It's all over and no cops were injured." I'm tempted to add the word physically, but manage to keep my big mouth shut for a change. "Any chance you can find Danny real quick?"

Danny's voice sounds in my ear a minute later. "You okay?" he asks. The boy knows me as well as anybody on the planet.

"Post-combat depletion, Danny. But I'm good. Vern too."

"You don't sound good."

"Be that as it may, I have to go. We'll talk when I pick you up later."

I'm generally open with Danny about the nature of policing, including the ugly and painful sides. But not this time. My head is still reeling as the Bradford rental comes into view. I'm expecting to find a dozen squad cars parked in front of the house. In fact, there are three vehicles parked at the apex of a curving driveway, a Mercedes SUV, a jet-black BMW, and a sleek, red Tesla with a translucent roof. The family cars, no doubt.

The home itself is imposing, especially compared to the small house I currently rent. Three stories high, with six evenly spaced dormer windows on the top floor; the wooden columns holding up the porch roof remind me of a southern plantation. The place was last occupied by an architect's family. They left Baxter more than a year ago and the place has been for rent or sale ever since. Almost certainly protected by an elaborate security system before the architect left, there's no sign of one now.

The door I approach has to be ten feet high and thick enough to withstand anything short of an RPG. But it slides open noiselessly when I push a buzzer lodged inside the mouth of a brass lion. The man who stands before me isn't wearing formal clothes, but the grim expression on his face leads me to conclude that I'm facing the butler. He stares at me for a long moment, at my dirty uniform and smudged forehead, but maintains a polite silence to admit me.

"Captain Mariola," I tell him without being prompted.

"Please, Captain. Wait here while I announce you."

Announce? I merely nod as he crosses the room and disappears through a side door. The Bradfords have been in town for about two weeks and the local media's been treating them as celebrity billionaires. So where's their security detail? Even if the move was too sudden to install a security system, human beings are always available.

My wait is short. Chief Black appears two minutes later, accompanied by a tall man wearing a navy suit that accents wide shoulders and a narrow waist. They start toward me, but then the Chief lays a restraining hand on the man's shoulder.

"Give us a minute," he says.

Routinely pessimistic, Chief Black's shaking his head as he approaches. The effect is striking because the Chief recently had a benign tumor removed from his brain and a row of sutures traces a straight line from his temple to the back of his skull. Now they appear to be crawling forward.

"Delia, what in the world . . ."

It takes me a second to realize that he's commenting on my appearance. "It went sideways, Chief. At Dwyer's. We've got three dead and one injured. Them, not us."

I don't have the energy to go into more detail. I don't have the energy to deal with a kidnapping either. The energy or the manpower. But sometimes you get lucky.

"The family's decided to wait for the FBI. Kidnapping's a federal crime anyway. I called you in for nothing."

"We're being dismissed?"

"That's up to the Feds, but I'll be surprised if we have more than a token presence on whatever task force they assemble. A liaison, maybe. Someone to sit behind a desk and keep his mouth shut. Or her mouth."

I know what the Chief's thinking, because I instinctively draw the same conclusion. If things turn out badly, the FBI will take the blame. Especially if I pass news of their takeover—anonymously, of course—to Katie Burke on the *Baxter Bugle.*

"Do we know anything, Chief?"

The several acres of lawn surrounding the house, though recently mowed, are more crabgrass than Kentucky blue. Stretching beyond the road, the lawn's broken by massive trees, a dry fountain, and a small, weed-choked pond. The trees, a mix of elms, maples, and oaks, look to have been planted when the house was built a hundred years ago. A child stands under one of the trees, a boy maybe ten years old. The right side of his head is shaved clean while the top and left side are long enough to fall below his ears. He's playing with a Frisbee, scaling it away from him at a steep angle that brings it back to his hand.

"Alright, Delia. Here's what I've been told. One of the security guys took a walk around the house about seven o'clock this morning and found a package leaning against the back door. The victim's purse and phone were inside, along with a ransom demand. I'm paraphrasing, but it went something like this. We have your daughter, Elizabeth. If you want to see her again, you must immediately accumulate ten million dollars in Bitcoin. You will hear from Elizabeth soon. Be ready to act. No delays will be tolerated."

"Clever, Chief. Very, very clever."

"Exactly."

Kidnappings usually go bad for the kidnappers at the exchange. The money has to be left somewhere. Somebody has to retrieve it. These days, the Feds have access to everything from satellite images to drones flying high enough to escape detection. Bitcoin, on the other hand, is virtual. Deposited in a virtual wallet, it literally becomes invisible to observers without a decryption key, yet can be rerouted through a dozen countries at the speed of light.

"One more thing. Did the note warn against calling the police?"

"That's the odd thing, Delia. It didn't."

Chief Black dismisses me at that point, the worried look having never left his face. I understand his worry. The coming of Nissan is too good to be true, an undeserved miracle that can be withdrawn in an instant. Say at the death of a billionaire's daughter. But I have other things to worry about.

The paperwork generated by the Dwyer raid and its bloody consequences will have the entire raiding party working for the rest of the day. We don't have a shooting board looking over our shoulders, as in larger cities, but that makes it even worse. Now speculators will take the lead, in the mainstream media and online. We've got to get out in front.

The weather seems to echo the changes. A freshening breeze tears at the sheet of gray cloud above me. The sky is now speckled with pale blue patches all the more vivid for the surrounding pewter. The afternoon will be clear and cool.

Chief Black gestures to the man waiting fifteen feet away and he steps forward. His confident expression doesn't change as he approaches and he doesn't offer his hand.

"This is Pierce Donato," the Chief tells me. "He commanded the overnight security team. Mr. Donato, this is Captain Mariola. Now, if you don't mind, Delia, I have to get back to the house. Mr. Donato will brief you." He winks. "I wouldn't expect a hell of a lot."

Donato and I watch the Chief walk away for a moment, then turn to each other. I gesture at my soiled appearance. "Sorry, I came directly from a crime scene that got out of hand."

"Not a problem." Donato slides his right hand into the pocket of his trousers. "There's not all that much to tell, not at this stage. We found a message claiming to be from Elizabeth's kidnappers early this morning along with several personal items. We'll hear from the kidnappers later today and speak directly with Elizabeth. They'll make their timetable known at the same time."

"That's it?"

"Pretty much."

"Was her bed slept in?"

"No."

"Tell me about her. Could she have set this up herself?"

Donato takes a moment to think it over, then says, "The girl's too smart for her own good, that's certain. If she had a motive, I might be suspicious. But she's already rich. Plus, she's only fifteen and doesn't have any friends in Baxter." Donato finally smiles, turning up one corner of his mouth. "Or anywhere else."

I'm curious, no doubt, but I'm tired and hungry, as well. If the case was coming to the Baxter PD, I might indulge myself. As it is, I thank Mr. Donato and head for Davey Cray and the Buick. Davey's still behind the wheel. He's holding a newspaper (the *Bugle,* no doubt, the only paper in town) at arm's length. Doing his job as he and his boss see it.

"Officer . . ."

I turn to find the boy, frisbee in hand, walking toward me. This close, I measure a confidence to the point of arrogance in his eyes, a look belied by a weak chin and a fragile physique. Danny would make two of him.

"My mother wants to speak with you."

"And you'd be?"

"Sherman Bradford."

"Elizabeth's brother?"

"Yes."

"And what do you want to tell me about her disappearance?"

The kid's arrogance betrays him. He's ten or eleven years old, too inexperienced for a sharp question he wasn't expecting. His eyes widen in surprise. What have I found out? Can he lie and get away with it?

"Tell me the truth and I'll protect you. Because you will tell me the truth, Sherman, sooner or later. Might as well get it over with. What do you know about your sister's disappearance?"

His uncertainty vanishes as suddenly as it appeared, replaced with anger. I've caught him off guard and he doesn't like it. But that's the way it goes when you're a child dealing with a woman who's spent a good part of her life interpreting body language.

"I didn't take her," he tells me.

"Who did?"

"I don't know. I swear."

"But there's something, right? Something you need to say? What is it?"

His nostrils widen as he draws a breath and I realize that he's been wanting to get this off his chest all along. "She sneaks out at night. Sometimes."

"Elizabeth?"

"Yes."

"And last night? Did she sneak out?"

"She could have." Now that he's revealed the big secret, his mouth tightens and his eyes again grow confident. "My mother's waiting, officer, and she doesn't like to wait."

"Lead on, Sherman."

◆

The boy leads me to a sunroom at the back of the house. The front wall of the room is glass and there's a domed skylight on the ceiling. As in the entrance hall, the room is almost unfurnished. A round wooden table rests in the center, surrounded by four upholstered dining-room chairs. A long couch in the back holds six or seven paintings. A dozen boxes, some full, some empty, lie before a potted ficus that reaches to within a few inches of the ceiling.

Facing away from me, a plump woman in her forties paces the length of the room. I watch her for a few seconds before clearing my throat and she turns to face me. She has an exceptionally round face and a full, yet narrow, mouth. Her blue eyes are large and marked by red lines that radiate outward to disappear between swollen lids. A thin gold chain circling her throat supports a pendant with a green stone I assume to be a small emerald.

"Excuse the appearance, Mrs. Bradford." I gesture to myself. "I'm Captain Mariola."

She waves my humility away, but doesn't offer her hand. "Can I assume you've met with my husband?"

"I haven't, actually. Chief Black intercepted me when I arrived. We've been consigned to a supportive role in the investigation. The FBI will take charge."

"And how does that make you feel?"

A middle-aged woman interrupts. Wearing the black-and-white uniform of a servant, she carries a tray bearing a coffee pot, cups and saucers, a pitcher of milk, and a plate of miniature cinnamon rolls.

"Would you like coffee, Captain?"

She lowers herself into a chair and I join her. "Desperately," I admit.

The maid pours for both of us. She hands me a cup, then retraces her steps into the home's interior. I add milk and sugar to my coffee and take a sip, barely suppressing a satisfied groan. It's only after another quick hit that I find my voice. "Nobody likes being dismissed, which is basically what's happening to the Baxter Police Department. But I don't think you asked for me because you're worried about my feelings."

The comment produces a smile that amounts to little more than a small expansion at the corners of her mouth. "My husband," she tells me, "can be manipulated, but not opposed. For example, I would have preferred to wait in Louisville until this home was properly secured before taking residence. Christopher decided otherwise and he insisted, without consultation, that his children come along. More than likely, he believed the conditions would toughen them."

"Excuse me for saying so, but I'm not seeing the tough part. Add a little furniture and I'd be looking at luxury."

"As I said, my husband can only be opposed by his brother. Whatever his reasoning, he made his decision and here we are." She brought the cup to her mouth, but did not drink. "I can't disagree with Christopher's decision to call in the FBI. Given the FBI's vast experience, they surely know how to . . . to bargain? No, that's not right. To negotiate, then. But there are no FBI agents in Baxter and whomever they import from the capital won't be acquainted with the local residents. The FBI will have to rely on their negotiating skills and that's not good enough." She draws a sharp breath through her nose before adding. "For me."

I nod agreement, though it's very unlikely that our "local players" have anything to do with Elizabeth Bradford's kidnapping. Our miscreants have mastered the necessary criminal skills to burglarize a home, deal a little dope, maybe even rob a convenience store. But a kidnapping with the ransom to be paid in Bitcoin is beyond their imagining. Way beyond. And the Bradfords have only been here for a short time. Most likely, the family was targeted in Louisville and followed to Baxter where they became vulnerable through their own negligence. Not to mention arrogance.

"Mrs. Bradford, I came here from an operation that includes three fatalities and there's a lot of work ahead of me. I don't want to be rude, but I have no idea what you want from me."

Cynthia Bradford rises from her chair. A tall woman, she displays an unconscious athleticism I wouldn't have predicted. "Please," she says, "let me show you something. I won't keep you long."

She doesn't wait for me to respond, but leads me through a pair of empty rooms into a room lined on all sides with bookcases. She gestures to a raised window at the far side of the room, but I'm already looking through the window at an overgrown rhododendron on the other side. The shrub is tall and thick enough to fully conceal anyone entering—or leaving—the house.

"Your daughter's room, Mrs. Bradford. Where is it?"

"Upstairs on the other side of the house."

"Her bed?"

"Made." She raises a hand to her mouth, then drops it to her side. "Tell me what you think, Captain. Because I believe our thoughts run in the same direction."

"Mrs. Bradford, the odds against a kidnapper discovering this shielded window, finding it open, climbing through, and navigating the route to Elizabeth's bedroom are astronomical. Even without the additional problem of getting her from her room back to the window. Most likely, we're lookin' at an exit."

"She left on her own?"

"That would be my assumption."

"To meet her kidnappers?"

"To meet someone." I know she wants more, but more of what? "Tell me about Elizabeth, Mrs. Bradford."

"My daughter is a senior at Phillips Exeter Academy, a feeder school for Harvard University. She has a tested IQ of 159 and a persistent thirst for romantic literature. Last year at school, she wrote an essay on the work of an obscure Romantic poet named Anna Laetitia Barbauld. The essay was judged worthy of publication in *Pendulum,* the school's literary magazine. Writing's become Elizabeth's primary ambition ever since. She wishes to be, simultaneously, a famous modern poet and Chairwoman of the Bradford Group."

She paused at this point, leaving me to close the gap. "Did you say that Elizabeth is a senior? Isn't she fifteen?"

"She's skipped two years. Another of my husband's command decisions. I opposed the advancement. Elizabeth is conceited enough without adding fuel to the fire. And that's the problem. For all her intelligence, for all her ambition, Elizabeth's an impulsive and at times reckless child. If she carries that attitude into her ordeal?" Cynthia Bradford pauses for a moment, but her eyes don't leave mine. "If my daughter snuck out of this house late last night, it was to meet someone and not for a stroll. I know it's a lot to ask, but in my opinion, federal agents from far away are very unlikely to find that someone."

CHAPTER SIX

DELIA

Work, and then work, and then more work. My day started before dawn and it's almost eleven before I leave the Bradford home and return to the station. The State Crime Scene Unit is already working the Dwyer location (we don't have our own CSU), counting the shell casings, measuring trajectories, investigating the fire that consumed the house. I have an interest in the results, obviously, but not in the procedure. I don't intend to revisit the scene until later.

Tucked behind City Hall on Polk Avenue, the Baxter Police Department is headquartered in a nondescript, single-story building universally called the House. Several officers greet me when I enter, but I merely nod as I walk through the reception room and into a corridor that leads to my office. Long wooden benches line both sides of the corridor. On one side, the benches are bolted to the floor and marked by steel rings, also bolted down. Four people sit on these benches, cuffed to the rings. Two are women and two are men. Speed comedowns in high gear, their eyes plead for release. In fact, they're right where I want them as I enter my office to find Danny waiting for me.

My son and I both contracted the Covid virus last year. By some quirk of fate, my illness was short-lived and my symptoms mild. Not Danny's. His fever remained at critical levels for many days and his cough barely responded to the codeine-spiked medication prescribed by his doctor. Danny eventually recovered, but the process took weeks in which I rarely left his bedside. And it's not that I loved him more afterward. No, his illness taught me just how much I'd loved him from the beginning.

Now he looks at me, eyes wide, probing for damage. I'm touched, but there's a lot of work ahead. I've just got time enough for reassurance.

"Danny, listen. I wasn't part of the shooting, not even as a witness. It took place on the far side of a house."

"But you're a hero, Mom."

"Huh?"

"Yeah, take a look." Danny's tablet rests on my desk, next to his backpack. He picks it up, pecks away for a few seconds, and finally turns the screen in my direction. And there I am, running toward the camera, the child in my arms, bright orange flames rising from the house behind me.

"Holy shit."

"Language, Mom." Danny's grin is always contagious and this time is no different. He gestures to the screen. "You've gone viral. I mean like *global* viral."

"Great."

The video was obviously taken by one of my cops. I'm seriously pissed, but sorting out the culprit is for later, as is retribution.

"Thanks for the heads-up, honey. There'll be a press conference this afternoon and the reporters are sure to ask about the girl. Meantime, I've got a mountain of work ahead of me and I need to get started. Abe Washington's the duty sergeant today. Go out there, tell him I need a favor. I want him to find some loose cop to drive you home, or back to the Taneys', whichever you prefer. We'll talk more if I get home at a decent hour."

Danny chooses door number two, the Taneys and his buddy Mike. At age fourteen, both expect to have Major League careers. Hall of Fame careers. They'll undoubtedly head for a nearby ball field and hours of practicing. Of course, the odds against even the most gifted fourteen-year-old eventually playing Major League Baseball are very, very long. I know that, and so does my son. But Mike and Danny are talented and determined, which has me thinking about college scholarships. College costs are out of control and I'm a practical woman. Danny will begin playing high school ball next spring and I'm going to send him to a summer baseball camp after school lets out next year. One noted for attracting scouts and college coaches.

Vern walks into my office a minute after Danny leaves. He doesn't have to be asked. Called away by Chief Black, I left Vern to run the scene. Now I need an update.

My office is relatively small and sparsely furnished, as befits any office in a city with a vanishing tax base. Faux-wood shelves on frames bolted to the wall. Two wooden chairs with rounded backs in front of my desk, an ergonomic chair (which I bought myself) tucked behind. A keyboard and monitor wired to a computer sit on the desk, alongside an intercom/landline old enough to be featured on Antiques Roadshow. The only personal anything is a photo of Danny in his Little League uniform after a game. He's covered with dirt and a tear at his left knee reveals dried blood beneath. As far as I could tell at the time, he was proud of both.

Vern drops his lanky frame onto one of the chairs in front of my desk. Nearly a foot taller than me, his features are Midwestern plain, his smile contagious, his dark, unruly hair only beginning to gray. And while his ears stick out a bit, they're a nice complement to an affable, hayseed persona he employs to good advantage. Vern grew up in Baxter. A high school football star, everyone seems to know him.

"You allowed to tell me what the Chief wanted?" he asks.

"No, but I'm gonna tell you anyway." I quickly describe the situation at the Bradfords', concluding with the welcome news that the Baxter PD will not be needed. "The Bradfords are going with the FBI."

"Bye-bye to the Baxter Police Department?"

"That's about it. And the whole deal's on the hush-hush for the present. Anybody speaking out of turn is likely to be held responsible if things go bad."

"And they go bad real easy with hostages. For some kidnappers, killing the hostage is no more than destroying evidence. Like shredding files in a swindle. If the FBI wants to shoulder the risks, so be it."

"My sentiments exactly. But I also spoke to the victim's mother and she's having second thoughts about putting all her eggs in the FBI's basket."

"So we're not out of it yet?"

"Exactly, but for now take me through your own adventure. What went on behind the house?"

Vern crosses his legs, laying his left ankle on his right knee. "They came through the back door, one after another, real fast. We stood up before they covered fifteen feet and ordered them to stop. Four hit the ground, three drew weapons and fired at us, pulling the trigger as fast as they could. Two officers returned fire, Goody and Mel Canning. . . ."

"Hang on, Vern. You didn't fire?"

"Nope. Maya Kinsley, either.

"Okay, go on."

"The firefight was over in a few seconds. Two of the three who fired on us were obviously dead. As dead as you can get. Maya administered emergency treatment to the third and we called in ambulances and backup."

"Right away?"

"Right away." Vern stops long enough to stifle a yawn. "I also photographed the crime scene before I came to you. I wanted to capture the scene undisturbed. Pristine, right? No misunderstandings?"

Grisly doesn't begin to describe the photos on Vern's phone. The first series is of the wounded shooter. Maya Kinsley kneels beside the man, partially screening the shot, but

Vern's caught a mini-fountain of spurting blood that appears in all but the last photo. The other two lie ten feet apart, their bodies having adopted the postures I associate with violent death. Arms, legs, feet, necks, and heads are twisted at opposed angles no living human can mimic. There's plenty of blood here as well, and the third shooter's jaw has been torn from his face.

I take in these details automatically, but they're not what I'm looking for. My attention is captured by three semiautomatic handguns lying next to the bodies, and by the spent cartridges visible in the dirt. All three were armed. All three fired their weapons.

"Vern, who did you say fired on our side?"

"Goody and Mel Canning."

Goody is Marcus Goodman, a new hire and the only Black man on the force. Mel Canning has been with the Department for more than a decade. He's conscientious, but I suspect that his main interest is in the paycheck he brings home to his family.

I reach out to the intercom on my desk and push the little button. I have a personal assistant named Martha with a desk in the administrative office. That's in theory only, because Martha has many other responsibilities. This time she answers right away.

"Yes, boss."

"Goody and Mel. Tell them to report to my office. Immediately, Martha. Like right now without delay."

"Got ya, boss."

The two men walk into my office a moment later. Goody, the younger, looks at me with pleading eyes. Like he can't process what happened even though he's seen the bodies. Mel Canning stands with his gaze fixed on the ceiling as he shifts his weight from side to side.

"Look, I know you're shaken up," I tell them. "And maybe it's my fault. Maybe I could have come up with a better plan. But for now, it's a done deal, so I'm putting the both of you on paid leave. Go home, hug your families. The regs allow you twenty-four hours before you give a statement. Take them and let me handle the rest. I've got your backs. And don't forget, it could have been you lyin' on the ground. It could be you in the morgue. No matter how you feel about taking a life, you have a right to survive."

The two start for the door, but then Goody hesitates. He looks at me. "You saved that girl, Captain. You and nobody else. And I just wanna say that I'm proud to be working under your command."

The compliment is well intended and I thank him for the sentiment, but not for the reminder. As it is, I keep returning to the girl, to that wail of abandonment, and I keep asking myself stupid questions that I can't answer. What happened to her? What *will* happen to her? I have to know and I don't want to know. There are too many bad endings to her story. Will she be returned to a family member? Is her mother or father one of the four sitting on the bench outside, a committed drug addict? Or will she have nobody and be put into foster care while a relative is sought? I've arrested foster parents for abuse and I know that many think of their foster kids as little more than paychecks at the end of the month.

I call in Cade Barrow, my sniper, next. Barrow probably killed John Dwyer, though I can't say for sure, but one look puts me at ease. As does Cade's smile and opening remark.

"What's up, Cap?"

"You okay?"

"Are you talkin' about Dwyer?"

"Yeah."

"All in a day's work. Been there, done that. On three continents."

I huddle with Vern for a few minutes after Cade leaves. My goal is to support the official version of what happened at the Dwyer house and that means dealing with the four tweakers sitting in the corridor. Once Vern and I are in accord, I quit my office and cross the corridor to the squad room. I find my detectives hard at work. I've ordered them to produce detailed accounts of their actions and observations. I'll review their statements later. For now, I enter one of the three interrogation rooms lined up on the far wall. The room is sparse, the blank walls dirty. There's a small table toward the back of the room with chairs before and behind. A third chair sits in a front corner. I take the chair in front of the table, my back to the door. A moment later, Vern leads our first witness into the room.

Her name is Amelia Giordano and she's twenty-three years old. Gaunt to the point of skeletal, her hair is brittle and thinning. She wears no makeup, not even to disguise the sores around her mouth, and when she opens her lips far enough to sneer, she reveals several missing teeth. Still, her dark eyes announce a stubborn defiance. I know what you think of me, they announce, and you can go fuck yourself. As the woman's not that far off the mark, I don't pretend to a sympathy I don't feel.

Trapped is not a comfortable state for a woman whose every nerve is twitching, but Amelia doesn't argue when Vern points to the chair on the far side of the desk. She sits and crosses her legs, her raised foot jerking up and down.

"I'm gonna be as plain as I can," I tell her. "First, you won't be charged with a crime. You didn't have drugs on you and whatever incriminating items you left in the house are toast. Burnt toast. Do you understand?"

Her chin comes up and she draws a long breath through her nose. Her eyes swap out the anger and swap in the hope. Most likely, she's already working her way through a list of meth dealers. Deciding which one to contact first.

"You're not gonna charge me with nothin'? Does that mean I can leave?"

"No, you can't."

"Why not?"

"Because I have a problem, Amelia. I've got a pair of bodies and a wounded man hangin' on by a thread. This you know, of course, since you were there. Which is how come I need your cooperation in the form of a written statement. Now, most people? I don't have to ask. That's because your average citizen is eager to help the police. So, what's it gonna be with you, Amelia? Are you eager?"

She taps a chipped fingernail on the table. "That don't answer my question, officer."

"Captain."

"Captain, okay. What I wanna know is how you can keep me here when you're not chargin' me?"

"Simple, you're a witness. A *material* witness. Now like I said, cops expect cooperation from Joe Average. But you, Amelia? You've been arrested twelve times in three states. That makes you a flight risk and there's no judge in this city who'll release you if I ask that you be held as a material witness."

"That's not right. . . ."

"Hey, I don't wanna hear your grievances." I slap the top of the table. "If you cooperate, you go home. If you don't, you'll be taken into custody. It's your move."

Amelia stares into my eyes for a moment, then shakes her head and laughs. "You are one serious . . . woman. So, what hoop am I supposed to jump through?"

I think she was about to call me a serious dyke, a compliment if ever I've heard one. "Let's begin with a verbal account of what happened. Then we'll move to a written statement. Start inside the house when Dwyer yelled the word 'cops.' "

Thirty minutes later, I have what I need. Committed to paper, Amelia's version has been read back to her with a camera recording every second. There can be no going back, or doubting that the Baxter PD fired in self-defense. I didn't prompt her either. I didn't have to because the facts spoke for themselves. After being awake for two days, and stoned out of her mind, Amelia panicked when Dwyer announced our presence. Along with the others, she fled through the back door, only to be confronted by Vern. Amelia hit the dirt, but not before the man next to her, the one in the hospital, fired off a few quick shots.

I dismiss her with a parting message. "I know you're gonna make a run for the nearest dealer as soon as you walk out the door. That's okay. I wasn't expecting better. Only I want you to carry a message from Captain Mariola. That's me, right? Tell every dealer you know that time is running short. Their time. I've got a list that includes just about every dealer in the city and I'm comin' for all of 'em. Tell them it's time to close the doors. Time for greener pastures. Otherwise, they can expect the same treatment John Dwyer got this morning."

Vern's standing behind Amelia, grinning from ear to ear. He doesn't speak, but merely steps aside. The woman's route will take her right past her handcuffed comrades. Past them and out the door, a free woman. I'm hoping they'll get the message and take the same deal without too much back talk. Of one thing I'm certain. There's a gravely injured man being treated at Baxter Medical Center. If he lives, he'll be charged with the attempted murder of a police officer. That will leave him with a single defense. The cops shot first.

CHAPTER SEVEN

DELIA

As I walk out the door, a patrol cop named Blanche Weber hands me a thermos of coffee I never asked for. Grateful doesn't begin to describe the emotion I feel at the moment. Blanche isn't an ass-kisser and I accept the coffee as a token of her admiration. Even though I'm not entirely sure of what I did to earn it. I don't have time to speculate either. I'm placing a call to Dr. Rishnavata as I get into my car. Arshan Rishnavata's the city's coroner. He arrived at the Dwyer scene shortly after I left and examined the two bodies as they lay in the dirt. I only have one question for him.

"All three of the men, dead and wounded, fired at the cops. That's a given. So, the only question is who fired first. Let me put it like this. Given the wounds these three men received, could they possibly have opened fire after they were hit?"

"The wounded man, possibly. He was taken to the hospital before my arrival. But for the others I would not think so.

Both were struck by multiple rounds and assault rifles do incredible damage. I believe they died instantly."

"I'm not telling you how to do your job, Arshan. But if you could make that observation part of the autopsy report, it'd be a big help."

Arshan doesn't exactly promise to honor my request, but I hang up feeling good. For sure, he won't claim that we fired first, which was the point of the exercise. Everybody on board, telling the same story, over and over again, until the public's tired of hearing it. I drive back to the crime scene, park behind a State Police CSU van. There's nothing left of John Dwyer's house, and not much, I suspect, of John Dwyer. What insanity ran through his brain when he decided to fight it out? Was it suicide by cop? The man had passed eleven of his thirty-five years in prison. He was facing another ten, at the least.

Sgt. Dunbar Hamilton, the State Trooper running the scene, spots me as I step out of the car and walks over. He's middle-aged and good-looking, with the kind of strong features and hard body that widows dream about. Being an out-front lesbian, I'm not interested, but when he made a pass at me six months ago, I was flattered. Now I'm remembering his smile when I turned him down.

"I was hoping you were bi," he explained.

The smile that accompanied the sentiment was engaging and now he displays it again. "Delia, how goes it?"

"Frantic doesn't begin to describe my day. I have a press conference to run and I need to get my act together. But I'm closing in now, so do me a favor. Take a quick look at these photos. Vern took 'em right after we got control of the scene."

I hand over my cell phone and watch Dunny examine the photos Vern uploaded. He takes his time, swiping at the screen with a huge forefinger.

"What're you after?" He announces. "Whatta ya need?"

"The scene was intact when you rolled up?"

"Except for the injured man, yes. He was already in the hospital."

"Okay, I want to know if the scene you found when you got here, the scene you surely videoed, confirms the photos I just showed you."

Another smile. "Yeah, it does. Exactly, as a matter of fact. The positioning of the weapons and shell casings demonstrate that all three discharged their weapons multiple times."

I don't need any more. This afternoon, at a press conference in front of City Hall, I'll communicate a simple story, with a beginning, a middle, and a tragic end. I'll back my story up with Amelia's statement, with the forensic evidence, with the timing of the call I made to John Dwyer (and which I recorded), with witness statements from Vern and Maya. Statements from the others who surrendered would amount to a bonus, but either way, my little story will have no rough edges. My answers to the reporters' questions will be specific and confident. I'll be able to protect my troops without having to lie. Or even fib, or exaggerate, or leave details out. The truth will protect us. For once.

My phone rings as I pull away. It's Danny and I reluctantly answer. "Hey, kid, what's up?"

"I have a paper due tomorrow and I need to get to my laptop at home."

"You have a paper due and you're just getting around to it?"

"No, it's not like that. My notes are ready to go. They're on the laptop, which is back at our house. I mean, I know you're busy, Mom, but Mrs. Taney's car won't start."

"Okay, I'm just leaving the crime scene. I'll pick you up on the way back to the station. Be outside. I don't have time to chat."

I'm close to the Taneys' home when I begin thinking about the child I pulled from the fire. I can't shake that helpless, abandoned cry and I'm hearing it again. Hearing it and asking the same question: What else has she endured in her short life? The glimpse I got of the living conditions inside the Dwyer house met my expectations. Decrepit? Dilapidated? It would take someone with a better vocabulary to describe the dirt and the chaos inside that kitchen.

My own parents were always good to me. We weren't rich, but I never lacked for any necessity, and never feared that I would. I felt safe. I felt protected. Mommy or Daddy would always be there to fix the boo-boo.

"Thanks, Mom. I can't turn this paper in late. Mr. Beaufort doesn't take excuses and I have to keep my grades up. I'm already not doing well in History." He glances in my direction from the corner of his eye as we pull away from the

Taneys'. Calibrating his mother's mood, no doubt. "So, what's happening, you know, with the investigation?"

Danny's already proven himself discreet. I can share with him and not fear his blabbing to his friends. I pass him my cell phone and give him a few minutes to review Vern's photos. They're grisly, of course, and not suitable for children as young as Danny. But I want him to know, especially when it comes to drugs. Danny's sure to face peer pressure in high school. Drugs are everywhere in Baxter. I hope to drive home two lessons. It's a lot easier to say no to the first taste of whatever's being offered, than the second. And the consequences of addiction are so severe that it's better not to risk becoming addicted. Better to walk away even if your so-called pals think you're a punk.

"I've pretty much established that we fired in self-defense," I tell him. "Beyond any serious doubt. The media won't have an angle to exploit."

Danny thinks about it for a minute, then changes the subject. "But you could have been killed. Going into that house."

"True, but it's nothing to worry about. If something happens to me, I'm sure we can find a nice pedophile to raise you."

"Mom, please. You could have been killed."

"Look, Danny, I knew there was a child inside a burning house. I couldn't leave her there. I'm a cop, for Christ's sake. I had to get her out." I give it a few beats, then say, "If you don't mind, I'm gonna make a quick stop. Right now, the girl's with a social worker named Zoe Parillo. I want to stop by Zoe's house and see how the child's doing. I don't even know her name."

I park in front of a single-story brick house on the West Side a few minutes later. The house is nicely trimmed. A blanket of English ivy clings to a fieldstone chimney, a few of its leaves already turning. Dark shutters frame the home's windows and I can see plants lined up on the inner sill of a picture window. The West Side is resolutely middle-class and Zoe's meeting neighborhood expectations. She's maintaining her property.

Danny and I walk to the front door along a flagstone path. I'm trying to decide how to approach Zoe, a woman I barely know, when the door opens and she steps onto a small porch. Her expression betrays a measure of uncertainty. What do I want? Why am I here?

"Hi, Captain." Her eyes shift to Danny. "What can I do for you?"

"Hi, Zoe. This is my son, Danny. I just stopped by because . . . Well, I was passing anyway and I was wondering how the girl's doing. I don't even know her name."

"Me, either. She won't tell me. But why don't you come in and see for yourself. She's sitting on the couch."

Zoe steps aside and I walk past her, followed by Danny. The girl's sitting upright, watching Sesame Street, her eyes unmoving. She's had a bath and her clean hair reveals its true color, a vibrant auburn. She's changed clothes, too, and now wears an oversized red jumper that hangs from her shoulders to her pink socks. A spray of pale freckles drifts from cheek to cheek.

I watch her for a long moment, not saying anything, until she finally looks up and sees me standing by the door. I don't know what I'm expecting, but I'm amazed and a little frightened when she leaps off the couch, flies across the room, and wraps her arms around my legs. I pick her up and hold her against my chest. Her continuing fear is evident in her rapid breathing and the strength of her grip. Does she still see the fire when she closes her eyes? Can she feel the heat? And what must it have been like for her before I made an appearance? Alone in that kitchen.

When Zoe offers coffee, I accept. There's no way I can just walk out of the house, and I find myself thinking maybe I shouldn't have come. Too late now, though.

Danny and I retire to a high-backed couch that's worn just enough to be comfortable. It receives our bodies gently, mine and the little girl I'm still holding. She loosens her grip slightly as we settle down, turning her head just far enough to see a television against the wall on the other side of the small room.

"Do you like Sesame Street?" I ask her.

She looks up at me, confused and even afraid. Is this a test? I pull her closer, imagining what it must be like as she tries to get a grip on her future. Miserable as it may have been, her old life was at least predictable. No more.

Zoe ends the conversation by lowering a tray of coffee and cupcakes onto a table in front of the couch. The home-baked cupcakes are topped with pink frosting and I can't resist. I pick one up and take a small bite.

"You want a taste?" I ask the girl on my lap.

A quick nod earns her a nibble that produces a broad smile and we finish the cupcake together. Ignoring the crumbs still clinging to my shirt, I take a sip of my coffee before pointing to the TV.

"This show is called Sesame Street. It's about a whole group of . . . of creatures living in a community."

Danny joins in without prompting. "The tall yellow one, that's Big Bird. And that other one, he's Cookie Monster. You have to be very careful because if you're not looking, he'll snatch your cookie."

The girl slides off my lap to sit between us. I don't know what she makes of my son, but they seem comfortable with each other and I let them go on as I quietly engage Zoe.

"Any family make an appearance?"

"Nope, not yet." She leans toward me. "Her mom's gone, an overdose about a year ago. I learned that from a neighbor. As for grandparents, aunts and uncles, if they're out there, they haven't come forward. And given the publicity, they should have."

"So where are you? Regarding her custody?"

"In a holding pattern. She'll stay with me for the time being." Zoe smiles as she spreads her hands. "You don't have to worry, Delia. She's a good kid and I intend to use my considerable powers to make sure she gets a break."

I stay for another ten minutes, my arm around the girl. Never having considered myself the motherly type, I'm surprised to find myself entirely comfortable with the feel of her slim body against mine. But I'm dog-tired, as well. It's been a very long day, adrenaline-filled, and I need rest.

When I tell her that I have to go, I expect to find the girl halfway panicked, but she doesn't react until I'm standing. Then she tugs at my sleeve, her head tilted back to look up at me, her expression earnest.

"My name is Emmaline," she announces. "My name is Emmaline and I'm three years old."

I flick the remote to open the car doors as Danny says, "I think she's still frightened, Mom."

"Hardly surprising." I take a moment to put my thoughts together, then add, "Emmaline was standing in a crib when I came into the house. Danny, she's three years old. That's more than old enough to climb out and run through the door. To run to safety."

"Why didn't she do it?"

"She was paralyzed. By fear, Danny. And that's the thing. Once fear takes over, you're totally lost."

CHAPTER EIGHT

ELIZABETH

Every student, male or female, at the various schools I've attended (except, of course, Deval Institute, which passes for a prep school in Baxter) has an ancestor story told in enough detail to guarantee its being as apocryphal as it is apocalyptic. Here is your founding father—never a mother—and what a dirty dog the originator of the family fortune was. It's only by the grace of God that he wasn't hanged before . . .

Could less be expected when a belief that every great fortune begins with a crime is proudly held by the families in our set?

The stories vary in detail, but hardly in content, and I can't help but understand them as origin stories of the sort told by hunter-gatherers the world over. Whether the earth rose from the sea on the back of a giant turtle or the first humans were carried from an unnamed region of the sky on the wings of a giant swan, the point isn't the story itself, but the willingness of the entire tribe to embrace the tale, a common myth being the glue that binds.

The founder of the Bradford fortune was not a Bradford. He was an Irish immigrant named Seamus Shaw who happened to reside in San Francisco when gold was discovered at Sutter's Mill, triggering a migration that quickly raised the population from less than a thousand to twenty-five thousand. Seamus worked the goldfields in that first year, 1848, when nuggets could still be dug out of the riverbank mud, but he was perceptive enough (the ancestor is always a genius) to realize that it couldn't last, not with hundreds of new arrivals every day. No, the real money, the steady money, the generational fortune, was to be accumulated by mining the miners.

Seamus sold pans, shovels, and picks at first, then rockers and Long Tom chain pumps, hoist engines and stamp mills, and clothing as well, and guns and knives. He diversified as the population of San Francisco exploded. They came by sea and by land, from the United States and Mexico, from China and Australia, from England and France, and they needed more than shovels and picks. They needed shelter, saloons and whiskey, available women, gambling dens. Seamus dallied in each of these entrepreneurial fields. Never the face of an organization, always an investor, he built much of the new San Francisco before moving to the goldfields when surface gold became scarce and the industry went underground. Deep mining is expensive, the owners generally consortiums that included Seamus even as the mines jumped in stages from the foothills of the Sierra Nevadas to the incredibly rich goldfields of Bannock, Montana.

Seamus migrated to Louisville after the Civil War, investing his money in rebuilding devastated southern cities and restoring cotton fields to prewar productivity. He had no interest in the fate of the newly freed men and women, instead backing the resurgent planters, economically and politically. Not that our ancestor was a racist—though he probably was—but only because Seamus knew there'd be a single winner in this battle and it wouldn't be the former slaves. In San Francisco, he'd backed the Committee of Vigilance over the Sydney Ducks in a successful effort to destroy an organized rivalry and stake his claim to a piece of the city's politics. That eight were hanged, before and after trials, that dozens were shot, that hundreds were driven out of the city bothered him not at all. As it did not prick his conscience—assuming he had one—to lend his capital to night riders who murdered thousands of Black men and women, who whipped and beat tens of thousands, who consigned generation upon generation of Black Americans to the most degrading poverty imaginable.

At dinner in our Louisville estate, my regular place at the table put me across from a portrait of Seamus Shaw by John Singer Sargent. I often studied that portrait, hoping, perhaps, it would reveal a family secret that would serve as a motivator to guide my life. The portrait remained stubbornly enigmatic, but I was nevertheless impressed by the ferocity in Seamus Shaw's small black eyes, by the aggressive posture, shoulders slightly forward, slightly hunched, by the massive chest, and by the gold-nugget stickpin in his satin puff tie. His beard, as thick and neat as it was full and dark, hung to the top of his collar, too precise to be anything but the creation of the artist.

At age nine, I discovered a Seamus Shaw biography in Father's study, along with a slew of newspaper stories. The bio was written by a commissioned genealogist named Powell Jenson in the early 1970s and it documented the antisocial behavior of which our family was so proud. More innuendo than fact, the newspaper and magazine articles allowed for many interpretations, the worst of which had been approved by Alexander Bradshaw, who commissioned the biography. Alexander stumbled onto the Shaw fortune when Seamus Shaw's grandson produced only a single child, a daughter, who took Alexander to wed.

I find myself thinking of my ancestor as the day progresses. I can't measure this progress, the high windows blocked, the edges sealed, daylight shut out, the darkness of night as well. And though it took some time, I now understand that Tashya is demonstrating my helplessness, my dependency. She knew I'd have to use that bucket, that I couldn't hold out forever, though she might be watching. By then, I'd discovered two small CCTV cameras and I tried to place myself in a (probably imaginary) blind spot between them. An act of defiance, pitiful but necessary. Seamus would understand. Father would not.

I believe that Father models himself after Seamus, thinks of himself as Seamus-like, lives a kind of what-would-

Seamus-do life. But he is not Seamus, and it's not a close call. Father is slim and unconsciously elegant, the product of an elegance-driven education that began at birth. His suits are elegant, his shoes elegant, his ties, the silk handkerchief in his lapel pocket, the Ceylon sapphire on his ring finger, the platinum wedding ring. And even as I try to imagine what Seamus Shaw would do, I know the answer is irrelevant. The issue, it goes without saying, is what Father will do. I exaggerate, of course. No man, no matter how stuffy, can remain forever suited, even bespoke suited, in the twenty-first century. But Father somehow maintains the aura, even in his tennis whites or his fitted golfing shirts, or even at the Farm where he trudges through the muck in handstitched Italian boots.

I'm still exaggerating. Father's closet includes a dozen pairs of designer jeans. Freshly pressed, of course.

We refer to Diomed Farms simply as the Farm, as if to diminish its place in the Bradford's claim to social status, but there's nothing more impressive than a thoroughbred farm that's produced numerous stakes winners, not in Kentucky bluegrass country. Yet even in the Farm's stables with the odor of horses and what they leave behind strong in his nostrils, Father maintains an elegance he won't (or can't) shed, right down to a tweed coat tailored by Anderson and Sheppard.

The same cannot be said of Uncle Henry, who will certainly inject his ultra-opinionated self into the rescue effort. He must take charge because the family, including Uncle

Henry, is cash poor, our expenses and revenue streams drawn from the Bradford Family Foundation, itself created from a gaggle of trusts and sheltered in the Channel Islands. The Foundation owns our home in Louisville, Uncle Henry's, too, and the Farm and the corporation itself.

The inescapable conclusion: Tashya will almost certainly have demanded a ransom greater than Father's cash on hand. And his assets? Even the family cars are owned by the Foundation.

Did I mention that Uncle Henry is the Bradford Foundation's Director and controls its funds? He can do anything except dissolve the Foundation.

I find myself reaching for a cell phone I no longer possess, as I have done a dozen times already. Habits die hard. Not that I'm one of those teens who pass hour upon hour bouncing between Instagram, Snapchat, and TikTok, and the rest of the mass congregation sites. These haven't been exactly forbidden to me, but some years ago, Mom and Father sat me down for one of those adult-preparation talks they foisted on me from time to time. Both my parents believed, absolutely, that the most popular social media sites store every keystroke. No matter their denials, their assurances of privacy. And they'd reveal every letter and punctuation point, if they could monetize private information without fearing civil liability or criminal prosecution. Even worse, should the wrong man or woman ascend to the presidency, they could be made to open their cloud accounts.

The consolation prize was one of the social websites catering to our set. The site allowed me to communicate with my peers, one-on-one or through groups centered on some field of interest. If I remember correctly, the designer-handbag group was especially popular with girls my age. And the best part? Membership accounts were, and are, by invitation only.

Phone aside, my thoughts run back and forth, skipping from Seamus to Father to Uncle Henry, though I make an honest effort to interest myself in the video games and the romance novels left by Tashya. I'm still at it when I hear the sharp clack of a withdrawn dead bolt and the creak of a door turning on its unoiled hinges. Then footsteps on the stairs, heavy footsteps, male footsteps. I'm instantly terrified, the emotion almost unknown to me, an evil spirit that's been waiting all these years to pounce. Its claws now sink deep, every cell on fire, my thoughts running rampant, rape, torture, death, my brave front collapsing on itself, a house of cards, a fairy tale more suited to a toddler.

Quentin appears in stages as he opens the door at the bottom of the stairs, legs, torso, dull, dull face, eyes somehow malignant and resigned. I know he'll hurt me if given the opportunity, but the set of his mouth tells me, Not yet, not yet.

"Upstairs," he announces. "Now."

I feel his eyes running over my body as I pass him, as I climb the stairs, him close behind, fearing his hands, but when I arrive at the top, I find a bucket of fried chicken and a side of mac and cheese, along with a small salad, on a folding table. There's a bottle of Coke and a pile of tiny napkins alongside.

The odor hits me, a solid punch, as unexpected and obtrusive, in its own way, as Quentin's thoroughly repulsive gaze.

"You wish to use bathroom?" Tashya's sitting next to a table ten feet away, a handgun resting in her lap. She points to an open door, then to a five-gallon plastic gas can. "Use water in can to fill tank for flushing."

I try to repress my first reaction, relief bordering on gratitude, but I can't, even though I'm sure this is again about dependency, about docility, about cooperation. I'm still at the center of this storm having not yet assured my parents that I'm alive, still in one piece and please pay the ransom before I'm not.

Tashya motions me to a chair and smiles a smile as cold as the winter light. Her gaze rakes my features, seeking an answer. Will I cooperate fully, or do I need further convincing, perhaps a taste of what Quentin might do to me if I prove overly rebellious?

"Eat."

A command, unquestionably, but that first taste, the spices, the grease, the crunch, seems miraculous, a reawakening of the desire for life, and I shift back and forth between the chicken, the mac and cheese, the salad, occasionally glancing (but not too obviously) at Tashya. I suspect that properly made up, her hair styled, her slanted eyes enhanced, in six-inch pumps and a little black dress that falls to mid-thigh, she'd be quite attractive. But as it stands, she appears utterly nondescript, the housewife you didn't notice in the supermarket checkout line, and I have to wonder if the drudge persona isn't the result of a major effort.

CHAPTER NINE

ELIZABETH

My stomach full, I lean back in the chair and shift my weight on the hard seat, from a numb buttock to a buttock soon to be numb. I'm not afraid now, my fear (irrationally because I'm pretty sure that Tashya murdered the Trooper) dropping away after Quentin steps outside.

"So, you are . . . accustoming?" Tashya asks.

"To what?"

"To the situation? I will not harm you if you play the part, yes?"

"I see. Once you're paid off, you'll just let me go."

"Yes, in a place very far from the nearest phone. In a place many miles from Baxter."

Most likely, I should keep my big mouth shut, but I don't. I'm too . . . bitter is the right word, a foul bitterness inspired by Tashya's patronizing tone. As though taking this murderess at her word is a perfectly natural thing to do.

"I've seen your face," I tell her. "I can identify you."

"Not to worry."

"If I'm not to worry, what am I supposed to do instead? I know how these things work."

"Then please tell me. How do these . . . things . . . work?" Tashya's smile is imperious, the smile of a boss instructing an underling. "You Americans, so naive, so failing in imagination. You think whole world is right here, playing by simple rule: if you have wrong done to you, then you call police and they ride to rescue. But what happens if police are the criminals? What if you call them and they do nothing because you are not rich and connected? Or because police have a . . . relationship? Yes, a relationship with your enemy? Then you have only family for protection. This I know from my own life. There is only family. Nothing else. But you Bradfords? From six weeks ago, on Bradford Group website, you brag about new project. One-point-six-billion-dollar car factory and Christopher Bradford will lead the team and whole family will relocate to bid on biggest private construction job in United States. That day I drove to Baxter."

"My family protects me too."

"So you think they did not call police or FBI?"

"No."

The windows are growing darker and I wonder if Tashya will turn on a light, or if the lights work. Stupid of me because there's no reason for Tashya to remain in the house once I'm safely confined. Even the CCTV cameras in my little prison can probably be monitored by phone or computer. I know something about the issue, thanks to my time with Paolo

Yoma. The cameras on our sites are encased in large metal boxes, their presence a deterrent. But much smaller devices exist, devices the size of a fly.

"I knew they would call the FBI," Tashya explains. "And I know the FBI will tell them to pay. That is safest course. Pay and we will let her go. And why? Because ransom is to be paid in Bitcoin to a virtual wallet that will vanish as soon as Bitcoin is received. Then I will also vanish. To Kazakhstan, Moldavia, Rumania, Uzbekistan . . . there is no end to this list of lands where cops can be persuaded not to look, even if I am somehow identified. So, there is no reason to harm you and your safe return encourages next victim to pay. Encourages FBI to advise payment."

"And if they don't?"

"Don't?"

"If my family doesn't pay. Or can't, at least not immediately."

"What do you say?"

Now I'm looking into Tashya's eyes but there's nothing there beyond mild interest. If it doesn't turn out, she'll still retreat to that same corrupt and familiar terrain. Leaving my body behind.

"How much," I want to know, "did you ask for?"

She decides to answer, perhaps because she senses that I'm willing to cooperate. "Ten million dollars."

"My father doesn't have ten million dollars, Tashya, or anything close to it. Our capital is controlled by the Bradford Family Foundation. The Foundation owns our home, owns our cars, owns the family emeralds Mother wears to the Foundation's galas."

Tashya takes a moment this time, then nods to herself, decision made. "Reward, yes, for ransom paid. Hostage is released. This is lesson for next family and for FBI. And if ransom is not paid? How could there not be punishment? You father must find money from your . . . Foundation. But he will do this for family. Family is what matters."

We're traveling at high speed along I-80, in the back of a minivan with darkened side windows. Tashya's voice fills the back where the two of us sit. Quentin's behind the wheel, his focus on the road. He hasn't uttered a word since ordering me out of the basement. Because he doesn't want to draw attention to himself? Because he was instructed to keep his mouth shut? Because he's too busy envisioning the treats he has in store for me? Either way, I'm having a hard time imagining Quentin vanishing into the Uzbek countryside.

"So, I will tell you this story," Tashya suddenly declares, "to show importance of family in this other world. I am fourteen years old, walking alone from school when a car pulls up and I am dragged inside. Where do I go? First, I am put in back of a truck with two other girls and we are driven three days to an ocean port. Then we go by ship to a place I don't recognize. We are there one day before being put in second truck and driven through desert to a brothel in Tel Aviv where I am made to prostitute myself for two years. Once I escape, but police return me to what they call my sponsor, Avram, so I am giving up, yes? I am wishing to be dead, but afraid to kill myself. Then one day Avram calls me into the front room and I find my cousin and uncle standing there. They have been searching all this time, never giving up, until they buy me back and take me home. This is family as most people in this world know it. Do you understand? To pimps I am not family. I am livestock, a valuable animal to be kept alive and healthy enough to perform. They will sell me over and over, drag me from one land to another, dump me when I am too old to be of use. In what country? This doesn't matter. Only family matters."

I don't necessarily believe a word she tells me—I'm not family, after all—but I can't see that it matters because I know she's essentially right. My family understands money and only money, financial transactions, and so they will eventually pay, if only to preserve an image, both internal and external. The Bradford Group employs twenty people in its PR department. I know this because they keep asking me to volunteer at some inner-city food bank, distributing off-brand corn flakes in oversized boxes.

"We're fifty miles out." Quentin finally speaks, his tone irritated, if not actually aggrieved. "How far do we need to go? Every minute on the road is a risk."

"Ah, business. And we were having such good conversations." Tashya slips a phone wallet out of her purse, the kind that blocks GPS signals, but doesn't open it immediately. "In here is throwaway cell phone. You are going to call your family on their house phone. I do not know who will answer but you will tell them you are unharmed and they must find money and pay ransom. You must do this quickly, so please think first what you are going to say."

I stare out through the darkened window for a few seconds, watching a tangled thicket of vines and shrubs rush by. Yes, I'm alive and being reasonably well treated. That's the easy part, and if the message was motivating, I'd leave it there. But it's not.

"Okay, I'm ready."

Tashya opens the wallet, removes my phone in its royal-blue case, punches in a number, and hands me the phone. "Quick," she says.

Father's voice sounds in my ear a few seconds later. "Elizabeth?"

"Yes, it's me and I only have a few seconds. I haven't been hurt, Father, and I know they'll release me if the ransom is paid. But if you don't, they'll dump my body next to some public highway where it's sure to be found. Please, Father. Please."

I hang up without being told. Tashya takes the phone from my hand and slides it into the wallet. Her smile is frankly admiring. "You have done well, Elizabeth. I could not have done better. Sure to be found? This is beautiful."

Sufficiently beautiful to earn me a privilege I might not have been granted. An hour later, having returned on dead-straight roads that ran between endless cultivated fields, I walk into the darkened house. Tashya hands me a tiny flashlight and points to the gas can filled with water. "Use bathroom," she tells me, "then downstairs."

I find my basement prison exactly as I left it save for two details. The bucket has been emptied and the nail I pulled from the drywall has been removed. There's one other player in this game. At least.

CHAPTER TEN

DELIA

Four-thirty in the morning and I'm up, showered, and dressed. No big deal because the Baxter Police Department is going to execute a pair of search warrants this morning and we need to be on-site before sunrise. No, what's different this morning is that Danny's with me in the kitchen. He's frying sausages and eggs for a breakfast on the fly. I think he's frightened. I was all over the evening news yesterday, me and Emmaline dashing away from the flaming house. Only a minute or two later and I would have been in the house when it exploded. That would have left Danny with . . .

I do this every couple of weeks, the guilt routine. Remembering all the times I left Danny with a babysitter while I worked overtime. And not to advance my career, but to pay our most basic expenses. Now there's enough for a few extras, like Danny's baseball camp. But I'm still renting and my car is six years old and I ran up my credit card last week buying Danny's winter clothes. The kid won't stop growing.

Danny's reached the age where he understands the economics of running a household, but that doesn't make up for when he was four, five, six and had no one to lean on when I wasn't around. Or when he spent more time in daycare centers or with sitters than he did with me. And it doesn't make up for the times he went to sleep with me at work, the mornings when he awakened with me still at work.

"Mom, what do you think is going to happen to her?"

My son's voice lifts me free of my pity party. "Her who?"

Danny turns back to the stove and begins to flip the sausages with a pair of tongs. I'm expecting a sarcastic response, but I don't get one. "Emmaline," he says.

"I won't lie to you, right? You know that." I wait a few seconds, but Danny's back remains turned. "Emmaline Dwyer's father was killed in the house, probably before the fire. Her mother divorced her husband three years ago, then died after an overdose. Zoe thinks Emmaline might have relatives back in Kentucky, but doesn't know who or where they are."

"That means she's all alone. Emmaline doesn't have anybody."

"She has Zoe."

"For how long?" Finally, the sausages flipped, he looks back to me. "It's not fair. She didn't do anything."

Danny's got it right. Emmaline didn't do anything. But in this case, innocence will not protect her. And me? I've come to believe that if life was really fair, I wouldn't have a job.

It's still fully dark when we take off, a pair of black SUVs headed for two destinations. I'm not expecting trouble at either one. Vern's crew is running up on a pair of brothers who deal kilos of marijuana, along with an occasional hundred-dose vial of LSD. My crew is headed for the home of Kevin Zeno, a major pill dealer. Neither target is violent, according to the informants who set them up, which is how Chief Black wants it. Enough drama, he explained, what with bodies in the morgue, me running through the litter with a toddler in my arms, and a secret kidnapping.

I've got Cade Barrow, Jerome Meeks, and Maya Kinsley with me. Meeks is behind the wheel, with Kinsley alongside. I'm sitting in the back next to Cade Barrow, wondering exactly what he's doing in our little town. Barrow was special forces in the Army and his assignments are classified. There's no way to find out what he did or didn't do, but putting a bullet in John Dwyer appears to have had no effect on him. Does that qualify him to lead the SWAT Team I plan to organize in the near future? Or disqualify him?

It's six o'clock when Meeks turns onto Packer Road in the Norwood section of Baxter and our target comes into view. Zeno's ranch home is dark, lit only by a streetlight at the end of the block. I can feel the tension building as Meeks pulls to the curb a hundred yards from the house. So many things can go wrong on either side when the guns come out.

"Okay, one more time. Jerome, you'll handle the ram. Once the door's open, we'll clear the living room first, all together. There's a master bedroom to our left, a kitchen in the back, and two small bedrooms accessed by a short hallway to our right. Maya and Cade, you'll secure the kitchen and bedrooms to the right. Hopefully, they'll be empty. John and I will secure the master bedroom. No hesitation, hear me? I ring the bell, I announce, 'Police,' John takes out the door. Then it's inside and right to work, like we rehearsed it last night."

I've reached the point where I expect things to go wrong, the instant glitch that obliterates all that careful planning. Not this time. I ring the bell, yell, "Police with a search warrant," John takes down the door with a single swing of the ram and we're inside. We burst into the master bedroom a few seconds later. Kevin Zeno is sitting up in the bed, hands already in the air. An unidentified woman lying next to him appears frozen, eyes wide and unmoving.

"On the floor. Now."

Zeno complies instantly, but I have to yank the woman out of the bed. She's wearing a T-shirt and panties and obviously not armed. Zeno's naked except for a pair of shiny blue boxers. I hold both of them on the floor while Meeks secures the closet and bathroom.

"Clear," he finally says.

His voice is immediately followed by Maya's. "We got a kid in here," she yells from the other side of the house.

"My daughter," the woman on the floor says.

"And you are?"

"Carol Sulottis."

"Do you live here, Carol?"

"No, I have an apartment on the West Side."

Her lucky day, though she doesn't know it and I'm in no hurry to tell her. "Okay, so here's what's happening next. First, you and Kevin will get dressed. Then you're going to walk into the living room and take a seat on the couch while the house is being searched. And no bullshit. I'm sure you heard what happened yesterday. Don't make me play that song again."

Maya's cradling an infant in her arms when the four of us step into the living room. By some miracle, the child is sleeping. Carol Sulottis instinctively moves toward her daughter, only to be restrained by Meeks, who waits for my nod before releasing her. I can't say that the mother-daughter reunion is all that touching, what with the child barely opening her eyes and Carol's pupils reduced to pinpoints. But a moment later, Zeno, Carol, and her daughter are on the couch and our guns are re-holstered. Friends now.

It goes quickly from there. First, Jerome retrieves a bolt cutter and a video camera from the SUV. He lays the bolt cutter on the floor and passes the camera to Maya. An inlaid cabinet sits atop a rug near the front wall. About four feet high, the cabinet has a skirt at the bottom that reaches almost to the floor, making it impossible to see underneath. I'm standing behind the couch when Cade and Jerome move the cabinet to the hallway and roll up the rug. The exposed trapdoor is exactly where the informant said it would be. Cade kneels to lift the trapdoor's lid, revealing a metal box between the joists. The box is over a foot long and secured with a combination lock.

"My sister," Zeno says. "My fucking sister."

I don't have to warn Zeno about keeping his mouth shut because we don't have any evidence. Not yet. But I read his rights to him anyway. With Jerome, Cade, and Maya as witnesses. "You wanna open the box, Kevin? Or should I use the bolt cutter?"

Zeno keeps his eyes on the carpet, but his tone is strong enough. "I'm gonna wait for a lawyer."

The Zeno house is far removed from John Dwyer's. The furniture's old and mismatched, and the walls need painting, but the place is neat enough. No dishes piled in the sink, no fast-food containers or liquor bottles on the floor. The same can be said of Zeno, Carol Sulottis, and her child. The girl's dressed in a clean onesie covered with pink and red butterflies. A chubby little thing, her eyes are clear and alert. Zeno looks healthy enough, too, and I have to think he's not so deeply addicted that he can't recognize his own interests. According to my informant, who is indeed his sister, Zeno holds an engineering degree from the University of Illinois. For all the good it's done him.

Meeks cuts the lock with the bolt cutter, lifts the lid, and pulls out vial after vial. "Percocet, Molly, Oxy, Xanax, Dilaudid, morphine . . ."

I wait until the vials are returned to the little box before moving on. "Cade, I want you to search the rest of the house. Maya, I want you to record the search. There has to be a second stash, one he used for daily transactions. Find it. As for you, Kevin, you are under arrest. Stand up, turn around, and put your hands behind your back."

I expect him to comply without any bullshit protests and he does. He's a good-looking kid, probably in his late twenties. Stoned, of course, his pupils no more than periods at the end of a sentence. Still, his eyes reveal a deep regret and I sense, as I listen to cuffs ratchet down, that he's seen this coming. He's seen it coming, but just couldn't face withdrawal. Or find a place to rehab. The waiting list for the only rehab facility in Baxter is longer than Kevin's likely sentence.

"Jerome, take Kevin outside and call for a patrol car with a cage in back. Put him inside and have him transported to the house. You ride along, Jerome, to make a hundred percent sure that he's properly booked."

My phone rings as Meeks leads Zeno outside. It's Vern. His raid has also gone well. They've recovered two kilos of weed, several hundred tabs of acid, and have three under arrest. I hang up without a lot of small talk. There's work to be done here and I'm standing directly behind Carol Sulottis and the child she holds in her arms. Neither of us speaks. We simply wait until Cade and Maya return.

"You find anything?"

"Yeah," Maya replies, "maybe six or seven vials in a dresser drawer." She taps the camera. "It's all in here."

"That's it? Only what's in the drawer?"

"Yup."

"Then we're pretty much finished here. I just need to speak with Ms. Sulottis for a moment, so . . ." I wait for Cade and

Maya to walk into the front yard, then lean forward until my mouth is a foot from Carol's ear. I'm still behind the couch and she's still looking away.

"I'm not going to arrest you," I tell her.

Her breath comes out in a guttural heap, "Uhhhh," and she begins to cry. The girl stirs in her arms, but then falls back asleep.

"I'm not going to arrest you and I'm not going to tell you that changes are coming to this city. Like good jobs with benefits and a pension to those who can pass a drug test. And I'm not going to tell you that if I did arrest you, there's a good chance you'd lose custody of your child. No, I'm not gonna tell you any of that because you already know it. What I'm gonna do instead is ask for a couple of favors. First, I want you to tell any other dealers you know, your junkie friends, too, that what happened yesterday and today is only the beginning. I've got a list of addresses that runs on for a couple of typewritten pages and I intend to raid every fucking one. So, if you don't wanna see Captain Mariola coming through your door with a gun in her hand, shut it down."

"That's it?"

"No, one more thing, a message to your boyfriend. Kevin doesn't have a record. Or didn't before today. That means he can help himself out by cooperating. A little courtesy will go a long way."

CHAPTER ELEVEN

DELIA

"Good work, Delia, you and Vern both," Chief Black tells me. "But I'm surprised that you didn't arrest the woman."

I'm sitting in the Chief's office, reporting on the morning's activities. "No drugs in plain view, boss, and she has her own residence. So there was nothing to arrest her for."

True as far as it goes, but most cops would have arrested her anyway. Bust her and let the prosecutors and her lawyer worry about the technicalities. Even if she was never indicted, I could have used the threat of prosecution to extract information. And I might have done exactly that, except for the baby.

"So, Chief, the kidnapping? Anything changed?"

"The kidnappers made contact last night. Or, Elizabeth Bradford made contact. She says she's unharmed and please be ready to pay the money. The kidnappers didn't speak."

"Who'd you put on it?"

"John Meacham's our liaison."

"The Dink? Are you kidding?"

"Delia, the situation is exactly what you anticipated. Meacham sat behind a desk all day. He wasn't briefed until early this morning and the Feds only told him what I just told you. We're out of it." He paused long enough to run the tip of his forefinger along the sutures in his head, as if surprised to find them there. "Anyway, there's good news too. The city's scheduled to receive the first inflow of federal money by the beginning of October. That'll mean expanding the force by fifteen officers. We'll be receiving a pair of armored vehicles as well, probably Lenco BearCats. No more headlong charges into enemy fire."

It's almost noon and I'm famished. I exit the station house on Polk Avenue and circle City Hall to emerge at the northern end of City Hall Green. More dirt than grass, the Green is roughly the size of a football field, including the end zones. Not exactly Golden Gate Park, true, but the Green is slated to be the center of our revitalized downtown. Just now, it's planting time and three eighteen-wheeler flatbeds bearing an assortment of trees are being unloaded by a crew of city workers. I stop for a moment to acknowledge their greetings. I've become a local celebrity since the video from the fire hit the air. The situation has left me with a bad taste in my mouth. The talk should be about Emmaline, about the child and her fate.

The red-brick shops bordering the Green range from three to six stories high. Long neglected, if not abandoned, they were the pride of the city when first built a hundred years ago. That era's due for a comeback. The soot-black facades are being power washed, a bay window has been pulled from one building, and masons are working on a line of columns above the top windows of another. I'm seeing the Green six months from now surrounded by thriving boutiques and trendy bars, and maybe one of those fusion restaurants, Filipino-Peruvian or Nigerian-Hawaiian. I'm also imagining a digital security camera attached to each building. The Baxter City Council has already passed the appropriate regulation. We're joining the twenty-first century.

Maxwell Plank, the Courthouse Diner's owner and host, finds me a booth in the back of the restaurant, away from the other diners. As he leaves, a middle-aged waitress named Haley, Max's cousin, drops a glass of water and a menu on the table.

"How you doin' today, Captain?" she asks. Haley was thrilled when I made Captain. She told me that she'd always wanted to be a cop, but she was afraid of guns and thugs. "And how's that little girl? Whole town's talkin' about nothin' else."

"All good for now. She's with Zoe Parillo." I watch her walk away, her ample backside swaying from side to side, the effect nearly insolent. Word out there is that Hayley suffers no fools.

A few minutes later, as I sip at an iced tea sweetened with honey, Vern slides into the booth across from me.

"Problem," I tell him, "in Maryville at the end of the week."

"About the Deputy?"

"Yeah, the funeral."

Our schedule calls for a task force of Maryville County Deputy Sheriffs and Baxter cops to raid a colony of bikers living on a derelict farm that straddles the border between us. Mostly Wolf Lowriders, the bikers are dealing meth from the farm, but not the home-cooked variety. The speed they sell is supplied by a Mexican cartel at a price well below the product offered by home-cookers. Our assault is designed to demonstrate our serious intentions. The farm is well guarded.

It's not going to happen, though. Not at the end of the week. A Maryville Deputy Sheriff named Powell York was shot to death last night, probably in the course of a routine traffic stop, though no one's certain and there are no suspects yet. Maryville's Sheriff, Martin Leland, has scheduled the Deputy's funeral for Friday morning. I'll have to be there, Chief Black too.

"I know Sheriff Leland," Vern says. "He coached my Pop Warner football team. Way back when. I knew Powell York too. A cautious man, far as I remember, and it don't seem like him to be caught off guard. But if he was killed in the course of a routine traffic stop, he never called in to his dispatcher. Leland told me there's no evidence. No shell casings, no tire impressions, no nothing."

It's the one you don't see coming that kills you and we all know it, Vern included. You're distracted, or someone comes out of a closet, or shoots from a darkened window, or you simply misjudge the threat. Then you get the Honor Guard Funeral with a couple of hundred cops in attendance.

We lapse into silence for a moment, then Vern looks up at me, smiling his lopsided smile. Never one to dwell on the depressing aspects of the policing profession, he's about to lighten the conversation.

"So, this morning, I take the husband to one side after we secure the scene. I've read him his rights and now I'm testing the waters. Will he turn? Become a CI? Meanwhile, he beats me to the punch."

"How?"

"He offers me two thousand dollars if I let him skate, five thousand if I let him take the weed and the acid with him. I'm tempted to ask where the money's hidden, which would mean another charge, but it's not worth the effort. The kid hasn't asked for a lawyer and I'll take another shot at him when we get to the house. So I dump him on a chair in the living room and take his wife into the kitchen. First words out of her mouth, she propositions me. And I'm thinkin', `What next, the fucking dog?' "

I'm smiling now, remembering a time back in Virginia when I was propositioned by a teenie streetwalker named Fancy-Nancy. I was semi-closeted at the time and believed I was successfully projecting a hetero image. Yeah, right.

"So, I walk her back into the living room and she shakes her head when her husband comes into view. 'Okay,' he says, 'I'm ready to cooperate if you cut my old lady loose. Whatever you wanna know.' "

"Did you take the deal?"

"Nope. I charged the both of 'em." Vern looks behind him for Haley. He's obviously hungry. "The way I'm thinkin', Delia, a couple of days in a cage and they'll beg for a chance to rat on their parents."

CHAPTER TWELVE

DELIA

I'm about to ask if there were children involved, when a man I've never seen before approaches our table. He appears to be in his late thirties and something in his bearing has me thinking ex-military. But he seems relaxed and his small eyes project confidence.

"May I speak with you for moment?"

He hands me a business card as he asks. I scan it quickly.

PAOLO YOMA
DIRECTOR OF SITE SECURITY
THE BRADFORD GROUP

I pass the card to Vern and nod to Yoma. As he fetches a chair from an unoccupied two-top, Haley walks up. Vern orders an open turkey sandwich and I settle for a Greek salad when I would've preferred a deluxe cheeseburger with a pile of the diner's garlic fries. I haven't found the courage to get on a scale, but my belt's getting harder and harder to buckle.

Yoma shakes his head when Haley looks in his direction. I appreciate the gesture. He hasn't been invited to join us.

"I've come from the Bradford house." Yoma's long face and longer nose seem vaguely mournful, but his tone betrays nothing beyond an eagerness to tell his tale. "From Mrs. Bradford, particularly. She tells me that's she spoken with you."

I glance at Vern, half expecting him to warn me off, but his expression betrays keen interest. He's a detective, after all.

"You'd be better off speaking with our liaison," I say. "That would be Detective John Meacham."

"With all due respect, Captain, Meacham's been kicked to the curb, which is exactly where he wants to be. He spends his time watching videos on his phone. The way he shuts it off whenever someone approaches leads me to believe he's watching porn."

"Does it matter? Is he somehow neglecting his duties? Or is nonfunctioning functionary the role assigned to him by federal investigators?"

Yoma takes a minute to think it over, briefly closing his eyes, then changes the subject. "I met Elizabeth Bradford at a construction site last year. Her father likes to bring his children to jobsites. Probably his idea of toughening them up. Anyway, the kids were given free reign while he was in meetings and for some reason they attached themselves to me. The girl . . ." He stops again for a moment. "Elizabeth's a high school senior, at fifteen. Brilliant? I'll concede that. But arrogant doesn't begin to describe her moment-to-moment attitude. And there's a sadness inside her, too, a loneliness and a yearning she can't conceal, though she tries hard enough. The girl has no close friends, at least according to her mother and . . ."

"Mr. Yoma," I interrupt, "worthiness has nothing to do with our response to kidnappings. To be blunt, the Bradfords have made their position clear. They're going with the FBI's hostage-negotiating team."

"You're wrong about the family, Captain. Henry Bradford made that decision. Elizabeth's mother feels differently and her father vacillates. But Henry Bradford, the older brother, must be obeyed. Henry commands the Bradford Group and he's a bully to his bones."

Yoma's gaze withdraws for a moment and I know he's reconsidering his approach. I haven't told him to get lost, but I'm finding it hard to believe that he expects me to launch a parallel investigation. Make that parallel and secret. Then he blinks twice and nods to himself.

"The FBI's putting all its eggs in one basket. Pay the ransom and Elizabeth's kidnappers will release their hostage. The Bitcoin's the key. Now I know that ransomware gets all the publicity, but according to Special Agent Smith, hundreds of kidnappings take place every year, mostly in Europe, South America, and the Middle East. These kidnappers are professionals. They know it's almost impossible to trace Bitcoin before it vanishes. Meantime, the perps retreat to countries like Albania and Georgia where they have large, extended families and the cops are for sale. Although I don't have details, I'm told this particular gang operates out of Georgia and their MO is well known to international police agencies."

"If the gang is well known, why haven't they been arrested?"

"How do cartels operate with impunity in Mexico? How did Mafia families operate in Sicily? Police corruption, payoffs to politicians, geographical isolation, a general indifference, all of the above."

Yoma stops abruptly as Haley approaches with our lunches. He waits until she smiles and says, as she always does, "Enjoy." Then he starts back up like he never stopped. "There's been no serious effort to locate Elizabeth's kidnappers. Not enough time, that seems to be the consensus. Pay and hope. If it goes bad? Well, you can't win 'em all."

Vern's sawing away at his open-faced sandwich, smiling to himself. I'm looking down at a stuffed grape leaf I'd prefer to be in my mouth. But I can't tell Yoma to kiss off. He's too well connected for that.

"How are they wrong?" I finally ask. "About there not being enough time?"

Yoma's grin tells me that I just swallowed his dangled bait. He raises his spread hands. "No way did Elizabeth's kidnappers target her *after* she got to Baxter. Like the Feds claim, not enough time. Not for meticulous professionals. And we have to hope the kidnappers really are professionals. If it's just a couple of local crazies, the odds against Elizabeth's survival are very long."

Vern breaks in, obviously intrigued. "If the kidnappers targeted the Bradfords in Louisville, how did they manage to snatch and conceal her in Baxter?"

Yoma fiddles with his phone for a moment, then offers it to me. "A good question," he remarks, "with a good answer."

I'm looking at a screenshot from the Bradford Foundation's Facebook page. The headline is plain enough: ON THE WAY TO BAXTER! The story beneath is equally simple. The Bradford Group will bid on the construction of a Nissan plant in the City of Baxter, along with the demolition of existing structures on the site. Winning the bid, given the economic turndown, is the Group's number one priority. So vital, in fact, that Christopher Bradford and his family will relocate to Baxter and lead the Group's bid team.

I'm looking for some bit of information I don't already know and it takes a moment to find the even smaller print beneath the headline. The posting is dated August 1, more than six weeks ago. I pass the phone to Vern, then finally dig into my salad. I think I know where Yoma's headed. Elizabeth's kidnappers had ample time to prepare. In fact, it's likely they were ready to snatch either of the Bradford children, or even Mrs. Bradford, whenever an opportunity presented itself. Right here in Baxter.

"The Bradford residence in Louisville is a fortress," Yoma explains. "I personally supervised an upgrade to their security system about two years ago. Gaining access would require a military assault. I expected to provide the same level of security for their house in Baxter. But the home they're in now wasn't their first choice. They originally bid on a home six blocks away. When that deal fell through a few days before the signing, they chose the house on Thornberry Street. That was only three weeks ago and I couldn't install the customized hardware before the scheduled move. I tried to convince Christopher Bradford to delay his arrival, but the man wouldn't listen." Yoma pulls back, smiling as he shakes his head. "I spent ten years in the military, an MP working perimeter security at overseas bases. I served under officers you could talk to and officers who demanded unquestioning obedience. Once he makes a decision, Bradford expects obedience, stops listening. Click your hells and shut your mouth, a technique he surely learned from his brother."

I've made it through the cucumbers and the shriveled black olives by the time Yoma rolls to a stop. I'm supposed to say something, but I don't know what it is. Yoma's plea should have gone to the Chief, the only cop in Baxter with the authority to buck the FBI.

"I don't wanna be rude, Mr. Yoma, but I'd appreciate your cutting to the bottom line. What do you expect from us? Us meaning the Baxter Police Department in general and me in particular."

"First, do we agree that no one came into that house and dragged Elizabeth out?"

"Yes."

"So, she must have left to meet someone she knew, however briefly."

Vern speaks up, surprising me. "Unless she left to meet her kidnappers. Unless she's in on the abduction." He jabs his fork into what remains of his sandwich. "Something that occurred to me this morning. If she went out to meet someone, why hasn't he or she come forward?"

"First thing, Elizabeth's the Bradford heir apparent. Her uncle has no children and Sherman's indifferent, not to mention unstable. Elizabeth also has a trust fund that puts four hundred dollars per week in her pocket. To spend as she sees fit. That amount will increase every year, in addition to compensation for just about every expense, from hair styling and pedicures to the car she'll drive and the dwelling she'll occupy. No, detective, Elizabeth left that night to meet someone and I think I know who that someone is."

CHAPTER THIRTEEN

DELIA

It's three o'clock in the afternoon. I'm in the front seat of Vern's Ford Explorer, headed for Baxter Medical Center. We're both off the clock, having signed out early, acceptable only because our day started before dawn. Paolo Yoma's in the back, responding to Vern's question.

"Yoma? That's an odd name. Where's your family from?"

"We've moved around over the past few generations, but we're originally from Syria. We left in 1951. More than thirty of us."

"At one time?"

"Yeah, all at once. The situation in Syria had become intolerable." Yoma's tone seems oddly wistful, though I detect a bitter note underneath. "We're Christians, Detective. We speak Arabic, French, Hebrew, and English to the outside world. Between ourselves, we speak Aramaic, the language Jesus spoke when he walked upon the Earth."

We stop for a light and Vern looks back over his shoulder. "Is that how long your family's lived in Syria? For two thousand years?"

"Longer, much longer. According to family legend, we survived the Assyrians and the Persians and the Romans."

"Yet you finally left?"

"Not all of us, and we didn't leave. We fled." Yoma's looking at Vern, but keeps glancing in my direction. "Islam generally tolerated Christians, especially in Palestine, until 1948, the year Israel became a nation. Bad break for Jews living in Syria. The smart ones moved over the border into Israel. The ones left behind were ruthlessly persecuted. To the surprise of not one citizen of the country, nor anybody living in Israel. Collective responsibility is what it's called. Every Jew responsible for the actions of any Jew."

A horn sounded behind us, a quick, polite beep, and Vern pulled off. Yoma wore his lopsided smile, but his eyes had turned inward. He settled against the seat as he continued his story.

"We were stupid. That's the heart of it. And I mean the entire family, including fourth and fifth cousins. We never expected our Arab neighbors to turn on us, but they did. Infidels of any sort became the enemy and the persecution never let up. My university-educated grandparents lost their government jobs and could only find menial work after that. Then, in late 1950, we lost our home too. That was the last straw and we knew we had to get out."

"To the United States?"

"No, under the quota system back then, immigrants from countries like Syria weren't welcome in America. Simple as that. We emigrated to Argentina, joining a small contingent of Yomas who'd gone before us. Juan Péron was the country's president at the time, a ruthless bastard if ever there was one." The smile again. "But you'll likely be more familiar with his wife, Evita."

"As in, 'Don't cry for me?' "

"Exactly. Now we did well in Argentina, no denying the fact, but the goal was always America. America meant safety, a chance to rebuild, a chance that didn't come until LBJ signed the Immigration Act in 1965. Even then, it took another six years before my parents secured their entry visas and left. I was born nine years later."

"That makes you an American, born and bred."

"And patriotic enough to join the army after high school, figuring I'd use my GI benefits to pay for college. Instead, my training in perimeter security, especially advanced electronics, led to job offers I couldn't refuse. Over the next few years, I made my way up to Assistant Security Manager at a Bradford Group site in Brazil where a road grader went missing overnight. Thirty-five thousand pounds, four hundred thousand dollars, vanished into the Amazon rainforest." Yoma pauses long enough to draw a breath. He's speaking fast, as if expecting us to shut him down. But I'm willing to indulge the man. Elizabeth's companion that night, he'd correctly reasoned, couldn't have been left to call for help ten seconds after they took off with her. He or she had to be taken out. Permanently? Yoma tried the morgue first, but the only admission in the past four days was a ninety-five-year-old woman. The hospitals came next, with Baxter Medical Center first on his list.

A twenty-dollar bill passed to an orderly bought him the information he'd carried to me and Vern. So, double kudos, enough for me to endure the charm offensive.

"When I was called back to Louisville, I knew the bosses at headquarters intended to fire me. The Site Manager was already gone. But I didn't wait for the axe to fall. I presented them with scaled drawings of a typical work site and a plan to cut the number of onsite security guards by two-thirds. Security guards are inherently unreliable, that was my argument. We can easily replace them with a carefully deployed system of high-tech cameras that can be remotely moved right and left, up and down. Augmented by sensors, facial recognition software, and lowlight capabilities, the cameras will feed data to monitors housed in a hardened onsite camper where they'll be watched twenty-four hours a day. You do this, I told them, nobody's gonna walk off with so much as a hammer. And the kicker, proven by a detailed spreadsheet? The entire system will cost far less than the manpower-reliant system in place."

If I'm enduring the bio, Vern seems well entertained. "Did you ever find the grader?" he asks.

"Never laid eyes on it again."

"How would they get it out of the rainforest?"

"I don't think they did. I think it was sold to illegal loggers or miners who need roads to move their product. One thing's sure, the Brazilian Federal Police were less than interested in recovering Bradford Group property. Most likely because the thieves offered a larger bribe."

Built in the '80s with federal money, Baxter Medical Center, at four stories, is sided with pale-blue panels. The panels are opaque, but efficiently reflect sunlight into the eyes of westbound drivers. We're on our way to interview Calvin 'Chip' McEwan. Chip's a superstar football player at Roosevelt High School. With a college scholarship on the line, I'm sure he'll talk to us. And he's got plenty of explaining to do, having been found unconscious in Baxter Park at five o'clock in the morning by a husband-wife team of birdwatchers. Baxter Park is a half mile from the Bradford residence.

I don't think the security guards working the visitors' desk in the lobby are happy to see us, but they dutifully forward a call to Dr. Susan Brennan, Chip McEwan's neurologist. I don't think Dr. Brennan's happy either. But it's our right to investigate crimes committed in our district and she deals with us in her office. Her patient, she informs us, has a severe concussion, the result of a blow to the parietal region of the skull. Fortunately, there's no fracture. Chip is only being held for observation. Just now, he's in room 303, two floors above.

Most cops dislike hospitals. Too much pain, too much death, too great a chance of their risky careers landing them in a bed with rails on the side. Myself, I've always been fascinated with the gleaming floor tiles, the white-on-white walls, the semi-abstract pastel prints. Maybe it's an illusion, but hospitals appear tightly organized, the staff in total control. A sharp contrast with the chaos at the House.

I bring my entourage to a stop outside Chip's room. "We're not going in," I tell Yoma. "Vern, do you know Chip McEwan?"

"Yeah. Him and the whole football team."

"Then you work him. Be careful, though. You need to find out if he was with Elizabeth without telling him that she was kidnapped." I don't have to spell out the obvious. If Elizabeth's kidnappers believe that the whole city's looking for her, they're liable to bury the girl somewhere she won't be found. "Call me now on your cell and put the phone in your pocket. If you stand close enough to McEwan, we should be able to follow the conversation."

Yoma looks disappointed. Tough shit. We need answers without appearing too eager and Vern's the man to get them. One football player to another. I nod and Vern steps through the door.

"Hey, Chip, bad break, man. How long you gonna be out?"

"I'll only miss three games. If I'm lucky."

"How you feelin' right now?"

"Okay when I lie here, but I'm having balance problems when I get up. You here to investigate?"

"Well, when you're discovered unconscious in a park at five o'clock in the morning with a cracked skull, it naturally draws police attention."

"Okay, man, I get it. But the thing that's driving me crazy? I can't remember what happened. The docs are tellin' me that's normal with head injuries, but I keep tryin' anyway. Like somethin' in me won't accept it."

"Well, what's the last thing you do remember?"

"I remember leaving my house around two-thirty. The rest is . . . it's weird, Vern, like I know something's there, only I can't get to it. Like I'm itchin', but there's no place to scratch."

"But you do remember leaving the house?"

"Yeah."

"Okay, and believe me, I don't get any pleasure out of sayin' this, but there's people downtown who think you were doin' some kind of drug deal."

"C'mon, man, I get drug tested every two weeks."

"I believe you, mainly because I know there are top-ten schools recruiting you and there's no way you'd fuck up your scholarship. So, let me cut to the point. Why were you in Baxter Park?"

"I was meeting someone."

"A girl?"

"Yeah."

"Name me a name, Chip."

"C'mon . . ."

"There's no c'mon. I have to know."

"This girl, she's new in town and real well connected."

"A name, Chip."

"And I swear that she came on to me. Yesterday afternoon, in town. She dared me to meet her. I didn't, like, drag her out there."

"Name her."

"Lizzy Bradford."

"Who?"

"Lizzy Bradford. You know, the Bradford Group? She's their daughter."

We're on the way back to the House, me, Vern, and Yoma. Yoma's expression seems to me almost triumphant, but I quickly bring him back to Earth. That's because Chip's story is irrelevant. We already knew Elizabeth snuck out of her house on the night she was kidnapped. To meet someone? Obviously. And if Chip's memory included a glimpse of her abductors, I'd be a lot more enthusiastic. As it is, we're back where we started.

"The best I can do, Paolo, is take it to Chief Black tomorrow morning. I gotta warn you, though. The Chief'll most likely tell me to bring it to the FBI. It's their case."

"Okay, I get it." Paolo's not one to give up, though his attitude remains pleasant. "But think about this. If the FBI's right, these kidnappers are from Georgia, a country on the border of Europe and Asia. More than likely, they've been in Baxter for the past six weeks. That's Midwestern, salt-of-the-earth Baxter. So, even if they're holed up now, they couldn't have conducted surveillance without being noticed." Another smile. "I could be all wrong, Captain. We could all be. The abductors might be locals. Or maybe they're Americans connected to some Mafia gang that's been here for generations. We'll never know if we don't look."

Yoma's theory is on point, but I'm not moving off my original position. I won't go behind the Chief's back, any more than I want my own subordinates going rogue when I become Chief.

Paolo shows no emotion when I shake my head, but I take it a step further. "You need to back off, Paolo. You won't get to her before the ransom's paid and you could put her in danger if you approach the wrong person. Think about where they took her. It has to be so isolated they can risk bringing her out when she's scheduled to contact her parents. So, yes, they needed the help of one or more locals. But can we find this location before those locals see us coming?"

My phone rings before he responds. It's Danny. He's at Zoe's and could I please pick him up on my way home. I agree. I don't have any choice. Zoe's home is several miles from my own and Danny's on foot. But I'm not happy because I can't imagine Danny's attachment to Emmaline having a positive outcome. I'd rather deal with a dead adult than an emotionally wounded child. And I'm a lot older than Danny.

Danny and Emmaline are sitting on the couch when I arrive fifteen minutes later. Danny's reading her a story with Emmaline's eyes moving from the illustrations in the book to Danny's face. She jumps up when she sees me, flying across the room to wrap her arms around my legs. Then she runs back to Danny and jumps on the couch, the two of them looking faintly ridiculous. At fifteen, Danny's only an inch below six feet, a ball player who prides himself on a take-no-crap attitude. Emmaline's no more than three feet tall and slim to boot.

"Cup of coffee, Delia?" Zoe's tone is sympathetic. My predicament's that obvious. "Freshly brewed."

I follow her into the kitchen, admiring, as before, a confidence she effortlessly projects. Her body is as solid as her attitude, wide shoulders matching wide hips, neither fat nor thin. She's wearing a Doctors Without Borders sweatshirt over white jeans.

"If Danny's being a pain in the ass," I say, "tell me and I'll call him off. He didn't ask for permission."

"He didn't call first either."

"Just showed up? That's not like him."

"I think he sees himself, maybe without saying it directly, as Emmaline's rescuer. Remember, he watched the same video everyone else did."

"Me running away from that house."

"That *burning* house." Zoe hesitates, but I'm not the social worker here and I keep my big mouth shut. "I find myself returning to the look on your face as you came toward the camera with the child in your arms. Your eyes were afraid, but your mouth was firm. You didn't just rush into that house without thinking. You understood the danger. You knew that you might not come back out."

"And Danny, of course . . ."

"I don't believe in long-distance psychological analysis, but it's possible that he's proud of you, on the one hand, and still feels that the risk you took amounted to a kind of abandonment. Where would he go if you weren't there to take care of him?"

"Actually, I have an agreement with Vern and Lillian Taney. They've agreed to raise him if something happens to me."

Zoe smiles as she motions to a seat at a tiny kitchen table, then lays out two mugs and a container of milk. "Equal or the good stuff?"

"The good stuff."

A moment later, we're sipping very hot mugs of coffee, looking at each other across the table. Zoe's eyes are steely blue, yet oddly yielding.

"If you want, I'll call Danny off," I tell her. "I'm sure you have enough on your plate."

Zoe shakes her head. "I spend most of my time investigating child abuse. Danny's company is a welcome break. He's a strong kid. You can feel his resolve. His confidence too."

"What choice does he have? I spend a lot of time at work and my hours are anything but regular."

"He has many choices, Delia. That's what comes of being alone. So far, I get the feeling that he's made the right ones." She leans out to lay her fingertips on the back of my hand. "I've dealt with many kids raised by single mothers who made bad choices. And so have you, I suspect."

I didn't argue with the obvious. "Danny and I were both infected with Covid last year. My symptoms were mild, but Danny was sick for a long time. I never left his side. And I've never been as afraid. I'd been inside Baxter Medical Center at the height of the pandemic and I couldn't imagine—and couldn't stop imagining—Danny on a ventilator. I blamed myself and still do."

"Did you wear a mask?"

"Always, but look, Zoe, I transported desperately sick people to the emergency room. We all did when there were no ambulances. Infection was inevitable. What I should have done is send Danny to stay with his grandparents. They would have taken him in a minute."

I stopped right there as emotions too powerful for Zoe's little kitchen welled up. "What if I'd lost him? My bright, beautiful boy, so full of life? What if he . . ."

Again, Zoe touches me, laying her hand on my shoulder. "But he did recover."

"Eventually, and it left us closer together. Bound, really, in a way I can feel but not name. Like there are no more questions. The chains can't be broken. Valyrian steel, Zoe. Like in Game of Thrones. Links that shatter diamonds." I smile as I feel my shoulders relax. "But I have to admit his focus on Emmaline's caught me off guard."

"You're right to be anxious. Danny thinks Emmaline's problems are unique, but she's a child of the drug plague, one of too many to count. As for Emmaline, she's in good shape physically, so I'm only keeping her while I try to locate her relatives. Assuming she has any. But that will have to end, Delia, and not far from now. In the meantime, how close do we want Danny and Emmaline to get? Because it's gonna hurt when they're pulled apart, hurt the two of them. Meantime, Social Services is being flooded with call from families wanting to foster Emmaline. Thanks to you, she's a celebrity, but . . ."

"But there's a hitch?"

"Not technically. See, the way I . . ." She pauses again. "From long experience, I've come to believe that infants and toddlers, even more than love, need to feel safe and protected. And if you imagine human beings a hundred-and-fifty thousand years ago, you can see why. But Emmaline has never known security. She's smaller and thinner than she should be and her hair was crawling with lice when you rescued her. And that's really the point. You rescued an unprotected little girl in her moment of greatest need. A little girl who doesn't know a damn thing about you just doing your job. She only knows that you're her savior, you and your son."

Zoe looks into my eyes for a moment longer, then walks over to a small microwave. Open, it reveals several loaves of bread and a white box labeled CurlyCue Bakery.

"I use my own microwave the same way," I tell her. "The seal's tight enough to keep the ants out."

Zoe grabs the CurlyCue box, as I hoped she would. She carries it around the table, lays it down, then hesitates for just a second before kissing me on the mouth. She holds the kiss long enough for me to yank my head away. I don't.

"I've been wanting," she says, "to do that for a long time."

CHAPTER FOURTEEN

ELIZABETH

Time and light. I've been a restless sleeper all my life, waking in the night, suddenly aware, as if dangerous predators roamed my too-large bedroom, fangs imminent, claws extended, nothing sweeter than the flesh of a child. I still awaken, though now unafraid, to stare at the ceiling for a few minutes until sleep returns, the odd thing that I know the time almost to the minute. Time and place, here I am at this precise minute, in this bed, in this room, in this house.

Safe.

No more. Earlier, after many hours alone (yet never alone, the cameras' unblinking eyes always upon me) I surrendered to a rage as powerful as it was self-defeating. This is not how it's supposed to work. Only a few years ago, I embraced a virtual vow, not unlike those nuns who embrace poverty, a life of knees-on-stone, swapping love of life for love of God. Never surrender is what it boiled down to. Withhold some part of yourself, maintain the decorous distance, never show your fucking cards. My thoughts belong to me, emotions as well, and I will not suffer from a need to share.

I lost it, nevertheless, my temper, my composure, my self-control. Two cameras and a bucket? Eyes on me every minute, every second? Figure it out for yourself. I smashed both cameras' lenses with the heel of my shoe, no easy job, pounding away until I heard the glass shatter. Satisfying for the moment, or for six or seven minutes before Tashya marched down the stairs, accompanied by the ever-faithful Quentin, and took my lantern.

The dark that followed was profound, the invisible hand before the eye, the black of a deep mine after a cave-in. And me the miner.

Now, only minutes later, I visualize rats slithering through cracks in the wall, rising on their hind legs, noses twitching. What do we have here? I imagine other dangers, too, beetles with armored bodies and mouthparts in constant, unceasing motion. I imagine things supernatural out of the movies Sherman loves to watch, the troll, the golem, the vampire, the demon.

I'm exaggerating, par for the course. But humans aren't designed for the night, our hearing not particularly acute, our noses entirely inadequate, and no bat radar to bounce off the cave walls. I experience a painful helplessness I've been successfully resisting for as long as I can remember, a surety that will never return. I'll pretend, of course, the facade long in creation and nothing to replace it.

Reality breaks through for the first time. There might not be a facade in my future because there might not be a future. Suddenly, I realize that I have no idea how long I've been sitting in the dark, mind wandering to no purpose. An hour? Two? Twenty minutes? Without my permission, time has become irrelevant, a buggy whip to be abandoned and replaced . . . by what? I listen, but cannot hear. I fumble for the table, find a Slim Jim, but it has no taste, even the water when I get to it unfamiliar. I want to scream, but I can't allow Tashya that victory. Get on my knees to her once, I'll never stand again.

I rise without planning, as though my sight has been restored, and knock over the rickety table. The crash slams against my ears, magnified somehow by the emptiness around me. A second later, I'm falling, balance suddenly gone, unable to anticipate the onrushing floor, the side of my head slamming into the concrete. I lie stunned for a time, the fear emptying out as I approach a precipice beyond which lurks a darkness even more profound. Then my thoughts begin to gently drift, paper sailboats on a tiny pond, rising and falling on ripples barely visible, prisoner of any breeze that happens along.

And then nothing.

I awaken from a dream to a time that's no time, to absolute darkness. In the dream, I wandered into one of our home's many unused third-floor rooms. I was looking for something I felt compelled to find, though I didn't know what. There was a bed in the room and I knelt to look beneath it, finding only the expected balls of dust. The drawers of a bureau followed, so light when I tugged them open that I knew there could be nothing inside. It's not here, that's what I told myself as I opened the closet door to find myself staring into the blue eyes of a murdered Deputy.

The dream fades quickly, despite the grisly image, my own reality an onrushing avalanche, and me on my back, a bump at my hairline in front nicely complimenting the one on top of my head. Which way is up? I know, of course, up being opposite to where I am, but there's no point to rising, even the food and water are on the floor.

Another time passes, equally unmeasurable, minutes or hours or seconds all the same until a tickling at the back of my consciousness becomes too intense to ignore. There's something out of place, revealed only by the darkness, and when my eyes find it, they lock on, as fixated as those of a marooned sailor on the prow of an approaching ship.

Light, at the top edge of the window furthest from me, a line of light, slender as a shoelace. I stare disbelieving, but it will not go away. And now I'm laughing because the same line must've shown itself twenty-four hours ago, unable to compete with the lantern I never shut off. It would still be invisible if not for the absolute darkness, the light barely able to illuminate itself.

I think of Mother insisting that luck plays a greater role in human affairs than humans want to acknowledge. And, she'd been quick to add, the rolling dice sometimes come up seven.

Sheets of plywood cover the two windows. What lies beyond the barriers? I couldn't know, but now I do. No concrete fill, no bricks, only glass.

I'm still lying on my back, gaze fixed, enraptured, when I hear footsteps on the stairs. I roll onto all fours, head spinning, and stand. The door opens a moment later and Tashya steps into the room, lantern in hand, effectively blinding me, and I know I'm being examined.

"You have done for yourself quite well," Tashya observes.

Her tone is devoid of emotion, yet her contempt washes over me, as material as the darkness before she arrived. She's reminding me that my best chance to survive lies in acquiescence, let Daddy raise the money and pay the ransom, let Tashya vanish. Unfortunately, there's still Quentin. Everything about him screams hometown and he can't be more than twenty years old. Can I be left alive to describe him? And what assurances has he been given? Because surely the matter's been discussed, my fate and his intertwined, the ultimate zero-sum game.

CHAPTER FIFTEEN

ELIZABETH

I'm led upstairs and told to use the water in the container to wash my hands and flush the toilet. We'll be on the road for some time and no pit stops. Obviously. The cold water stings the side of my head and I cry out. I'm hoping, now, that Tashya hears me. Submission is the best move on the board—Father will be pleased, assuming I survive—but the effort needed to suppress my rage surprises me.

There's no food on the table when I return to the kitchen, no mac and cheese, no fried chicken. More punishment? Tashya rises and leads me to the door.

"Your foolishness has already killed one man," she tells me. "Are more to come? Will one of these be you?" A hand on my back guides me through the door. Quentin is already outside, standing by the van. "Do not be more trouble than you are worth," she tells me.

Ten million dollars is a lot of worth. That's what I'm thinking, though I'm not foolish enough to speak the words aloud. Tashya's eyes are as cold as ever and Quentin's baby blues shift effortlessly from my breasts to my butt as I climb into the van. Tashya follows and Quentin slides behind the wheel and we're off. I now have a part to play, one more (final?) contact, another touch of home base before the crucial moment. Money or no money, life or death. Because I don't doubt Tashya's simple explanation for how these things work, reward for compliance, punishment for any failure, but how do you know whether the victim's family can't or won't, and why the fuck should it matter?

"I'm sorry," I say. "For the cameras. It's just hard . . ." My voice drops to a whisper. "You know, going to the bathroom with somebody watching."

"This is trivial nothing from what others go through. They give me drugs to make me . . . enthusiastic. When you are addicted and your pimps control the supply, you will do whatever necessary to guarantee the next dose."

Another poor-little-me lecture? I'm starting to believe that's who she is beneath the lizard-eye facade, that's how she explains herself to herself, always the victim.

When I don't respond, Tashya continues. "Do you doubt your family will pay?"

Do I? There's no payoff without Uncle Henry's signature on the bottom line. I'm pretty sure he'll go along—motivated by the family's reputation if nothing else—but Uncle Henry is Father's polar opposite. Foul of mouth and temper, he can transform a five-thousand-dollar suit into a rag lifted from a thrift-store rack inside of an hour. Uncle Henry claims that volatility is an asset in business, as is unpredictability, but I've long believed that both are ingrained in his nature. As I believe that my father's cool control is how, as a child, he neutralized his older brother's aggression.

"My family will pay," I tell Tashya. "But timing could be a problem. As I've already told you, the Bradford fortune—and I won't lie to you, it's immense—is controlled by the Bradford Foundation and . . ."

Tashya's already shaking her head. "Family can borrow emergency cash from their bankers."

"That's what I'm hoping. But there's the Bitcoin too. Is it possible to purchase Bitcoin worth ten million dollars as easily as buying a book from Amazon?"

"No, is not as easy as using debit card in banks, but it can be done through online brokers. The FBI knows how." She raises a finger, shutting me down. "You must trust that I am professional. You must trust that FBI is professional. This is how you survive."

Yes, but for how long? Tashya hands me a piece of paper with my instructions printed out in large, emphatic letters. She illuminates the page with a tiny flashlight.

"Read carefully," she tells me.

Tell parent you are UNHARMED!

Parent will be contacted ONCE more only.

Next contact will contain ALL instructions for delivery.

Bitcoin MUST be transferred within two hours!

You will be RELEASED one day after Bitcoin is received.

There will be NO further contact.

Use value, as Father might say. I still have use value. Okay, fine, but the part I don't like is the last line about no further contact because uttering the words instantly transforms me from an asset to a liability.

We're moving with traffic along a state road of some kind, two lanes in each direction, an occasional intersection, an occasional stoplight. There's a crescent moon above, strong enough in a cloudless sky to reveal cornfields reduced to stubble by the harvester.

"You are very quiet," Tashya says.

"I'm watching."

"Watching what?"

"The world go by. This little world, anyway, maybe the last world I'll ever see."

Tashya takes my shoulder, gently, and turns me toward her. "You go through much, I understand this, and you are young, only fifteen. But I make this prediction: many years from now kidnapping will make you more interesting to your peers. You will tell your story again and again, adding this, subtracting that. So, yes, your peers will have diamonds and emeralds and wear designer gowns to galas, just like you, but they will not have a story of rubbing their shoulders with vicious kidnappers."

Quentin can stand it no longer. "Give her to me for an hour and the bitch'll beg to obey you. No more back talk. She'll fuckin' beg."

Tashya smiles and shakes her head, but doesn't correct him, only shifting back in her seat, allowing the darkness, cut by oncoming headlights, to settle in.

"When I speak to . . . to whoever answers the phone, am I supposed to read the message exactly?"

"No. Your parent must know that your voice is not recorded. That you are currently living. But do not stray from instructions. You will not be speaking to them again before you are exchanged."

Quentin turns onto a two-lane county road and now there are only the shorn fields and the occasional farmhouse.

"Prepare yourself." Tashya removes a pair of gloves from a box on the floor, dons them, finally produces a cell phone and hands it to me. "Now."

A few seconds later, I'm talking, not to my father, but to Uncle Henry, his gruff, "Hank Bradford here," a trademark. The man cannot step out of character no matter the situation.

"What are you doing there, Uncle Henry? Where's my father?"

"Asleep."

"Then my mother?"

"Right here. Now, listen, you tell those bastards we're putting the money together and we intend to pay the ransom. But if they harm a hair on your head, I will track them down. I don't care if I have to spend my last penny. I don't care if they retreat to the ends of the earth."

The phone's on speaker, so I don't have to relay the threat. I look at Tashya, but she only smiles and signals for me to go on.

"You need to stop being an asshole, Uncle Henry, for the first time in your fucking, battle-scarred life. This is not a war, it's a kidnapping. A transaction. This for that, me for money. So, keep a civil tongue in your head. These people are professionals and once they get started, they never stop coming. Christ, it's no wonder a judge granted your wife a divorce and all that money. They should have given her a medal for putting up with you."

Nobody speaks to Uncle Henry this way. Most likely, nobody's ever spoken to him this way. But I'm not waiting for him to explode. Time to get it over with.

"You'll receive one final message. This final message will include the web address where the ransom needs to be sent. If you don't send the ransom within two hours, they'll kill me. If you do send the ransom, they'll release me within twenty-four hours. But either way, there will be no further contact. It's do or die."

That's enough for Tashya. She pulls the phone from my hand, shuts it off, rolls down the window and tosses it into the brush at the side of the road.

We're done.

They don't kill me on the spot, a contingency that hasn't escaped my imagination, me lying in the stubble of a harvested cornfield, strangled, shot, stabbed. Father would pronounce these musings a product of my overactive adolescent hormones. But if I'm not to survive, if some unforeseen impediment prevents the ransom's delivery, or if I wasn't intended to live from the outset, my decomposing flesh will have to be put somewhere.

The drive back is uneventful except for an oncoming Sheriff's car that rolls past as if I wasn't there, didn't exist, wasn't a keystroke away from being murdered. I can't take my eyes from the window, can't get enough of the world, the moon's reflected glow in a pond, a pair of dogs or coyotes far in the distance, a single cloud hanging on to the horizon as a drowning sailor might cling to a straw. A will to survive I didn't know existed rises to meet a swelling despair. Tashya will be apologetic, this gives her no pleasure and she really, really wishes it could be otherwise, but Quentin must be protected. Obviously.

My dungeon's been restored. The table and chair upright, the floor clean and dry, popcorn, jerky, chips, tablet, lantern, water, and paperbacks neatly arranged on the table. Someone's been here in my absence, not Tashya and not Quentin, a third party unwilling to join Tashya in her third-world refuge.

Tashya allows the situation to speak for itself, closing the door behind me, sliding the bolt home, climbing the stairs. She doesn't speak because there's nothing more to be said, only the waiting. And me not knowing how long, I can't sit still, neither food nor water, nor even the games on the little tablet, hold my attention. Some part of me I can't recognize demands that I seek a way out, that I at least try, and not recklessly either.

What would Seamus do?

I finally take a drink of water—not too much, the bucket ever in mind—then begin a meticulous inspection of my dungeon. I'm looking for any security cameras in addition to the ones I destroyed. They haven't been replaced and, after thirty minutes or so, I'm pretty sure there are no others. Except for my little niche, the room is apparently empty.

Confident that I'm unseen, I turn my attention to the windows, especially the one at the far end of the room. Even standing on the chair, I won't be able to reach its top edge. The table would bring me closer, but if someone came down the stairs while I was standing on the table, I wouldn't have time to return it to its original position.

I carry the chair to the far window and quickly test it. The wooden legs are tightly joined to the frame, round seat firmly set, stiles and splat solid. It will hold me. As predicted, I can't reach the top of the window, but the chair does answer two important questions. Standing on the seat, I can shake the lower part of the plywood panel covering the window. It's nailed into the window's frame, which has to be wood. If that frame is as old as the house, and the wood has dried out and the nails are not too long, the panel might loosen. And I have to assume whoever put it up was in a hurry because it could have been screwed into the frame, in which case I'd be securely encaged for the duration.

I move the chair back to its original position and settle into a thoroughly unhealthy dinner, a bag of corn chips, two Slim Jims, a chocolate bar, and a bottle of berry-flavored water. Father would be appalled.

◆

The last of the adrenaline finally out of my system, I fall asleep despite my aching head. I'm tired enough to sleep through the night, but when the dead bolt on the other side of the door snaps open, I'm instantly awake and alert. Then Tashya strolls into the room, fixing me with her dead blank eyes and my pulse skyrockets. She's carrying a gun in her right hand.

"Come."

I can't move and yet I must, the muzzle of the gun trained on me, unwavering, the wand of a magician, the drum of a voodoo priestess. Tashya follows me up the stairs and I'm thinking, Turn on her, push her down the stairs, hope you land on top, hope the gun flies out of her hands.

In fact, seized as I am by an impulse-crushing fear, I simply obey. At the top of the stairs, Tashya again directs me with a single word, "Outside."

Her hand finds my back as the door closes behind us, her touch as gentle as it is insistent, an irresistible force. She shuts down her little flashlight and she pushes me toward the forest without speaking. The moon's gone, but the stars are bright enough in a cloudless sky to light our way. The trees and brush, even the forest floor, glow faintly, the whole as beautiful as it is eerie, no place for humans here, go back, go back. Only there's no going back and the pressure of Tashya's hand increases whenever I hesitate. We're following a faint trail, no more than a shadow, deeper and deeper into the forest, skirting thickets, passing into and through a grove of pines, the forest floor barren beneath.

"Tashya . . ."

"Move."

"Please. Give my parents a chance to pay the ransom. If they don't, you might need me again."

"Move."

Now I can hear it, the solid thump of a shovel digging into the earth, the hiss of dirt sliding off the shovel's blade. Then a shadow, moving, lifting, throwing. Finally, Quentin standing in a chest-deep hole, throwing down the shovel when he spots me, a triumphant smile on his face, he at last the victor after a life of losing. He lays a hand on the edge of the hole and vaults up and out, rising to his full height.

"About time," he says an instant before Tashya pulls the trigger three times, the shots oddly truncated, the pop of a firecracker, short and sharp. All three bullets strike Quentin's chest, producing three red dots that quickly expand. I watch him look down, watch the fingers of his right hand go to his wounds, watch them come away bloody. Does he finally get it? Does he realize that it wasn't Elizabeth Bradford who became superfluous once the final call was placed? I half expect him to say something when he raises his head, but he merely falls backward, tumbling into a grave he's dug for himself.

CHAPTER SIXTEEN

DELIA

We smell it before we climb the porch steps, the putrid stench of a decomposing corpse that assaults our lungs as well as our nostrils. I've been here before and I know I'm not going to vomit, which is fine. But some corner of my lizard brain is demanding that I turn and run.

It's early morning, still dark, and we're keeping the vow I made to Carol Sulottis yesterday. Warrant in hand, we're raiding a tiny home on Grove Street at the northern end of the Yards. Decrepit in the extreme, the home's shutters hang to one side, the roof has shed half its shingles and the concrete foundation has crumbled away in several places. Nevertheless, the house is occupied. Joanna Young, who lives in the house with her boyfriend-of-the-month, is a heroin retailer with a habit that consumes every penny she makes. Our informant described her as "terminal."

"She's overdosed three times in the last two months," he'd explained. "Naloxone pulled her out of it, but me, I don't think she was all that happy to be alive."

I have a degree of sympathy for the addicted, a sympathy that reaches most retailers. Higher up, the dealers are as predatory as any mob enforcer, but most of those at the bottom are only in business to support a habit. If there was a way out, I believe many would take it. There isn't.

"Your turn," Vern says.

Vern and I share a binding rule. We never ask our subordinates to do anything we'd refuse to do ourselves. That means I can't ask Cade to go through the house with a video camera while I call the coroner. I have to go inside with him. But I do have an ace in the hole. After rioters sprayed the Capitol police with bear spray, the Baxter PD added gas masks and face shields to the equipment we carry to raids. I'm not expecting to be sprayed inside the house. I'm only hoping the mask cuts the stench.

"Here ya go, Cade." I toss him a mask, then put on my own. Cade's the cop with the video camera, probably not his best use, but the Dink isn't here and Maya carried it yesterday.

The odor of death and rot lingers in my nostrils as Cade and I cross the front porch to find the door unlocked. I've drawn my weapon, but the odds against finding a live person in that house are as close to zero as odds can get.

"You ready, Cade?"

"Yup."

We go in together, me first and Cade right behind. The masks help, but the stench remains powerful. I pause in the doorway to process a scene I've witnessed many times in the past.

There are two bodies in the room, a woman in a stuffed chair, a man on a couch. The woman is bent forward, her face between her legs. Her hair, originally blond, is now dark with the liquefied remains of her scalp. It's moving as well. The man's lying faceup on the couch, but no features are visible through the maggots and the mini-cloud of attending flies. Rough calculation, given the heat wave, the man and the woman have been dead for about three weeks. The bloating and liquefying, along with insect and maggot activity, are at their peak. Neither body, of course, is recognizable.

"You seein' this, Cade." I gesture to a pair of syringes, one still in the woman's arm, the other lying at the feet of the man on the couch. Unless the pair injected at exactly the same time, one saw the other die, then slid the plunger home anyway.

"Yeah." Cade's a step ahead of me. The camera's already going. He'll have to record each room, in this case a living room, bathroom, and bedroom, before we can retreat.

"Quick and thorough," I tell him. "In and out."

In both cases, the victims' wallets and ID are on the floor. No money, though. The home's been thoroughly ransacked, every drawer pulled out, kitchen closets emptied. The bedroom's in even worse shape. There are no more bodies, thank God, and no evidence that a child lived here. But mattress and box spring have been torn open and I have to cross heaps of piled clothing to open the door of an empty closet.

"Whatta ya think?" Cade asks.

"About what?"

"Was whoever tossed the house present when the other two bought it? Did he watch them die, then steal anything of value he could lay his hands on?"

"He? What makes you think it was a man?"

A cop I knew back in Virginia, a sort of mentor, once described junkies as feral. I'm seeing that here. Whether the thief was present when the two overdosed, or happened on the scene later is pretty much irrelevant. Predators never turn down an opportunity to feed, and no junkie turns down a chance to pick up a few easy bucks. Heroin addicts don't have two-hundred- or three-hundred-dollar-a-day habits. They have whatever-I-can-raise habits. As in every penny, every day, the need unrelenting. Junkies will do anything to avoid what they call "getting sick."

One more task ahead, I break out the evidence bags and collect any identifying items on the floor. Cade videos my every move and we're out of there. I've been through this before, usually with somebody who died alone of natural causes. It's like reentering the world after a time spent in another dimension. I rip off the mask and draw a deep breath, then another. Cade seems less affected, standing almost casually after removing his mask. Again, I find myself wondering about Cade's suitability. Too cold? Or merely efficient?

My speculation ends there. I've got work to do, here and back at the House. "Maya?"

"Yes, boss."

"We've got two bodies inside. Until the coroner pronounces the manner of death an accidental overdose, house and yard are a crime scene. I want you to preserve both. You and Abe." I point to Abe Washington. "Vern, I want you to take charge. You know the drill. Process any evidence the coroner uncovers, identify the bodies, notify the next of kin, write up the bullshit." I gesture to the house. "You can go inside if you want to look for yourself. Personally, I wouldn't recommend it."

I might have taken some of this on myself, but I'm the highest-ranking officer on the Baxter PD and running behind is part of the job description. Recently, I've been getting flak from the Chief, who's been getting flak from Mayor Venn. We're not writing enough traffic tickets, parkers or movers, and I need to light a fire under our patrol division. ASAP. And what about arrests for the other crimes Baxterites commit, from domestic assaults to burglaries? Arrests have been made, but our assistant prosecutors have yet to be fully briefed on the evidence. Arraignments, hearings, and trials await my input.

"You want me to call Arshan?" Vern asks.

"No, I'll handle it myself." Removing and autopsying the two bodies is Arshan's job, his and his little team of morgue assistants. And welcome he is to it.

"We collected whatever ID we could lay our hands on," I explain when Arshan comes to the phone. "Otherwise, nothing's been touched."

I'm including the two bodies in the untouched category and Arshan's smart enough to know it. "Did you call in a Crime Scene Unit?" he asks, his tone vaguely hopeful.

"No, and I won't unless you determine a crime's been committed. We'll process the house ourselves." I can't help rubbing it in. "After you remove the bodies, of course."

Time to catch a ride back to the House and go to work. I've spent most of my cop career as a low-ranking patrolwoman or detective and I have to resist micromanaging the entire department. Like right now, when I'd rather be elsewhere, but won't be going anywhere. Three vehicles are approaching our location. A large van belonging to WBAX, a battered Chevy Impala bearing the station's go-to reporter, Katie Burke, and a motorcycle piloted by the *Baxter Bugle*'s own Basil Ulrich.

They're here because I invited them through a trusted third party. They'd done me a big favor by giving Emmaline room when their bosses were likely demanding candid photographs. I wanted the child left alone for obvious reasons and they'd honored my request. Allowing them on scene to record what I expected to be a routine perp walk was meant as payback. Now, the perps would come out in body bags. Even better.

I chat with Basil for a good fifteen minutes while Katie and her cameraman set up. Never faint of heart, Basil wants to know if he can take a few shots inside the house. I won't let him contaminate my scene, debt or no debt, but I do suggest that he sneak around to the back of the house where he'll discover a very dirty window that looks into the death chamber.

"Of course, if you leave a shoe impression and it turns out to be a pair of homicides instead of ODs, don't bother with the subpoena. I'm not gonna testify in your defense."

"Wouldn't dream of asking." Basil's nearing his fiftieth birthday and is at least thirty pounds overweight. I suspect that once upon a time he looked great on a motorcycle. No more, but he can't give it up in favor of an SUV. His vintage Harley's become so tightly associated with his image, he'll be riding it until he's eighty.

"Ready, Captain."

Katie Burke's twenty-five years old and looks younger. She came to WBAX from Northwestern and Baxter's a first stop for her. It's an I-paid-my-dues assignment she'll reference in her social media posts. Personally, I like her. She's always cheery and she can take a joke. Right now, she's wearing enough rouge to eclipse a sunrise, with neon-blue eye shadow to match. But if the footage is aired tonight, I know she'll appear naturally stunning while yours truly will have the complexion of a slug.

I straighten my cap and my uniform blouse, remember to stiffen my spine, finally take a position where the cameraman points. He squints through his viewfinder for a moment, then raises a thumb. Basil's standing out of the shot, notebook in hand. I'll only have to do this once.

Under Katie's direction, I review the limited facts at hand: "We arrived with a search warrant. The residence is a known center for heroin sales in Baxter. We didn't find heroin, though. We discovered a pair of bodies, a man and a woman. Right now, I suspect both overdosed, but the coroner will make a final determination." Then I repeat a message I try to send every time I speak in public, whether at a press conference or a Rotary Club lunch. I'm hoping it'll penetrate if Baxterites hear it often enough. "Katie, there are jobs coming to Baxter, lots of jobs, lots of high-paying jobs with benefits. If the companies handling the demolition and construction phases can't find enough drug-free Baxterites, they'll hire outside workers. We have to get it together and we don't have a lot of time. This is our seventh and eighth death from an overdose this year. We can't go on this way."

I'm back at the House a little before eight, early enough to meet some of the cops scheduled to appear at upcoming trials. One of them is Patrolman Harry Green, who responded to a husband-wife domestic dispute about six months ago. The woman spent two months in the hospital and her face is now permanently lopsided, despite multiple surgeries to repair broken bones. Her attacker-husband's sitting in our jail a floor below me. Thus far, he's been unable to raise the twenty-thousand-dollar bail imposed by Judge Young, who deemed him a flight risk. And why not? The man's spent more than half his life in prison for a series of violent assaults, on men and women alike. My goal is to keep him in prison until he comes out in a coffin or a wheelchair.

I brace five cops over the next ninety minutes, delivering a consistent message. Report to the DA's office tomorrow afternoon at one. Bring any notes with you and review them ahead of time.

My request is pretty much routine and I'm wrapping up when Martha informs me that I'm wanted in Chief Black's office. I've been hoping to grab a cup of coffee and a toasted corn muffin while I give some thought to yesterday's kiss. Zoe Parillo was married (to a man), for a decade no less, a relationship that dissolved about a year ago. That doesn't surprise me, not really. Gay men and women jump through some amazing hoops to blend in. Still, the kiss leads to a pair of questions. Why me and what am I prepared to do about it?

Except for a single detail, Chief Black's office is pretty much as you'd expect. A decent wooden desk with matching upholstered chairs in front. A couch against the wall, fronted by a glass-topped coffee table. Framed awards from Baxter's various civic organizations and private clubs on the wall, along with photos of the Chief with any politician or celebrity willing to shake his hand.

The exception, about two feet long, lies on a credenza behind his desk. The *Flying Cloud*, a clipper ship, holds the record for the fastest all-sail voyage between New York and San Francisco. At least according to Chief Black. The scale model on display in Black's office is amazingly detailed, from its copper-clad hull to a forest of unfurled sails hanging from its three masts. The rigging is intricate, every twist of the rope clearly defined.

Black follows my gaze to the ship as he hangs up. "That's what I want our growth to be like," he tells me. "Fast and smooth. The *Flying Cloud* transported forty-niners to the goldfields of California, and gold from the mines back to

New York. Humans to the land of riches and riches back to the humans."

I'm not all that impressed, but I nod agreement. "So, what's up?"

"First, about this morning. You've got bodies?"

"Yeah, a pair. Likely overdoses. The syringes are right there."

"But no sign of trauma?"

"I didn't look that close, boss. The pair have been dead for a good three weeks."

The Chief draws away. Being that close to a rotting corpse is not something you forget. "It's not on us, anyway," he observes.

"No, it's not."

Black touches the line of stitches in the side of his head and winces. Then he leans back in his chair and drops his folded hands to his lap. "The kidnapping, Delia, is why I've called you in. There's a lot of conflict out there between the mom and the dad and the uncle. We may have to get involved."

"They've got Meacham, boss. Isn't that enough?"

"I know what you think of John, but the family likes him. The problem is that he's not enough. The family thinks their situation deserves more attention. One lowly detective's not gonna do it."

"That'd hold more weight if they hadn't decided to go with the FBI. The father made it clear. We have no role to play."

"That was before the uncle showed up. Anyway, as John told you, they've heard from the kidnappers. The family's expected to forward ten million in Bitcoin within two hours of notification. The instructions came in the form of a phone call from the victim, Elizabeth Bradford."

"No negotiations possible?"

"Nope."

"And no way to contact the kidnappers."

"Same answer, Delia." Black rises from his chair and turns to his clipper ship. "Sometimes, when things get rough, I think about stepping aboard one of these beauties and setting sail for some distant port." Again, he touches the line of stitches and I'm thinking that the worst thing about cancer is the inescapable fear that it'll return. That it's just waiting for an opportunity. "I want that port to be thousands of miles away. I want to take six months to get there."

"Sorry to be a killjoy, Chief, but the closest ocean is fifteen hundred miles from here. You'd have been better off with a covered wagon."

The remark earns me a smile, but not a laugh. There's no sailing away for cops. The bodies this morning prove that much. Chief Black runs a finger along the rail of the *Flying Cloud*.

"You think you can make a constructive contribution, Delia? Something the FBI can't accomplish on its own?"

"I do, actually. The current theory is that the Bradfords were originally targeted in Louisville, but no opportunity presented itself. Most likely because security was just too tight. Then a piece appeared on the Bradford Group's website announcing that Christopher Bradford was coming to Baxter and he was bringing his family with him. Six weeks ago, Chief. That's when the story appeared. The kidnappers reacted by moving the operation to Baxter."

"What I'm getting out of this, Delia, is: so what?"

"So, they—meaning the kidnappers—had a lot of work to do in a totally unfamiliar locale. Could they cover all the details without being noticed? I'm thinking no, Chief. I'm thinking I'll find some trace of their presence if I stir up enough dust."

"So, what's the downside?"

"If the kidnappers get wind of the investigation and think I might be getting close, they'll likely kill the victim and bury her where she won't be discovered."

"That would make prosecution almost impossible, even if we caught them before they left town." Black returns to his desk, his expression set. The short-term is not under consideration. "Look, Delia, the family's holding a meeting this morning and they've asked me to send someone. I want that someone to be you. Let Vern handle the squad for the time being. It seems the victim's uncle could present a problem. Find out for both of us. It's your department too."

CHAPTER SEVENTEEN

DELIA

I get in through the front door this time. Through a front door overseen by two security guards, including Pierce Donato, and into a large hall. Winding stairways at the back of the hall ascend from both sides to a second-floor balcony. I don't have to imagine a lord of the manor reviewing his company from that balcony because a man I take to be lord of the manor is up there. Checking me out. I'm guided here by Paolo Yoma's description of the older brother, Henry. He's staring at me, his gaze as indifferent as it is evaluating. Like I wasn't staring back at him. Like he was in a blind, observing the behavior of some unsuspecting animal.

The attitude's very familiar. I've seen it on the faces of some of the higher-level dealers in the county. I can disrespect you from morning to night. You can never disrespect me. And he's right in this case. The city needs the Bradford Group too much. Them and other businesses like them.

"Samuel, please show Captain Mariola to the study."

There's a man standing next to me, a servant. He could be anywhere between sixty and eighty, wearing a gray suit with a gray tie and a gray handkerchief in the outer pocket of his jacket. The shoes are black, though, and his wispy hair is chalk white.

"This way, Captain."

I'm expecting to find the FBI's command center in the study with its built-in bookcases and dark wainscoting. But there are no FBI agents in the room. Instead, Cynthia Bradford sits on a cornflower-blue love seat next to a man I assume is her husband, Christopher. He's wearing a camel-hair jacket over a white shirt with a button-down collar. In contrast to his wife with her red eyes and mussed hair, he projects a calm demeanor that I'm not foolish enough to associate with competence. The Dink's standing next to Paolo Yoma near one of the empty bookcases. He's holding an open laptop. Yoma's sipping at coffee in a cup thin enough to pass for tissue paper. He straightens when I come in, but leaves the only necessary introduction to Cynthia Bradford.

"Captain Mariola, this is my husband."

I nod to him and he nods back. Now what? Meacham makes the first move. He gestures to a computer printout on a glass-topped coffee table.

"Transcripts of the two contacts," he explains. "Or you can listen to them, if you want. There's a recording."

"I'll listen first."

Meacham inserts a thumb drive into the laptop, then hands me a pair of earbuds. I listen to the recordings twice, struck by the difference in tone. Elizabeth's voice is steady in the first, despite the overly dramatic "left by the side of a highway." In the second, her tone is vicious as she attacks her uncle. What to make of it? That's for later. But if Cynthia Bradford's been straightforward about her daughter's intelligence—a girl who's skipped two grades—the inconsistency demands examination.

Finished with the laptop, I return the earbuds to Meacham and gather a copy of the transcripts. Henry Bradford chooses that moment to enter the room. He ignores brother, sister-in-law, Meacham, and Yoma, walking up to shake my hand. I think he's planning to put my knuckles in a death grip, but something in my eyes stops him. Or maybe it's the captain's bars on my shoulders. Or maybe I'm just being paranoid. Maybe he's a sweetheart with a gruff exterior.

"Henry Bradford," he announces. "Thanks for coming."

"Glad to be of help."

Cynthia Bradford speaks without raising her head. Nevertheless, I hear defiance in her voice. "Would you like coffee, Captain, or something to eat?"

"No, thank you. I'm fine."

Henry sighs—there she goes again—before speaking. "You've been briefed by Paolo. Tell me what you think we might do besides remain passive . . ." He pauses here to look at his brother. "Besides remain passive and hope for the best, which is the only option the FBI has to offer. Now, at the moment, I believe their assessment is essentially correct. We are more likely to achieve the only important goal, Elizabeth's return, by paying the ransom than by opening an investigation. But there's another side to the FBI's recommendation. There's not a single agent on the team who works closer than a hundred miles from here. They can't launch an investigation because they don't know the players. So, please, give us an alternative to just waiting. If you have one."

There's not all that much to be said, not really. Nevertheless, it's certain to be distressing for Cynthia and I'm not going to launch into an assessment until she gives me the okay. Head still down, she doesn't speak for a moment. Then she folds her hands in her lap and says, "I need to know, Captain. Please."

"Alright." I take a moment to find a beginning. I've given some thought to the basic question of how to locate Elizabeth, but drawn no conclusions. Too many unknowns. "I'm gonna take as fact Paolo's theory that your family was first targeted while you were still in Louisville. You were targeted, but security was too tight and the conspirators never found an opportunity. Then word leaked out: Christopher Bradford was bringing his family to Baxter. What form that word might have taken doesn't really matter right now. What matters is that the conspirators must have come to Baxter weeks ago. Finding a place to take their victim? To hold her for days, to bring her out and back from time to time? Baxter's a small place. Most of its residents have been living here for generations and strangers are noticed."

I stop for a moment, looking from face to face. Anybody disagree? We all on the same page? Meanwhile, the scenario I'm describing is only the most likely.

"Okay, as a detective, I often try to see events through a criminal's eyes. So, I'm imagining myself in Louisville, waiting for an opportunity that hasn't presented itself. Then I learn about the move to Baxter and I take off, probably with my co-conspirators. First thing, I need a place to stay, which turns out to be harder than it sounds. New people are coming to Baxter every day, looking for their slice of the Nissan pie. Land prices are through the roof and the few hotels and motels are usually full. So, even if I manage to book rooms without using a credit card, I'll be far from isolated. Alternatives might include short-term Airbnb rentals, but most of them are rooms in somebody's house. There are also a few homes for rent, but if I go that route, I'll have to deal with a landlord who's likely to run me through a background check. I'll have to sign a lease agreement as well."

"You're suggesting . . . exactly what?" Christopher Bradford speaks up for the first time. "They had to be noticed? They would have stuck out?"

"Maybe, and maybe they're locals and we've got it backward. A small chance, even a tiny chance, isn't no chance. But I'd start with the cheaper hotels and motels. Between me and my Chief of Detectives, Vern Taney, we know most of the proprietors anyway. From there, if we have no luck, I'd review *Baxter Bugle* and Airbnb rental listings in the ten days after your move became public. I'd also work the neighborhood we call the Yards, where the Nissan plant will be located. It's drug heaven down there, with dozens of abandoned homes, small businesses, and factories. At first glance, it seems like a perfect spot, a proverbial skid row, but we're in the early stages of a crackdown and the neighborhood's heavily patrolled. And those drug dealers? They're always on the lookout for cops and they don't miss changes in their work environment. Worse yet for the kidnappers, ten or fifteen of those dealers are confidential informants who regularly trade information for time. They'd like nothing more than to curry favor without having to rat on their fellow druggies."

Paolo manages a smile. "But they must have taken her somewhere," he observes.

I know I'm supposed to respond, but the obvious being the obvious, I have nothing to say. Uncle Henry cuts me off in any event.

"Do you think you could find them?" he asks.

"Before they see me coming? Or after?"

Cynthia Bradford draws a sharp breath. Maybe I've gone too far. Still, I'm glad it's out there. Christopher, on the other hand, seems relieved and I have to assume that he's for waiting it out. The underlying psychology is simple enough. If you pay the ransom and things go bad, it's not your fault. But if you send me to hunt the kidnappers down and they see me coming and kill your daughter? Now it's on you.

"Look, I really don't have any more to add." I turn to Uncle Henry, my gaze direct. "And I don't have the authority to make a commitment either. That would come from Chief Black."

"I get the point." Though Henry Bradford's smile lifts his jowls a fraction of an inch, it's devoid of humor. "But it's obvious that you believe you can run them down if you have enough time."

"Run them down or get them running."

Though I don't ask for his company, John Meacham follows me outside. He seems nervous, but determined.

"Okay, John, what's up?"

Meacham's blue eyes are clear, his sandy hair full and freshly styled, his shoulders broad, his waist narrow. He'd be on our recruitment posters if he wasn't the Dink.

"I've been spending most of my time in the Feds' command center on the other side of the house," he tells me. "Doing nothing, right? Like nobody pays any attention to me. Like I'm not there. That's good, Captain, because I've got big ears and there are a few things you definitely need to know."

"Let's hear 'em."

"The agents have identified the gang that took Elizabeth. Or they think they have and they seem pretty convinced. Problem is, it doesn't help them."

The day is rapidly warming as we approach noon and we're standing in direct sunlight. I can feel the sweat just beneath the skin on my forehead as I walk the Dink into the shade cast by a nearby maple.

"First, tell me how they've made this identification. Are they guessing? Do they have hard evidence?"

"They've identified a dozen past kidnappings that follow the same pattern. A written note that announces the kidnapping. The ransom to be paid in Bitcoin within two hours of a final demand. Two contacts with the victim, then a final notice with an address on the web. The other cases were in England, Ireland, Greece, and Germany. Eight cases altogether."

"Who's supplying this information?"

"The basic source is Interpol, but the pattern's been entered in the National Crime Database. Also, they caught one of the kidnappers in Belgium. He died on the night they arrested him, probably a suicide, but they identified him through DNA. Kamaz Didiani from Georgia. The country not the state." Meacham takes a breath, more relaxed now that he'd gotten my full attention. "So, here's the general thinking. Not mine, the FBI's. Mobs in Georgia are families, like the old Sicilian mobs. Only these families stretch out to fourth cousins and there's no birth control. The FBI thinks the Didiani mob numbers about two hundred members. They're into everything from smuggled Chinese antiquities to . . . well, to kidnapping."

"Hold on a second, John. I don't see how any of this applies to us. Not if all the victims were released after the ransom was paid."

"They weren't. In one case, the ransom was paid, but the victim—a GE executive—disappeared."

"How long ago?"

"That I don't know, Captain, but not yesterday. They were talkin' about him like he's dead." He stops for a second, then nods to himself. "One of the agents, a profiler, thinks the kidnappers are branding themselves. Like the victims are carefully managed by a foreign woman who makes no effort to disguise her appearance. She constantly reassures the victims. Don't worry. You'll be home soon. No chains or closets, either. Good treatment and release after payment, the ordeal over in less than a week."

"Then the kidnappers can be identified. Some of them anyway."

"In theory, yeah. But they used a different woman each time and while the victims spent days examining mug shots, there were no positive IDs. But even if there had been, finding them in Georgia would be almost impossible, not to mention dangerous."

"Got it, and good work, John. Seriously. And you should run this by the Chief as soon as possible."

"Already on my to-do list."

"Great. Anything else I need to know?"

"Two more things. According to the victims, their female managers mostly spoke English, but had foreign accents. Russian or Polish is what the victims thought, but the FBI's sure they're Georgians. They made the victims do all the contacting because they didn't want to be voice printed. But the accents were there in every case."

"And?"

"The gang wants to be recognized. At least that's what the profiler thinks. They're hoping the cops will play it smart and advise the family to pay up. And that's just what the Feds are telling the Bradfords. You want your daughter back and paying the ransom is the best way to make that happen."

We exit the house to find Sherman Bradford playing on the lawn with a small dog. A terrier of some kind. He straightens up as we approach.

"Hey, can I talk to you for a minute?" The lopsided haircut doesn't hide the toll his sister's kidnapping has taken. No longer arrogant, or even pretending to be, his gaze is imploring. I'm in a hurry, but there's no way I'm walking past the kid.

"Hey, Sherman, how are you doing?"

"Mom bought me a dog." He hesitates for a moment, his head tilting to the left as he considers what he should say next. "Does that mean Elizabeth's not coming back?"

"C'mon, Sherman. How can you think that?"

"Because nobody tells me anything. Because I don't know what's happening." The boy ignores the puppy jumping up on his legs. He looks as if he's about to cry. "I read a lot of books about crime," he insists. "I could help."

I reply with the obvious. I have no choice. I'm not at liberty to reveal what the boy's family has decided to withhold.

"They're trying to protect you."

"Why didn't they protect Elizabeth?"

"Didn't you tell me she snuck out on her own?"

We both stop when the dog spots a gray squirrel working the base of a maple thirty yards away. The little terrier's fast, but the squirrel merely darts up the tree, leaving the dog to growl in frustration.

"Why her?" Sherman asks. "Why Elizabeth? Why did they take my sister?"

"Money, Sherman. They took her because her family's rich enough to pay the ransom."

"But why Elizabeth? Why not some other rich kid?"

"Only the kidnappers can answer that question. But you say you study crime, so wouldn't asking *how* work better? How is a lot more useful."

"I can't ask how, because nobody will tell me what's going on."

I nod agreement. "Can I suggest a strategy?"

"Yes?"

"Nagging." That draws a smile. "Who's easier to work on, your mother or your father?"

"My mom. Father never listens to anyone but Uncle Henry."

"Then keep at your mom, alright? And don't give up. Now, give me a hug."

CHAPTER EIGHTEEN

DELIA

I'm driving away from the station house, Vern at my side. We're off duty and headed to a baseball game. Danny and Mike are playing in a fall league designed to prepare Little League standouts for high school play. Both kids expect to make their high school team, but the tryouts won't come until spring and they want to stay as sharp as possible.

I've briefed Vern on the developments in the Bradford kidnapping and I'm pretty sure we're focused on the same tidbit. The kidnappers who spoke with the victims were all women and they spoke with "Russian or Polish" accents. As I listened to Meacham, I'd flashed to Boris Badenov from the old Bullwinkle show. At age eight, Danny found his accent hilarious. But the comedic aspects aren't the point. No, the point is that anybody with that accent negotiating Baxter's housing options would surely be remembered.

Chief Black agreed with us—or me, at least—when I pointed this out an hour after we left the Bradfords. The Chief's been a cop for the past forty years. A cop's instincts are the only instincts he has. Strike that. The Chief's also a politician with a politician's instincts. That's why he didn't instruct me to investigate. And probably why he didn't forbid me either. No, Chief Black leaned back in his chair and grunted. "Do you really think Meacham got his facts straight? John Meacham?"

"Yeah, Chief, I do."

I don't want to discuss any of this with Vern, but I can't think of a way to fend off his curiosity that I won't have to apologize for later. We've been on the clock since five this morning and watching our kids play ball is a pure pleasure. Family time, right? Like you can't be a cop every minute of every day?

"It's the victim who didn't come back that got my attention," Vern says.

He's talking about the GE executive who vanished after the ransom was paid. Funny thing about human beings, give them a fact and they want to surround it with details. They want to make a story out of it. But there's no story here, only the inescapable. Paying the ransom doesn't guarantee the life of the victim. Usually, yes, but not always.

"Did they search for him before they paid the ransom?" Vern asks. "Or did they pay and hope?"

"Don't know. Don't know whether he was killed before or after the ransom was paid either."

"But paying the ransom doesn't guarantee the hostage's life."

"You read my mind."

He did, as far as it went. But he's yet to happen on the little voice telling me to let it go until I'm ordered to investigate. We're talking about a world of bad choices here. Shut up and pay? Go all proactive? Your decision will be judged by the outcome, not the reasoning that brought you to it. If we investigate and Elizabeth doesn't come home, blame will fall on the Baxter Police Department in general and its top commanders in particular. This is a fools-rush-in situation if I've ever seen one.

The baseball field at Goldman High mimics just about every other high school baseball field in the region. It is far less grand than Goldman's football field, the browned grass so unevenly maintained that the ball throws up a little cloud of dust every time it hits the ground. Rows of mostly unoccupied bench seats run in tiers on both sides of the plate. I'm expecting to find Lillian Taney and I do, three rows up on the third base side of the field. But I'm not expecting to find Zoe Parillo sitting next to her. Nor Emmaline, who's standing behind the fence protecting the fans, her eyes riveted on the shortstop. That would be my son, Danny.

Zoe's apologizing almost before I sit down. "I'm not crowding you, Delia. Really. That's not me. But Danny came over this morning and . . ."

"Danny?"

"Yes, and he told Emmaline he was going to play this afternoon and did she want to watch?"

"Which, of course, she did."

"Which, of course, she did."

I accept the comment as I settle down to watch Danny and Mike play ball. Baseball isn't the fastest game out there and I'm not all that much of a sports fan anyway, but when it's your kid, you pay attention. Danny's in his usual position at shortstop, but Mike's been moved to the outfield. Both are intensely involved in the game, despite a pitcher who can't seem to throw strikes and batters who aren't stupid enough to swing. That leaves the fielders to stand around waiting for something to happen. Danny keeps up a constant line of chatter while he waits, critiquing the batter's fitness to hold a bat, encouraging the pitcher, until an easy ground ball finally heads his way. He takes it on the second bounce and throws to first. Inning over.

As Danny returns to the players' bench, he looks up and waves to me. Emmaline notices the gesture and turns around. If anything, her expression becomes even more serious as she runs up the stairs to stand in front of me. Zoe was right and I can't help but see it. Emmaline's hazel eyes grow quizzical. What now? What's supposed to happen? I reach out and haul her onto my lap. A second later, her head's resting against my chest and she's grown quiet.

Lillian Taney's smiling as she leans across Zoe. "She's gonna be a stunner. The hair, the big eyes, even the freckles. She's gonna be a stunner."

I'm not about to argue the point. In fact, I'm having second thoughts about taking her onto my lap. But all that's for another time and place, maybe with Danny after dinner. I'm proud of his emotional reaction to Emmaline. The girl's gotten nothing but bad breaks, probably from the day she was born. She deserves some good luck. Only the Mariola family isn't the place she can hope to find it. Not long-term.

"Oh, by the way," Lillian continues, "Mike asked if Danny can sleep over tonight. They have a science project they're working on together."

Beside me, Zoe's hand finds mine, her fingers lightly grazing my palm. Am I being set up? Or maybe fixed up? By my own son? And my partner and his wife and . . .

"Good," I tell Lillian as my fingers curl around Zoe's. "You'll get them to school in the morning?"

"Without a doubt."

I return to the game when Danny steps to the plate. Over time, Danny's drilled a baseball reality into my nonathletic brain. In baseball, you can do everything right and still fail. That's the case here. Danny takes the first pitch inside, leaning, but not jumping, back. Then he inches closer to the edge of the batter's box and I know he's looking for an outside pitch to drive the opposite way. The pitcher obliges and Danny steps into a mediocre fastball, catching it on the sweet spot, hitting it about as hard as a fourteen-year-old can hit a baseball.

When the second baseman, a Little Leaguer no more than thirteen, realizes the line drive is headed right for his face, he jams his eyes closed and jerks his head away. The boy's pleading for mercy and he receives it. The ball cracks into the center of his glove and somehow doesn't fall out. Now he's a hero.

Danny looks up at me and shrugs as he trots off the field. I spread my hands. That's baseball. Then I hear Emmaline muttering something into my shirt, over and over again. I have to lean down and cup my ear before I understand what she's saying.

"Mommy, Mommy, Mommy, Mommy, Mommy . . ."

CHAPTER NINETEEN

ELIZABETH

"Bury him."

Spoken with no tone, the words lost in the shadows, as casual as a pair of aged slippers tucked beneath the bed. Did it stop raining, should I spread jelly or marmalade on my toast, shall we go shopping or to the gym, does someone need to be buried? Yet the words repeated themselves, as though waiting to be embraced, believed, accepted, affirmed. Anything but the forgetting my brain insisted on. Ram these words into the darkest corner of the darkest room in your brain. Bolt the door on your way out.

"Bury him."

"I can't. Please."

I begged her, voice quavering, knees shaking, but the silvery gleam of the revolver in Tashya's hand made its own demands: no bluff here, I've killed once tonight, blood already on my hands and at least one other in the past and perhaps many more.

Bury him-Bury him.

The words echoed like the echo on a poor cell phone connection.

Bury him-Bury him. You must-You must. Bury him-Bury him.

The shovel's handle still slippery with Quentin's sweat, the blade sliding into the piled earth, the rattle of small stones, the shovel full and me raising the piled earth, my back to the grave, half-paralyzed.

"Bury him-Bury him."

"I can't."

"Bury him or join him."

The sound that came from my mouth, too thin to be a wail, rose from some despairing place I didn't know existed. It moved Tashya not at all. Her features remained veiled, as the gun remained steady, as the message remained constant. There's a lesson to be learned and you will learn it even if you don't know—even if you can't imagine—what it is.

My back was to the grave. I had to turn, to look, to cover what a minute ago was a living human being with dirt, to watch the hole fill as though taking life for a second time, as though erasing life altogether.

Tashya shifted her weight from one side to the other, the gun moving with her, and I turned in a panic, fear for my own life overwhelming every consideration. I was alive, after all. Quentin was dead, after all. Tashya held the gun, after all.

Dug in a little clearing, as far away from the roots of the surrounding trees as possible, the grave was fully exposed to the intense starlight. Quentin lay on his back, open eyes bright enough to scream, to accuse. I moved the blade of the shovel over his grave, turned it face down, watched the dirt fall beside his right leg. Unable to look for a moment longer, I pivot back to Tashya and the piled earth. If only I'd listened to my father, my mother, the security detail I so carefully avoided, Quentin would be as alive and threatening as he was only a moment before.

"You must do this," Tashya insisted. "You must bury him." She raised the gun. "I cannot hold this gun and the shovel too. You must bury him."

And who will bury me? I didn't—couldn't—say the words aloud. Tashya had killed without evident effect, the deed not all that important, a means to an end, a bare necessity. Take a life and sleep a dreamless sleep and maybe have a snack before retiring. Murder makes me hungry.

My life vanished at that moment, every privilege gone, elderly maître d's addressing me as Miss Elizabeth, an armed chauffeur ferrying me back and forth to school, fawning saleswomen in trendy boutiques, an elderly instructor who voiced his disdain for precocious girls silenced by a phone call from Mother.

Tashya didn't give a flying fuck about my pedigree. She had a pedigree of her own and it didn't allow for deference, not to law, not to governments, not to borders, and certainly not to fifteen-year-old girls who expect every complaint to be addressed.

"You must move quickly, Elizabeth. Before daylight comes."

I dug the shovel into the pile, thinking I could maybe toss the earth into Tashya's face and then overwhelm her. Just like in the movies. Instead, without turning, I flipped the dirt into the hole behind me. Again and again and again. I hoped to find a heaped mound of earth when I eventually dredged up the courage to once more look. I found, instead, Quentin staring up at the stars as though following the progress of his spirit.

I covered his face. Quickly. I tossed dirt into his eyes, onto his parted lips. I removed him from sight. I left his relatives, the police, his friends to search fruitlessly, endlessly, as though seeking a figment of their imaginations. As though seeking an invisible friend.

I labored until my hands blistered, until sweat dripped from my hair, faster and faster, grunting, swearing, brain whirling, my heart ready to explode, until the grave was full, until I'd covered it with dead branches and leaves, until Tashya led me back to my prison.

Safe in the kitchen, dawn showing though the windows, she first ordered me to wash in a bucket of cold water in the bathroom, then ordered me to sit before a rickety table and eat the hamburgers and French fries provided by that still unknown co-conspirator. I'd never before truly hated, the emotion seeming inappropriate, but I hated then. I hated and I wanted to tell her to go fuck herself, that I wasn't her puppet. Fear was also a stranger to a life dominated by confidence born of privilege, but hate and fear now tumbled through my brain like wet towels smacking hard against the sides of a clothes dryer.

I washed. I ate. I looked into Tashya's eyes, as blank as Quentin's in his grave. I listened while she justified killing Quentin, as she explained that she only shot him to protect me.

"Quentin had no retreat. He could not take refuge with family in the mountains. He is local. . . ."

"Was." I stopped chewing for a moment. "He's dead now."

"Better what? Him? Or you? He would never agree to let you live."

"And you? You will? And don't just say, Yes, I will."

"You are young and your father is in construction business, not retailing. You know little of branding. Yet this is what we do. Always the same. Two contacts with victim speaking directly to family, ransom in Bitcoin, two hours to make transfer after third anonymous contact. And here is most important part. The victim is released after the ransom is paid. Our brand, yes? Recognized by cops, which is why we don't tell family not to contact police. We want them to bring in the FBI because FBI will tell them everything I am telling you. The FBI will tell them to pay."

I knew I should keep my big mouth shut because I had nothing to gain by speaking out. I couldn't. "Is that what you told Quentin? That you were going to let me go? Or did you tell him that he was digging my grave?"

For once, Tashya's face revealed an emotion, even if it was mere curiosity. "Why does this matter? You are alive and he is dead. This is how life is. One wins, another loses. Quentin's family lived in this house as caretakers. Then new arrangements were made and they had to leave. The house has been empty since then, but Quentin still has a key. Very useful, yes? We needed a place to keep you and this one is perfect. Very isolated, very safe. For you as well as me."

This time I managed to control myself. I didn't say, "But not for Quentin."

"You must trust me for this," she continued. "Police coming is the worst thing for you. Here you are safe, where they cannot find you. So, there is only the waiting now. Two days, three at most, then home again like nothing happened. The only requirement is patience."

I shoved a handful of French fries into my mouth, unwrapped another burger, took a bite. Tashya sat on the other side of the table, the revolver close to her right hand. I could throw the hamburger in her face. I could overthrow the table. We could scramble for the gun, alternately grabbing each other's heels, throwing punches, biting, kicking. . . . But I can't fool myself. My life had prepared me to ace the SATs at age fourteen, which I'd done. Fighting, though, was not in my basket of skills and Tashya knew it. This part of the game, the lesson, was glaringly obvious. Settle down, wait it out, don't challenge your fate. We don't intend to harm you. You have our word for it.

I needed to go on the offensive. I was tired of being helpless, manipulated, a trapped rat in some exotic behavioral experiment. Move the girl here and there and everywhere, until her brain fogs and she embraces a befuddled acquiescence. But I'm not befuddled and my fear of an hour before is melting away. Not the rage part, though. I felt as though I'd been invaded, my life twisted into a knot I'd never untie. I was changed forever, against my will, and Tashya's reassuring tone hasn't come close to reassuring.

I lifted the top of my bun and removed the sour pickle slices, then took a bite and chewed. Very casual, like my tone when I finally spoke.

"My extended family, besides our home in Louisville, owns a chalet in Aspen, a villa in St. Tropez, and Diomed Farms where some of the fastest thoroughbreds in the world are bred. Our collection of Muzo Mine emeralds has been appraised at sixteen million dollars. Our collection of ancient telescopes and microscopes is among the finest in the world. We travel often, of course, usually by company jet, but sometimes on the family's yacht. The suites at the hotels we visit are larger than most homes."

"What is point of this?"

"Well, I was just wondering. Our money is ours to enjoy freely, but what will you do with the ransom money, and the ransom money from the other kidnappings? Can you vacation on Lake Como? Buy apartments in London? Or do you have a big room somewhere in the Caucuses filled with dollar bills and euros?"

I expected outrage, but Tashya found me amusing, though her dark blank eyes revealed nothing. As usual. "I have daughter, yes? In Georgia? Very young, only three, but I am hoping she grows up to be exactly like you."

CHAPTER TWENTY

ELIZABETH

I found an addition to my basement prison when Tashya followed me down the stairs, an extra blanket on the mattress, compliments no doubt of the other or others involved in Tashya's scheme. A lesson too. Even if I succeed, an attack on Tashya will not result in my freedom. Others are watching and who knows if they're committed to Tashya's branding strategy, committed to the life of a girl more trouble than she's worth.

"I do not know if you will see me again before ransom is paid. This will take two days at minimum. Time will seem very slow to you, unable to tell night from day. Anxiety, yes? You are sure to be anxious, maybe thinking nobody will come, that you will be left here to die. The mind plays many tricks when you are afraid. I know this from my own life. But this is your final test and you must endure."

And how should I have labelled this attitude? Maternal? Concerned? The compassionate kidnapper anxious to reassure, so sorry but my hard, hard life justifies all, and you'd do precisely the same if you were in my shoes?

But there's no more to be said and, a moment later, Tashya's climbing the stairs with the door shut and bolted behind her and then there's just me. Me and my bucket.

It's morning, Wednesday, three days after I was taken, but it might as well be three years. So much to consider, a future of choices based on missing pieces and no way to fill in the gaps. Still, I'm compelled to make the attempt, not least because I can't allow myself to dwell on the eyes, on Quentin's, on the Trooper's, on my own if Tashya's been lying all along. I open a bottle of water and drink, then shut off the lantern for a moment and look up at the light at the top edge of the window furthest away. Still there.

My uncle is a very rational man, despite the bluster and the bad temper. He once told me that his displays of temper were purely indulgent, but he didn't give a damn. He enjoyed the role of bully, especially because no one had the courage (or the integrity) to confront him. But all that—the self-indulgent displays, the cowed subordinates—was beside the point. Uncle Henry wasn't out to make friends, or enemies for that matter. Uncle Henry was out to make money, an end that could only be achieved by carefully measuring costs and benefits, risks and rewards. Underbidding can turn a profit into a loss. Overbid and the contract goes to someone else.

"Success in life often depends on outcomes that cannot be determined in advance." We were celebrating Christmas in Louisville when Uncle Henry sat me down for this particular lecture. It was about an hour after dinner and he'd been drinking pretty hard. "The best you can do is estimate the costs of failure and the benefits of success, then put them on a scale. Are the potential costs catastrophic? The benefits astronomical? In any given society, the vast majority care little for the analysis required to separate costs and benefits, much less for weighing them, one against the other. Instead, they choose on impulse, driven mainly by the fear of loss. We call this overwhelming majority losers. We call them ordinary. We call them 'the salt of the earth.'"

Bradfords, it didn't need saying, weren't losers. Or ordinary, or even salty. We are, however, made of flesh and blood, as the bumps on my head, a pair of half-buried golf balls, more than prove.

I have to occupy my brain because the eyes lurk out of sight, only waiting for me to relax. I have to keep moving and this one decision, if I commit to it, carries enough risk and reward to command my complete attention. At least for a while.

For a while I can forget the blisters on my palms and the dried sweat that leaves my hair in clumps. And I can forget that shovelful of earth, the one I tossed onto Quentin's face. I half expected a reaction, expected him to jump, but he didn't move at all and his eyes remained open.

So the issue to be resolved: flee or wait it out. Costs and benefits, risks and rewards.

Assuming success, the reward is too massive to need description. The costs, assuming failure, are unknown. I don't believe Tashya will execute me if I try to escape, not right away at least. Despite her insistence on two contacts only, she can't be certain I won't be needed a third time. Ten million dollars is an awful lot of money, enough, perhaps, to make even my Uncle Henry blink.

But there's a question that needs answering before an effort to escape can be made. Is Tashya sitting upstairs in the kitchen? Perhaps with her accomplice? I don't know if I can remove the panel covering the window, but I'm certain that an attempt will be noisy enough to alert Tashya if she's remained in the house. But has she?

I find myself thinking like Uncle Henry or Father as they'd assemble a bid, say for demolishing the structures in a neighborhood called the Yards. The knocking down part is child's play, the equipment, the manpower, the time from standing up to fallen down. The rubble presents a far greater challenge. For example, used brick can be sold if it's not too badly weathered, and brick was the construction material of choice when the warehouses were erected. Thus, evaluating the condition of the brick, building by building, is a necessary first step. The same principle applies to the steel girders that support the structures. They also have value, depending again on their condition. Sell off the brick and the girders, transport them to the buyers, and you're finally left with worthless rubble.

By state law, construction debris must be transported to Construction and Demolition debris landfills. So where is the nearest Demolition landfill? Is it large enough to accept everything we send its way? If not, how far to the next landfill, and the next, and the . . .

I don't know I'm crying until the tears run over my lips and onto my tongue. This is all too much for me. I'm only fifteen years old and, for all my pretending, too soft and weak to deal with murder, with bullets fired into the bodies of human beings, with the sure and certain end to life, every dream gone, what you are, what you might become. It's all too much.

I need to hide and I do, dropping to the mattress and covering myself with both blankets. I'm shaking, overwhelmed, but there must be a merciful god somewhere because my body takes the only way out and I fall asleep.

My sleep is fitful, up and down, in and out, frozen in space, swept along by a current I cannot see or name or resist, an eye for an eye, Elizabeth's for Quentin's, Quentin's for the Trooper's, all for Tashya's. At one point, I'm lying on my back, not in a grave, but in my bed at home, as earth tumbles from an unseen shovel onto my face. At times I lie awake, staring up at a heating duct that passes directly overhead and I'm reminded of a jet's contrail, or the trail left by some burrowing household mole. Our gardener in Louisville, Mike, hunts moles across a lawn vast enough to engulf a football field. Mike favors traps over poison, monster traps that smash the heads of unwary animals, including the rabbit I found where the lawn gives way to a forest cut by a horse trail that runs above the Ohio river.

Despite everything, I don't want to wake up. I don't want to decide, to take any risk, though risk is already here, tangible as a pile of dirt heaped on a shovel's blade. But wake up I do, driven by necessity, a bucket in my future. Another humiliation, another reminder.

I don't know what time it is, have literally no idea, thinking I might have slept for an hour, or three or six, as if it matters because I'm already on notice. Nothing will happen today, or probably tomorrow, or even the day after, but that's the key. The family must be given time to collect the money. A premature demand might result in a loss for all concerned. My time is accounted for, at least in Tashya's eyes. But what of her time? This house is supposed to be unoccupied, and while the area doesn't seem especially popular with hikers—the road leading to the house is marked by a NO TRESSPASSING sign—there's always a chance that somebody will happen by, always a chance that some hiker, driven by a larcenous impulse, or mere curiosity, will examine the house, trying the door, looking through a window. If they discovered Tashya at the kitchen table, perhaps sipping at a mug of coffee, would they report her presence? Say, to the police?

More to the point, with me safely tucked away, will she take the risk?

I have only Tashya's word for her so-called "branding," the hostage always released, the family reunited, the only loss monetary. It's surely possible, even likely, that she designed her story to keep me quiet, every element a fiction, including the family in Georgia waiting impatiently for her return. Money first, of course.

No, what's real is Quentin, the Deputy lying in the road and Tashya's deader-than-dead eyes.

The day drags on, seeming endless, the sun frozen in the sky, as it was for Joshua in his battle with the Amorites. And, yes, I received a certain amount of religious instruction, but not too much, the part about serving God or mammon scrupulously avoided. Just as well anyway, the slow, slow pace, giving me time to think, to formulate, to strategize, because I can't bear the thought of awaiting my fate, a good girl of the old school engaged in her needlework. The probabilities are on my side if I wait it out. The Bradfords are almost certain to pay the ransom and Tashya, in my judgment, when I strip away my justified rage, is very likely to release me. Being an unbeliever in crystal balls and the entrails of sacrificed birds, I can't demand certainty, but Tashya could have chained me to the wall, or locked me in closet or the trunk of a car and I'd have made that phone call anyway. Driven by fear, I would likely have done about anything she asked me to do. Nothing like that happened. Tashya was even so good as to eliminate the largest impediment to my release, a boy named Quentin.

So one certainty and one (very) likelihood. Maybe it's enough, but not before I explore the alternatives. I'm feeling stronger now, and angrier. Tashya wants me to believe that she forced me to bury the man she murdered because she couldn't wield a shovel and a handgun at the same time, the sequence entirely pragmatic. She can't understand why I'm not pleased, there being no room in her psyche for regret or shame.

Work is a concept beloved to us Bradfords, as if we earned our bread by the sweat of our brows, instead of other people's brows. I take up the lantern and begin a close-up inspection of the walls. I'm searching for a camera or a microphone and wishing Paolo was here to share his knowledge of the technology. Maybe there's a new device so tiny it can barely be seen, or so perfectly disguised it can't be recognized. I don't think so, but I'm not taking any chances, and I have plenty of time because the strip above the window shows daylight and I won't make a move, if I make a move at all, until after dark.

The walls finished, I examine the mattress and box spring, the table and the chair, even the little packages of jerky in case one has been opened and resealed. I turn finally to the ceiling, moving the table as I go, climbing on and off, my neck craned, paying the same attention to detail Father brings to his estimates. Again, I find nothing, no audio or visual device, and when I stop to think about it, I'm not all that surprised. Tashya as much as admitted that she'd adapted the space on the fly, fully illustrating the old cliché that beggars can't be choosers.

I look up at the window, the strip of light appearing no different than it did this morning, or an hour before. But time does not stand still, not for me, not for Tashya, only for Quentin. The afternoon will pass, night will follow. I don't know if the plywood panels covering the window will loosen, but I intend to find out. I intend, if at all possible, to determine my own fate.

Uncle Henry will be so proud.

CHAPTER TWENTY-ONE

DELIA

It's five o'clock on Wednesday morning. Hump day, the middle of the week. Get past this hurdle and it's clear sailing until the weekend. But this particular Wednesday is anything but ordinary. It's been more than two years since I've awakened beside a woman, and that was a one-and-done hookup that I stumbled into. Now, beside me, a sleeping Zoe Parillo breathes softly, her chest barely rising. I touch her gently, so as not to rouse her, and she doesn't stir. Last night, as we lay beside each other, she more or less admitted that her pragmatic approach to her job was protective. And me, I'm sailing in the same boat, actively cultivating a protective coat of emotional armor. That's because I spend my days wallowing in a misery I usually manage to worsen.

I slide out of bed. I'm supposed to pick Vern up at six and I'll have to stop at home for a clean uniform. Now I pull on yesterday's uniform and head for the bathroom. When I come back out, Zoe's sitting up in bed. Her expression's hard to read, a bit on the grave side, but curious and apprehensive as well. Our lovemaking was ardent, to say the least, but still more than simply physical. And now?

"Can you stay for breakfast?" Zoe asks.

"Can't. I have to meet Vern at six and I'm gonna be late as it is."

"Emmaline will miss you."

I've got a talent for saying the wrong thing and I prove it. "What now, Zoe, a guilt trip?"

Zoe's face registers her surprise. I've got it all wrong, but getting it wrong in relationships is my specialty.

"Hey, I'm sorry." I try smiling. "It's a cop thing. Always suspect the worst."

"And I need to get used to it?"

The question hangs in the air, the unspoken part louder than the spoken. Zoe wouldn't have to get used to "it" if last night wasn't the beginning of something. And I'll say it again. It wasn't just about the sex. Last night, while Zoe and I sat on the couch, watching a movie I can barely remember, Emmaline worked on a coloring book. She glanced up at me from time to time, projecting a message I readily understood. I'm being a good girl. Don't abandon me.

I indulged her, of course, praising her efforts, reminding her to stay between the lines, contributing to her choice of crayons. And thinking of Danny when he was three. At one point, I couldn't help it, I picked her up and hugged her against my chest. A series of little kisses followed, pecks really, tickle kisses. Emmaline's delighted laughter was reward enough.

"Yeah, Zoe, you will."

I have the door open, about to step through, when Zoe finally says what she's wanted to say all along. "I'm going to foster Emmaline. I don't think she can deal with moving into a strange environment when she's still processing this one." Zoe's smiling when I turn toward her. "Hey, Delia, I'm a social worker. Giving guilt is what I do."

That earns her a kiss. Then I'm out the door, my attention already turning to the day ahead.

Sunrise is still an hour off and the streets are predictably quiet, the exception being the site of a long-closed Radisson Hotel, which is being transformed into an upscale Hilton. A pair of eighteen-wheeler flatbeds are parked outside, both loaded with drywall. This is a scene being repeated almost everywhere in Baxter except the Yards, where the building part can't begin until after the demolition.

I take my time, despite already being late. My thoughts keep running between Danny, Emmaline, and Zoe, with occasional visits from Elizabeth Bradford. I don't need the distractions, but there's nothing I can do about them. I'll have to make it right with Danny if I continue to see Zoe. And if Zoe fosters Emmaline, the girl will remain in my life, along with the attachment. Maybe it'll be good for Danny. He's been sticking his nose in at every opportunity, his concern genuine enough, a brother to a sister. Well, commitments require sacrifice—of time, at the least—so let's see what he does when Emmaline's demands interfere with his training schedule. When he knows she's hoping to see him, but his buddies want to go to the movies.

Vern's waiting outside when I pull up. He begins to speak as he slides into the car. "You heard?"

"Heard what?"

"The kidnapping. Katie Burke led with it on the late news. It's out in the open now."

"Who leaked it? No, wait. It could be anyone. The FBI task force, that's eight people right there, and the Bradford's private security team, and maybe even one of the Bradfords. Meantime, Katie Burke will never reveal her source."

"Exactly right, Delia. And it doesn't change anything. Not for us."

"Except that it's sure to make the kidnappers more paranoid. Now the whole city's involved, looking for any sign of the girl."

Vern has nothing to add and we drive in silence to a small house in Dunning, the neighborhood closest to the Yards. Word here is that the mostly ramshackle homes are being purchased at rapidly escalating prices. The buyers hope to accumulate blocks of property, tear down the existing homes and erect high-occupancy housing in their place. Baxter has never had much in the way of apartment buildings. That's about to change. You can walk to work from just about anywhere in Dunning.

I bring my Toyota to the curb in front of a home rented by Cameron Carlyle. The house, though small, is in surprisingly good shape, but then Cameron has a way of landing on his feet. Not today, though.

"Hang on a second," Vern tells me as I'm about to open the door. "Something else. Lillian's pregnant."

"That's great, I know you've been . . ."

"And she wants to adopt Emmaline."

I try for a poker face, but only burst out laughing. I'm imagining Lillian Taney and Zoe Parillo on a field somewhere, battling for the right to parent the girl. Maybe with broadswords.

"You good with that?"

"Yeah, sure, we've been wanting more kids for a long time. I'm just afraid that Emmaline has family somewhere and they're gonna show up and claim her. I don't want Lillian to be disappointed. She's pretty much fallen in love with the girl. Mike too."

Vern and I pound on the door and announce ourselves. A voice from inside, a man's voice, shouts, "Don't break it down. I'm coming."

Cameron Carlyle opens the door a moment later and Vern pushes past him. Rumor has it that Cameron's involved with underage girls. He's handsome enough, smooth as well, and his soft brown eyes look into yours as though you were the last human on the planet. Meanwhile, he has the conscience of an amoeba.

Vern comes out a moment later. "He's alone."

"So, what's with the bad attitude?" Cameron asks. "I thought we were friends."

Cops don't like snitches any better than the mutts they rat on. Snitches are necessary, of course. Indispensable, actually.

Which means you have to put up with them and the deals they cut. Until the day they lie to you.

The search warrant we obtained before yesterday's raid was based on an affidavit from Cameron Carlyle. He swore that he'd done business with Joanna Young within the last week. Only problem is that Joanna Young and her companion had been dead for at least two weeks by then. Most likely, Cameron was about to pull off some deal and needed us out of the way.

"How long have you known me, Cameron?" Vern asks.

"Long time, detective. In fact, pretty much my whole life."

"Then you also know that if you don't stop fucking with me, we're gonna make a stop on the way to the station. Like in a quiet cornfield where I can beat the crap out of you without anyone seeing."

Cameron looks at me, but I'm keeping my expression neutral. We don't ordinarily abuse the men and women we arrest, but snitches are different. At some point, most will try to play you. This is a test you cannot fail.

"C'mon, guys . . ."

"Guys?" It's my turn to play the bad cop. "Is that some sort of homophobic comment?"

"What? Hey, no." Cameron's brown eyes turn inward for a moment as he collects himself. "Please, can we start over? I'm saying please. What have I done?"

Vern shakes his head. "I told you right out of the gate. You fuck with us, we're gonna charge you with selling heroin to an undercover cop. Did you think we were bluffing? Hope not, because you're under arrest. Turn around and put your hands behind your back."

Cameron finally gets it. He crossed a line by pointing us to Joanna Young, a line he probably didn't know existed when he perjured himself. Tough shit. I watch him turn around.

"You're pissed about Joanna," he finally says.

"We used your info to get a warrant for Joanna's house." I take my time cuffing him. "You claimed that you purchased heroin from Joanna less than ten days ago. By that time, she'd been dead for at least two weeks."

Cameron flashes a radiant smile. "Okay, so I fibbed about the deal. But Joanna's a straight-up dope dealer. . . ."

"Was a dealer, Cameron. She's dead, remember?"

"But I didn't know that."

Vern steps up as I close the cuffs around Cameron's wrists. Vern's a very large man, much larger than Cameron, and I detect fear in Cameron's eyes for the first time.

"Two overdoses, plus a third party ransacks the house, and you didn't know? When are you gonna stop lying, Cameron?" Vern doesn't wait for an answer. He takes Cameron's arm and says, "Alright, let's go."

"Wait, wait. Gimme a chance." That smile again, so confident, so assured. In his own eyes, he can do no wrong.

"Make it quick."

"Okay, you know the kidnapping thing? Been all over the news?"

"You're gonna claim you know where the victim is?"

"No, but listen to this story and tell me if you think it's important." He doesn't wait for the go ahead. "Maybe three weeks ago, I'm in a club, Palacio. I'm standing at the bar, waiting for somebody, and there's this couple next to me.

The guy's twenty-five at the most, but the broad? She's gotta be like fifty and she's got a mass of neon-yellow hair piled on top of her head, Dolly Parton style. Meantime, he's comin' on like she's Megan Fox, tellin' her that he's in on the biggest deal ever seen in Baxter. It's gonna be the news story of the year. Only he can't talk about it because it's not exactly on the up-and-up. But when it happens, it'll blow the lid off."

I stop him right there. "Was the word kidnapping used? Even once? And you lie to me again . . ."

"I'm not lyin'. He never said kidnapping. But what else could he be talkin' about? Believe me, there's nothin' big happening in town. Nothin' illegal. If there was, I'd know. And by the way, the woman called him Quentin."

"Quentin what?"

"I don't know."

"You're tellin' me that you weren't part of the conversation. You just happened to overhear what this guy said."

"I'm always listening, Captain. Always."

This I can believe. Cameron's brain works like a CIA computer, storing irrelevant information just in case. But what does it mean? A guy bullshitting a woman in a bar isn't exactly news. And the conversation took place three weeks ago.

"Not good enough, Cameron. You have anything else to trade?"

He runs off a series of names, but most of them are already on my to-raid list. The rest are too small to bother with at this stage of my crusade.

I guide Cameron to my car and into the back seat. He slides inside willingly, but flinches when Vern slides in beside him.

"Listen," he tells us, "I still think the story's good. But if it can't get me off the hook altogether, can you at least ask for a low bail?"

CHAPTER TWENTY-TWO

DELIA

It's still early, only seven-thirty, when I settle Cameron into the booking process. There's plenty of additional work to be done on our end. Paperwork, naturally. We have to dig up the report filed by the undercover who bought from Cameron, make sure the heroin is still in an evidence locker, and prepare the case for prosecution. I assign the job to Vern with the understanding that he'll reassign it to one of our detectives, probably Maya Kinsley.

The squad room's empty when I pass through on the way to my office. The Chief's not in yet, either, which gives me time to make a quick phone call to Danny. One night away and I'm already anxious.

"Hi, Mom."

"Hey, I missed you last night."

"Missed you too. Did you get to see Emmaline?"

This is not the question my son wants to ask and I love him enough to answer the one he did. "I spent the night with Zoe. Emmaline was there too. She went to bed early."

"Good. I mean really, really good. I mean I've been worried. What will you do when I go away to school? You'll be all alone."

"Like Emmaline?"

"Yeah, like Emmaline."

"Danny, my son, are you parenting me?"

That earns me a laugh. "Well, somebody has to. And thanks."

"For what?"

"The straight line." Danny hesitates, but I've got nothing to add. "Ya know what I was thinking?" he asks.

"No, tell me."

"I was thinking we could adopt Emmaline."

Now I'm trying to remember where I left my broadsword. "Let's have this conversation tonight. I'll be home for dinner, pizza in hand, half pepperoni and half mushrooms. If you get home first, you can make garlic toast and a salad."

"Okay."

The quick assent is followed by a long pause I refuse to interrupt. I know what's coming next and I don't mind, not in the slightest.

"Mom, can we talk about the kidnapping later? It's all Mike thinks about. Like it's the biggest crime in Baxter, maybe ever. On the news, it said the kidnappers are demanding ten million dollars."

"Sorry to disappoint, kid, but the FBI's taken over. The plan now is to pay the ransom and hope for the girl's release.

There's no investigation. At least not one I know about. And please don't forget. This conversation is strictly between the two of us."

"Okay, but what I heard on the news this morning? People are thinking the kidnapping might screw up the deal with Nissan. Have you heard anything?"

"Not a word."

Ten seconds after Danny hangs up, the phone rings again. My Caller ID reads Unknown Caller, and I almost let it ring out, only sliding my finger across the screen at the last minute.

"Hello."

"This is Sherman Bradford. Is this Captain Mariola?"

"It is, Sherman."

"Your nagging strategy worked, Captain. Not right away, but when Mom saw I wasn't giving up, she let me read the transcripts. You know, of my sister's calls? And the last one? That's not the way she talks, Captain. Not to Uncle Henry. The two of 'em get along great. They're like a two-man gang. She'd never talk to him that way."

"So . . ."

"So, there's a message. There has to be."

"Any idea what it is?"

"No, but the message is a piece of a puzzle. You get one piece of a puzzle, it doesn't make sense. But then you get two and three and four and suddenly message number one tells you everything you need to know. That's the way Liz explained math and she's the smartest kid in the country."

Sherman runs on, his words coming so fast they're almost slurred. "My sister's really big on measuring. Like she knew there was a risk in improvising, that the kidnappers might figure out that she was trying to communicate. So she must have been pretty desperate. I mean, she doesn't know that we've decided to pay the ransom, that we're not looking for her. Maybe they've got her locked up in the dark. Maybe she's really scared. My sister's always been the brave one."

I tell Sherman that she's still the brave one. Her attempt to send a message proves it. But I know, even as I hang up, that the role of the Baxter PD will be determined by Chief Black and Mayor Venn. Most likely, they've already discussed the various possibilities. For sure, we'll hold a joint press conference later in the day, us and the FBI.

I'm hungry and I have a long day ahead of me. I need to fuel up, but it's not to be. Seated on a bench outside my office, Christopher Bradford, Elizabeth's dad, rises as I approach. I find myself wondering if he's aware of my contacts with his wife and son. Not that it matters. Christopher Bradford is a visitor who cannot be denied a welcome.

"Mr. Bradford." I extend a hand which he gently shakes. "Are you here to see me?"

"Yes, if you can spare me a few minutes of your time. I know you have a division to run."

The man's features convey the anguish I felt when Danny was sick. His blue eyes are sunken behind the dark shadows that surround them. His lips are slightly open, as if he is having trouble breathing, and his shoulders slump. But his inherent formality hasn't completely deserted him. Christopher Bradford's wearing a blue blazer over sharply creased charcoal trousers and a white shirt. No tie, which for him is probably halfway to naked. A wedding ring circles the fourth finger on his left hand. A class ring with a sparkling green stone, which I'm guessing is an emerald, circles the matching finger on his right.

I open the door to my office, then step back to let him enter first.

The chair in front of my desk doesn't come close to meeting his standards. It's padded, true, but it's been around for a decade, a narrow parlor chair from a time when the Department struggled to pay the electric bill.

"Please, have a seat, Mr. Bradford." I circle the desk to drop into my own chair. "Has there been a new development?"

"No, but . . ." He drops his eyes to his lap for a moment, then brings them up to meet my own. "My brother has spent a lifetime measuring probabilities. Myself as well. Henry insists that guaranteed outcomes are as scarce as dinosaurs. One can never guarantee outcomes because outcomes are always in the future and the future cannot be known."

I nod my assent, though two-headed coins exist and loan sharks will put a gun to your head while you sign away the deed to your home.

"I don't doubt the FBI," he continues. "I believe it's very likely they've identified the gang that took Elizabeth and its operating strategy. I believe, too, that on the face of it, her kidnappers are likely to release Elizabeth when the ransom is paid. Unfortunately, Elizabeth knows nothing of this. She only hears what her kidnappers tell her and she has no reason to believe them. Perhaps they only mean to keep her quiet until they collect the money."

Bradford pauses, his gaze expectant. I'm supposed to make some comment, though I'm not sure what it is. Or what Christopher Bradford wants.

"What you've said, Mr. Bradford? It's obviously true. But I'm not sure what you want from the Baxter Police Department."

"Ah, what I want." He tugs at the creases in his trousers before crossing his legs. Not the sign of a man who intends to rush. "The FBI has oversimplified. They speak as if each kidnapping by the gang were identical. No variables, do you see? The Bradfords, on the other hand, know that factoring in as many variables as possible is key to success. You can't foresee every turn of the screw, but you must still consider as many as possible."

One part of my brain is screaming: coffee and breakfast, right now. Meanwhile, I suck up.

"The main variable, would that be Elizabeth herself?"

"Yes." Bradford finally smiles. "That's why I came, I think. To portray my daughter as an individual, and not as a number in the FBI's calculations."

"That's a very good idea." Now intrigued, I settle back to listen.

"As you probably know, the Bradford Group is a family-held business. That obligates each generation to provide the leadership necessary to maintain our independence. There's another way, and many a privately held corporation has chosen it. We could simply go public, diversify into unfamiliar fields, and hire managers with the expertise to run a diversified organization. The resulting IPO would make us very, very rich, of course, but very useless as well. Neither I, nor my brother, care for that label. The Bradford Group is our creation. It belongs to us and always will."

"Can I assume Elizabeth has a part to play here?"

"She does, Captain. You see, my brother cannot father children, and while there are cousins out there, none have demonstrated the necessary talent."

"And Sherman?"

"Sherman was born prematurely. He had a hard time of it for the first two years, and while he did recover physically, the ordeal left him far too . . . too fainthearted to head the Bradford Group. No resentment here, by the by, and no jealousy. Sherman understands and accepts his role. As I believe Elizabeth accepts hers. With the approval of my brother, Elizabeth's grooming began before she started school. I'll not bore you with the many facets of her grooming, but I would like to relate a single example. If I may."

I don't have a good deal of choice, but I'm hoping he'll get to the point before my blood sugar drops below detectable levels. "Sure, go ahead."

"One summer, when Elizabeth was nine or ten, memory fails me here, I hired a contractor to build a one-room house behind our summer cottage. The house was to include a half bath and a mini-kitchen, with all the attendant plumbing and wiring. Elizabeth didn't argue when

I required her and Sherman's participation. I think she understood even then. From the trenching for the foundation, to the raising of the roof, to the drywall on the interior, Elizabeth participated. She not only worked on the project where her physical strength allowed, she peppered the contractor, and whoever else would listen, with questions. By the time, the house was finished, she thoroughly understood the basics."

"And Sherman?"

"Sherman lost interest early on. He would attend the construction when directly ordered, but after a few weeks I gave up. The project wasn't intended for him in any event."

Bradford folds his hands and glances up before continuing. "One more anecdote. More to the point, actually, the point I need to make. My reason for interrupting your morning. Elizabeth was twelve years old when I discovered a short story she'd written as a birthday present to her brother. Elizabeth had filled her tale with the goblins and ghouls her brother loved, revealing, I believe, a romantic sensibility appropriate to her age. Her prose, on the other hand, was stunning. I minored in English Literature at Harvard, Captain, so you can be assured that I'm not playing the role of a proud papa. The words flowed across the page and the images she evoked were striking. I knew, after reading the story twice, that absent her family obligations, Elizabeth would have a place in the Arts. That won't be possible, I'm afraid, and again, I believe she knows and accepts."

I can't say I wasn't fascinated, but Christopher Bradford's tale was irrelevant at this point. Did the entire Bradford family want the Baxter Police Department to investigate? Or did they still believe that waiting it out was the best option? There were no other relevant questions.

"I spoke of Elizabeth as a variable, Captain, and you didn't disagree. How will she react to her capture? A romantic fifteen-year-old who believes, and not without reason, that she's the smartest person in the room? And how will her captors react if she tries to escape? Elizabeth has a great regard for innate intelligence, but much less for genuine expertise. She has no experience with the art of escape, but we can be sure that her captors are experienced at taking, hiding, and holding their captives."

Bradford stopped then, stopped suddenly. His blue eyes grew more intense and I recognized a pleading quality to his gaze. Unfortunately, I wasn't the answer to this prayer.

"What are you asking, Mr. Bradford? If anything. Has the family changed its mind? Do you want an active investigation?"

Another smile, this one rueful, almost embarrassed. "There's a reason my brother heads the company, a reason beyond his simply being the elder. I'm good at details, at tracking the numbers, whether they be dollars or cubic meters of cement. But decisions that involve the fate of the company? I vacillate, not unlike my son."

He stands, rising quickly to his feet, as though he's done something shameful and needs to get away. "I should never have brought my family to Baxter," he tells me as I escort him to the door. "Our security precautions weren't in place. If Elizabeth is harmed, I don't think I could bear it."

"More security wouldn't have helped. Elizabeth wasn't taken from the house. She left on her own."

"I know. I've seen the window she must have climbed through. Still, given another week, the windows would have been alarmed."

"Then she'd have found another way."

I head out before some other pressing duty arises, to Lena's Luncheonette across the street. In contrast to the Courthouse Diner where lawyers gather to talk of settlements and plea bargains, the Luncheonette's all business. The tables are Formica-topped and a long, scarred counter is fronted by torn stools repaired with duct tape. Lena opens her restaurant at six in the morning and closes at four in the afternoon. What with its limited menu—eggs in the morning, sandwiches in the afternoon, doughnuts all day long—it'd be called a food truck if the place was on wheels. Cops and workers at City Hall form virtually the whole of its customer base.

I find a stool at the far end of the counter and plant my butt. I was hoping for a nice, quiet breakfast. That's not going to happen because I still can't stop my brain as it jumps from one compelling topic to another. The kidnapping, first, but also Zoe, Danny, and Emmaline.

"Hey, Delia." Lena strides up to me. She's tall and still imposing in her sixties. "Coffee?"

"Yeah, and keep it coming."

"Anything else?"

I'm about to order eggs and bacon, heavy on the home fries, when I check myself. I've put on a good fifteen pounds over the past couple years. That didn't matter much before Zoe, but now . . . now I'm thinking twice. Not that Lena serves yogurt and fruit salad.

"Let's just do a toasted corn muffin."

"Gotchya." Lena makes a note in her order pad, then looks back up. "About this kidnapping, Delia. If the girl doesn't make it, do you think it's gonna hurt us with Nissan? Because I went to the bank yesterday and applied for a loan. I've already had two offers to buy the place, but I think I'm gonna go upscale."

"Sorry, Lena, I forgot my crystal ball."

"That's okay, Delia. I got tea leaves instead."

We laugh together, but the question hangs in the air as she moves off. My anti-drug campaign is designed to show that Baxter won't stand for crime and disorder. Now we've got a kidnapped girl, the fifteen-year-old daughter of one of the wealthiest families in the country. Call it a wild card with a yet-to-be-determined value.

The coffee arrives a moment later and I find my thoughts turning to Sherman Bradford and the two calls made by his sister. I've read the transcripts several times and the radical difference in tone is inescapable. But her message, if there was a message, eludes me. Vern read the transcripts, too, and he laid the disparity to an elevated level of stress. Elizabeth can't know about the gang's freeing hostages (all but one) in the past. Plus, she's only fifteen and time's passing, the endgame drawing closer and closer. So, yeah, she's freaking out. What would you expect?

Then there's Cameron Carlyle and a lounge lizard named Quentin. I'm pretty sure that Quentin exists. Cameron wouldn't send me on another wild goose chase, not after the Joanna Young fiasco got him arrested. But I can't make myself believe the story amounts to anything, even if accurate. And none of it matters until the Chief decides on what we do next.

My thoughts are still running in circles as I work my way through an enormous corn muffin that probably has as many calories as the bacon and eggs I originally wanted. Lena's one of those people whose life is all about work. I don't think she comprehends the purpose of downtime. True, she closes up at four, but she bakes the muffins and doughnuts she sells, starting at three in the morning. And when it comes to the doughnuts beloved to cops everywhere, you can forget the chains. Lena's Luncheonette is at the head of every cop's list.

The restaurant is busy, as usual, with a knot of customers gathered by the takeout counter near the front door. That's why I don't register the presence of Paolo Yoma until he's almost on top of me. I find myself glad to see him, or at least intrigued, but my phone rings before he can begin whatever spiel he's brought with him.

It's Katie Burke from the *Baxter Bugle*. I'm tempted to let it ring out, but I know that won't help me. Katie's a bulldog. She'll be calling me every ten minutes.

"Hi," she announces at the sound of my voice, her tone as chipper as ever. "I'm calling to allow you a chance to comment."

"About?"

"About the kidnapping."

"My comment is no comment. We'll release an official statement, probably this morning, but don't hold me to it."

"Okay, had to try."

I hang up and turn to Paolo. He's a homely man, his face narrow, his nose too long, his mouth too wide. At the same time, he continues to project the self-assurance that impressed me the first time we met.

"I think," he tells me, "I found where the kidnappers stayed when they first got to Baxter."

"You take the location to the FBI?"

"Nope. Took it to Henry Bradford instead. He's the reason I looked in the first place. Henry's been having second thoughts about waiting it out. He instructed me to investigate."

"And who gave Henry Bradford the authority?"

"A private citizen hires a private investigator. It's not against the law."

"Not if the private investigator is licensed in this state. Are you licensed in this state, Paolo?"

"Nope."

I'm sure Paolo can't wait to describe his investigation, but Vern calls before he gets started. The Chief requests our presence. Like immediately. I think I'm relieved as I cross the street and head directly for the Chief's office.

Chief Black's not alone when I step inside, followed by Vern. Adrienne Hope, Mayor Venn's top deputy is sitting off to one side. There's also a man in the room, a man the Chief quickly introduces. He's Special Agent Eli Carson. Carson nods to us, expression neither friendly nor combative. An older man in a suit that's become too small for him, he's here to do a job.

Chief Black speaks first. "Let's bring everyone up to date. Agent Carson."

Carson's sitting in a chair that usually rests before the Chief's desk. He's pulled it to one side and turned it to face the three interested parties, me, Vern, and Adrienne. He begins with a description of the Didiani gang, relaying the same information provided to me by John Meacham, then shifts to the main reason he showed up today.

"We're in a holding pattern," he tells us. "The ransom money's been secured and converted to Bitcoin, but the kidnappers have yet to demand the transfer. This is par for the course. The Didiani gang has been operating for about a decade and their strategy doesn't change. The final demand is made two to three days after the second contact with the victim."

Chief Black glances at me, raising a finger, then speaks. "The kidnapping is out in the open now. Does that change your calculations?"

"Not at all." Carson has the reassuring smile and direct gaze of an insurance salesman. "The gang's modus operandi is consistent. The ransom is paid and the victim is released, unharmed. Whether or not the kidnapping becomes public knowledge. The reasoning, I assume, is that next time out, law enforcement will recommend payment as the best option. As we do now."

"I see." The Chief rolls his chair back a few inches. "Can I assume the Bradford family supports your recommendation?"

"A hundred percent."

Agent Carson's pretty good. I know he's lying, but his eye contact, as it jumps from one of us to another, remains firm and direct. He should have been a con artist. On the other hand, that's exactly what he is. First, there's the GE executive who never came home. Second, there's Paolo Yoma. Yoma's an executive with the Bradford Group. Director of Security, if I remember right. No way is he operating without the family's knowledge and approval.

"So, where do we come in?" the Chief asks, his poker face every bit as composed as the agent's.

"A reassuring press conference this afternoon. Local and federal agencies involved, situation under control, negotiations ongoing. I'm sure you know the drill. All smoke, no fire."

"Sounds good to me. How about you, Adrienne? You on board?"

Adrienne Hope smooths her skirt. She's been operating behind the political radar screen for decades, a true survivor. "I'll discuss it with the Mayor, but I can't see how our presence adds anything."

"What," Chief Black wants to know, "if someone from the Mayor's office moderates the presentation? Without, of course, committing herself to a particular course of action."

"That could work."

Agent Carson stands up and straightens a tie that's ruler straight. "I admire your model, Chief." He points to the *Flying Cloud*. "I keep a model ship in my own office. British warship, *The Sovereign of the Seas*. Fully outfitted, she carried one hundred two guns. Next time we meet, I'll show you a photo."

Carson's out the door a minute later, leaving me, Vern, the Chief, and Adrienne to chew over his wake.

"Pardon my French," Chief Black declares, "but that prick was lying through his teeth. We know one of the gang's victims never came home. So, what else is he lying about?"

As Paolo Yoma's still at Lena's waiting, I quickly describe our brief conversation. "Yoma claims that he was told to investigate by Henry Bradford. There's no reason for him to lie. I think it's pretty obvious. The family wants more than the FBI's willing to give."

"What about the other part? About his knowing where the kidnappers stayed when they first came to Baxter?"

"No opinion, boss, not unless I check it out for myself. But Yoma's not stupid. In fact, he's a little too competent for my taste. Or maybe too smug."

Adrienne Hope raises a hand as she speaks out. "Cynthia Bradford's touched base with our office. Of course, the family's prepared to pay the ransom, but they'd like to see some sort of an investigation on our part. Discreet, naturally. Very, very discreet."

"Does she admit to being aware of the risk as I explained it to her and the rest of the family?" I ask. "Of what might happen if the kidnappers see me coming? Discreet or not, there's still a chance that I'll get too close. That I'll get too close and won't know it."

"I'm only certain that wait and hope isn't good enough for Cynthia Bradford. And we have to be pragmatic. We have to look at this from the city's point of view. If the ransom's paid and Elizabeth released, everybody wins. But if she's not, if there's a hitch somewhere, it'll look bad if we've done absolutely nothing. Personally, I think the Feds will find a way to blame us."

There being no challenge to this prophecy, Adrienne rises and crosses the room on her way out. Well into her seventies, she's another of those Baxterites who claim their families arrived in covered wagons.

The Chief walks her to the door, then closes it and turns to me and Vern. The stitches on the side of his head have been removed and his hair is growing back. In a month, the scar will be invisible.

"I want you to handle this, Delia. Nice and quiet, like the lady said. Me, I'm not convinced there's anything to find, but let's give it a couple of days. Vern, you run the in-house show while she's gone. I'll be in touch with both of you when we set a time for the press conference. Now, I've got a statement to write."

I make a stop in my office before taking up the task assigned to me. I keep a pair of jeans and a sweatshirt in the closet. Clothing of choice when I watch Danny play ball, or when I'm investigating a kidnapping that can't be investigated.

CHAPTER TWENTY-THREE

ELIZABETH

Even as Sherman struggled through a difficult first year of life, I realized that my obligation to my brother would be lifelong, a Bradford commitment, unyielding, irrevocable, to continue through eternity if only genetic research could solve the immortality problem. Sherman was quiet and distant from birth, an ailing infant who didn't cry, who seemed always surprised. What's happening with this new life? How did I get here? Would you kindly put me back?

We made natural companions, Sherman without friends because he couldn't make them and didn't need them, me because my peers didn't like me. And Sherman took instruction, believed in me, a fountain of all wisdom, although I was in most ways more ignorant than my gecko. I took Sherman through his first years by the figurative hand, he willing, even eager, to be led.

"Your brother trusts you," my mother told me. "You know what that means?"

Uncle Henry had a different take on the matter. "Your brother can't make it on his own, but he's still a Bradford and it's important that he act the part."

"Or at least that people believe he's acting the part?"

"Well put, Lizzy. In our world, it's the show that counts."

On this afternoon, the show is all wrong. I doze off, drift into a dream of my brother, his voice, begging for help and me unable to find my shoes or my phone or my coat, then wake suddenly. Unwilling to risk another dream, my duty shirked, I throw off the blanket, rise, and begin to pace. I drink a little water, chew on one end of a Slim Jim, the chemicals foul on my tongue, use the bucket strategically placed in a corner, try to interest myself in one of the movies on the tablet, an old comedy, every laugh-line telegraphed.

I want the night, escape, imagining myself slipping through the open window, tracing the miles to Baxter, knocking on the door of our temporary residence. Hey, it's me. I'm home.

Implacable, almost defiant, the day will not retreat, the light over the window a thin line, unchanging, eternal. I've knocked hard on the stairway door with no response and I have to think I'm alone in a house that's supposed to be unoccupied, Tashya unwilling to chance a visitor to the park glimpsing her through a window. Not with just days to wait before the payoff. Right?

Wrong. Tashya's footsteps on the stairs are all wrong. They lack her customary deliberation, that display of self-control, I'm in charge here, no detail untended. She's rushed now, frustrated, her concern visible in her tight mouth and raised shoulders, the first sign of emotion yet displayed. Yes, Tashya does have feelings. Not compassion, surely, or empathy or kindness or generosity. Fear, though, or at least anxiety, some domino that failed to fall.

"We must leave."

The gun in her hand precludes any protest, or even negotiation, off you go and keep your big mouth shut. For once.

And I do go, and do keep my big mouth shut, up the stairs, through the kitchen and out the door. There's a U-Haul van parked close to the house, side door open, the man behind the wheel turned away so I cannot—and better not—see his face. I clamber aboard without being asked, into a closed space without windows, a bulkhead between the cargo area and the front seat hiding the driver.

Tashya climbs in behind me and slams the door. From overhead, a small light provides a thin illumination that's somehow as threatening as total darkness. The van moves before I find my balance, tipping me onto a thin mattress that covers most of the metal flooring.

I want to remain silent, the ever-brave Bradford refusing the consolation of speech, but the obvious interruption in the plan Tashya and family have concocted dissolves my reserve. I am no longer Sherman's protector. I'm a fifteen-year-old girl out of her element, dropped into the very world the Bradford fortune was meant to preclude.

"Tashya, what's going on?"

No answer, only the insect hiss of revolving tires on dry pavement, the sudden silence of the van stopped. At a light? A stop sign? I'm as blind to the outside world as I was in the basement, even more so with no streak of light to offer hope, however slight. The van picks up speed, accelerating onto what must be a main road, and we're both rolled about, me and Tashya and her gun. She sits with her back against the bulkhead as I cling to the mattress, feeling the metal floor of the van through the thin material. The words come back to me, the toddler's prayer: And if I die before I wake.

The van moves to the right and slows, traces a series of turns, finally stops altogether. A moment later, I hear the latch on the driver's door snap open, then the door slam shut. We're alone.

"It's out there," Tashya announces.

"What's out there?"

"Your kidnapping. It's gone . . . viral, yes? Entire city looks for you."

I'd already concluded that everybody was looking for me. Stupid, actually, if quietly paying was the intent from the outset. If Tashya told the truth about her family's past, if the FBI identified the pattern.

"When will you demand payment?"

"There is problem."

The fear that grips me centers in my gut, the tightening claws of a raptor. Do I at some point become more trouble than I'm worth, an infected appendage, amputation the only remedy? This is a question I've asked myself before and will probably ask again. Assuming I live long enough.

I listen quietly for a time. We're in a parking lot, no doubt, probably at a rest stop on the interstate. I can hear the voices of people walking by, a child crying, a woman talking rapidly with no returning dialogue, a horn sounding, an engine starting, revving up, dying to an idle. And only the thin wall of the van separating me from normal life, the everyday, taken-for-granted world I rejected as too ordinary to acknowledge.

"Tell me about the problem, Tashya."

"There will be a delay."

"Why?"

"Does that concern you?" Tashya's face continues to betray her anxiety and I realize that just because she's the face of the crew that took me doesn't make her it's leader. Or even very important, and it's possible that she fears Quentin's fate. I can't bring myself to believe she's worried about Elizabeth Bradford.

I should do it. That's what I tell myself. Pound on the side of the van and scream for help. There's no one behind the wheel, no one to drive away and Tashya won't shoot me. Not with no hope of escape, not in a death penalty state, kidnapping, however vile, the lesser offense. Yet when Tashya's eyes narrow and she raises the barrel of the gun in her hand, all that Bradford resolve peels away and I'm a three-year-old child, afraid of the dark, the devil under the bed, the skeleton in the closet.

"Tell me, Tashya." I want to ask what she's so afraid of, but I don't. "Why the delay?"

"Always in life things happen at random. You cannot anticipate everything, no matter how long and hard you are planning."

"You sound like my mother."

That gains me a thin smile. "First stop for ransom Bitcoin . . . closed down by police in Albania. For why? It does not matter. We must find a new first destination. Safe destination, yes? This will take some days."

"How many?"

"We are hoping two or three."

The driver's side door unlocks and I hear our driver slip behind the wheel. A few seconds later, Tashya's phone rings. A heated conversation follows—I can hear only Tashya's end—but I find myself asking a question. Is the person on the other end, almost surely the driver, so familiar as to be unwilling even to have his voice recognized?

Then we're moving again.

"You are going to call parents. You will say this."

Tashya takes a sheet of yellow paper from the inside pocket of her jacket and passes it over. The hand-printed message, written as lines of dialogue, seems oddly foreign, as though even the roman alphabet has been learned, not imbibed.

I am good.
There will be a small delay.
Remain patient.

"You will not wait for reply. You will not add anything. You will not respond to anything that is said. So far, Elizabeth, I have been . . . considerate. This does not have to continue. I have troubles and do not need more. Say the words, hand me the phone. That is what you will do."

My mother answers the family phone, likely because no more calls are expected and she's the only one to persist. I stumble at the sound of her voice, reality now my gecko's tongue curling around a cricket. I may never see her again.

I catch myself up, read the message, hand the phone to Tashya, who slides it into a phone wallet. Mom's voice lingers, hers the arms to which I fled as a toddler, no longer a safety net, only a memory of another time that might have been another lifetime. I've got it now, I tell myself, it's Quentin they fear and not his body discovered by a hiker's beagle. Tashya and her crew followed us to Baxter because Louisville didn't present the opportunity they sought. A long shot? Undoubtedly . . . until they happened on Quentin and his hideaway in Ulysses S. Grant State Park.

"You are thinking what?" Tashya asks. "To escape?"

"No. I'm still hearing my mother's voice. What she said before you took the phone away."

"And what is this?"

"We have the payment ready." I'm lying, but Tashya only shakes her head. "Nothing to say, Tashya? What happened to the tried-and-true formula? Two demands, payment in Bitcoin, ransom sent, hostage released?"

"This is still to happen. Only the delay."

The delay is in her response and I know what troubles her and her unseen allies, the family gangsters here and abroad. Maybe Tashya and Quentin came together in a private situation, nobody the wiser, his role in this drama unknown and unsuspected by friends and acquaintances. But its far more likely that they initially found each other in a public setting, that there followed a brief courting based on sex, money, or both, that they were seen together, Quentin and this older woman with her foreign accent.

And now he's vanished.

I'd been imprisoned in a cottage occupied once upon a time by Quentin and the kidnapping is public knowledge, my photo on every TV set, on every phone screen, the entire city looking for me. That must include the official lookers, the police.

We're on the interstate again, the unyielding buzz of the tires especially loud. The van isn't insulated and the composite panels covering the sides and the back rattle softly. Trucks seem to pass in slow motion, the roar of their engines felt as well as heard.

We ride for another twenty minutes, from the interstate, over a pair of lesser roads, finally onto a dirt road, the van's hard suspension jolting through the potholes. The van slows, then stops, and the man in front shuts off the engine, the constant hum replaced by the chitter of crickets. The door opens, shuts, and I hear footsteps retreating. Tashya sits across from me, her expression firm. Nothing's changed here and I'll do what I have to do.

"I know what it's like," I tell her, "to live for a family. You can't fuck it up. You just can't. There are, after all, expectations, especially for the entrusted."

"You are misunderstanding, Elizabeth. Mistakes, yes, but not by me. I am here for repairs. And for making decisions others are afraid to make. Two days, three at most. Then we are gone."

Not all that long ago, Tashya would have added, "And you are released." Not this time, and I have to wonder if the message she's sending is a threat. Become a pain in the ass and the joke's on you. Or is she simply tired of my voice, of my repeating a message already looping through her mind? But I'm sure of this, though I can't put a finger on the probability: if the cops stumble on Quentin's relationship with a suddenly arrived foreign woman fifteen years his senior, it's only a hop, skip, and jump to my prison. And that, for Tashya, would be the worst outcome imaginable, me rescued, the ransom unpaid, and her to explain the failure. Assuming her future doesn't include spending the rest of her life in an American prison.

Five minutes later, the driver's side door opens, closes, and Tashya's phone rings. I think I know what they're doing. I think they're looking for a new place to keep me until the ransom is paid. Tashya's tone is sharp, impatient, anxious. The truck starts an instant after she ends the connection and the vehicle begins to move, retracing steps, the rutted lane first, then a back road, then some sort of intermediate highway, then the interstate, the van moving faster with each transition. Tashya doesn't speak, most likely because there's nothing left to say, but I watch her gradually relax and I know we're headed back to Quentin's cottage, to my basement prison. And I know that Tashya has resigned herself to whatever course of action keeps her safe.

I have to get out.

CHAPTER TWENTY-FOUR

DELIA

Paolo's right where I left him, at Lena's, the only change being the empty plates in front of him. I glance in Lena's direction as I sit down. She's holding a carafe of coffee which she raises along with her eyebrows. No words necessary, I nod once and she comes over.

"Anything to eat, honey?"

"No, thanks." I'm not offended by the familiarity. All Lena's customers are honeys. I wait until she fetches a mug and fills it, then take a sip. It's not rancid, like the coffee inside the squad room, but it'll have to do.

"Okay, Paolo, first thing. You investigate on your own again, I'll arrest you. I'll arrest you and convince a judge to keep you locked up until the . . . the situation is resolved. From this minute forward, you don't do anything without my okay."

Paolo's interested expression doesn't change, but I don't think he's all that impressed. If arrested, he'll undoubtedly be represented by the kind of lawyers who got OJ off the hook. "Got it, Captain."

"You think I'm bluffing?"

"Not for a minute."

"Good." I lean forward. "You told me that you discovered where the kidnappers stayed when they first got here. That's kidnappers, right? As in more than one?"

"As in two." Yoma's gaze never leaves my face and I assume he's trying to impress me. "Two that I know of."

"Hold on, Paolo. There's something else I want to explore before you tell your story. Something that's been running around my brain for the last couple of days. According to Chip McEwan, Elizabeth was taken from Baxter Park around four o'clock in the morning. And that was after she snuck out through a back window in her home about three-thirty. You with me so far?"

"Yeah."

"So how did her kidnappers know she'd sneak out on that day at that time?" I run on before he can offer an opinion. "Did the kidnappers have eyes on the home twenty-four seven? Was someone hiding behind a bush, peering through night-vision binoculars? That sort of operation would indicate serious numbers. One or two people couldn't bring it off. Is that what you found? A large group of conspirators?"

"No."

"Paolo, you're Director of Security for the Bradford Group. That correct?"

"Not exactly. I'm Director of Site Security. I work on the company's projects, wherever they are."

"What about the family's security team?"

"Contracted out. Same with security at our offices."

"Nothing to do with you?"

"Outside of me supervising the electronics, nothing. In fact, my team is relatively small and completely mobile. You can find us wherever the Group has an ongoing project, in the bidding as well as the work phase."

"What about the guards assigned to the various projects?"

"Broken into two parts. The tech personnel are company employees who work under me. The rest are supplied by local contractors at prevailing rates, which saves the Bradford Group a lot of money when it operates overseas. Remember, we rely on cameras, not people, to secure our sites."

"You've already explained the part about the cameras." I signal Lena for a refill, then point to a doughnut display and mouth the word *glazed*. Lena nods and I'm back to Paolo. "I want you to obtain the files on the security personnel working in the house on the night of the kidnapping. The staff as well. Because if there was nobody out there to spot her when she climbed through the window, somebody must've spotted her while she was still inside. According to her brother, she'd snuck out before."

"Don't you need a search warrant for the files, or at least a subpoena?"

"I might, but not you." I sit back as Lena walks up with my doughnut and lays it in front of me. Sorry, Zoe. "You work in the company's security division. Surely, if you suspected an employee of stealing, you'd have access to their employment records. Especially if Henry Bradford personally approved the search."

Paolo stares at me for a moment, then smiles. "Damn, Captain, if you're not as devious as I am."

I ignore the backhanded compliment. "I want to take a look at anyone in the house on the night Elizabeth was snatched. Check that. I want Paolo Yoma to look at anyone in the house. Just the paperwork for now. Anything that looks suspicious, you bring it back to me."

"No problem, Captain. My password allows access to those files."

"Great. But let Henry Bradford know what you're doing and why you're doing it." I wait for a nod that's quick in coming. "Now, you claim you know where the kidnappers stayed when they first arrived. Let's hear it."

"When you visited the residence, you raised a question. Where did the kidnappers first live after they moved to Baxter, a city presumably unknown to them? Then you mentioned the seedier hotels in town and that got me thinking. Better yet, it got me working. I started by assuming the probabilities we've already established. That the kidnappers' move to Baxter was sudden, that the city was unfamiliar to them, and that the gang would include a woman who spoke with a strong accent. They'd need a place to stay while they got their bearings and they wouldn't be eager to use a credit card. True, the Holiday Inn by the interstate accepts cash, but a cash payment would surely draw attention. Along with a likely request for identification."

Paolo stops long enough to frame his thoughts. "If I had to bet, Captain, I'd bet the kidnappers didn't expect to succeed. Not given the time pressure. I'd bet they got lucky somewhere along the line. They stumbled onto an opportunity that pulled everything together."

"Let's stick with the hotel for now."

"Okay, so I'm looking for bottom-tier dives that take the money and don't ask questions. Whatever you write in the register, it's alright."

"How did you locate them?"

"Google, how else? I couldn't network because I didn't know anyone who'd visited Baxter. So, I accessed the usual suspects first. Yelp, Hotels.com, Booking.com, and Priceline. I found a few one-star joints and saved the addresses. Then I did a general search for Baxter and found a website named BaxterBoosterGirl."

I'm laughing despite myself. The site's operated by Deirdre Venson. According to biography long enough to pass for a memoir, she worked the gig economy until she discovered that her annual income didn't cover the rent. Then she jumped to entrepreneurship and developed BaxterBooster-Girl after the Nissan deal became public. Where to eat, where to stay, where to rent, where to buy prime real estate. Half the brokers in Baxter advertise on the site. She's a rising city oligarch.

"You've heard of it, Captain?"

"I've been interviewed for the site."

"Then you know about the page Voyager Beware?"

"I don't."

"Places to avoid in Baxter. Now, here's the beautiful part. Rather than face defamation suits, she encourages site visitors to post anonymous reviews." Paolo hesitates long enough to register my impatience. "Okay, to the point. I found three hotels listed, all three accused of being havens for prostitutes and drug dealers. I visited all three, claiming I was looking for a runaway wife who not only abandoned her children, but looted the family savings before she and her lover fled to Baxter. And, oh yes, she speaks with a Polish accent."

"Not Georgian?"

"I wanted to keep it simple. A foreigner, not a southern belle. As it was, I struck out at the first two, the Harmony Inn and the Power Lodge. That left the Prairie Hotel, where I caught a break. The clerk—or maybe the owner . . ."

"Describe him?"

"In his sixties, probably, with a really sparse gray beard that he's let grow too long. His eyes are a pale green, almost watery, and the left one has a lazy lid. It comes within a few millimeters of being closed."

"Yeah, he's the owner alright. Lives there, too. Name is Donald Grogan. So, go on."

"Donald seemed half-asleep when I walked through the door, but he woke right up when he spotted the fifty I held between my fingers. After a little back-and-forth, he told me that a woman with a heavy accent, accompanied by a younger man without an accent, stayed at the hotel for two nights in early August. He remembered because he doesn't get out-of-town guests. The date, by the way, coincides with the article on the company website."

At that point, I remind myself. Time is not on our side. But at least Yoma's provided me with a starting point.

"Okay, let's get moving. You grab those files and review them. Who might be working with the kidnappers? Who might have spotted Elizabeth leaving the house? Let's try to catch up around noon."

"And you, Captain?"

"I'm going to have a conversation with an ex-con named Donald Grogan. See what else he might know."

I haven't told Paolo that the Prairie Hotel has been on the Baxter PD hit list from the beginning. Based on multiple informants, the affidavits we presented told the same story. Grogan rents to numerous independent drug dealers and prostitutes. The dealers conduct business inside the rooms. The prostitutes service their johns inside other rooms.

Our preparations were meticulous, but not enough to secure a warrant for the entire building. That's because we couldn't put a particular dealer in a particular room at a particular time. Grant us a general warrant and we were likely to bust in on somebody's fiftieth wedding anniversary, or so the judge reasoned. But that reasoning didn't apply to Donald Grogan. We had informants claiming he kept ecstasy behind the counter and in his office. The information was precise enough for a warrant to search those spaces.

I place a call to Vern from Lena's. Paolo's lead isn't much of a lead, which we both know without saying it aloud, but it's all we have. "By noon, Vern. We'll go in quietly. Five of us, three in uniform. Use Cade if he's available."

"Got it."

"And if Caitlin's working today, could you send her a message? I'll see her in my office in . . ." I bite into my doughnut, then mumble, "a half hour."

Caitlin Capuano's our in-house computer expert. A good-looking girl in her midtwenties with a quick, bright smile, she doesn't look at all like a nerd. But in the macho-cop world, all civilian workers are nerds, while civilian computer experts are supernerds.

CHAPTER TWENTY-FIVE

DELIA

It's almost one o'clock when our caravan settles down a block from the hotel. Besides myself and Vern (and Caitlin, who'll remain in the car until I need her), I've got three uniformed cops under my command: Jerome Meeks, Maya Kinsley, and Cade Barrow.

I ask the obvious question once we've exited the vehicles: "All ready?" I don't wait for an answer. I herd them, weapons drawn, through the Prairie Hotel's main door and into what passes for a lobby. A stairway to my right leads to the upper floor, a hallway directly ahead provides access to the other rooms on the first floor. The registration desk is to our left and Donald Grogan is standing behind it.

My informants, interviewed separately, were in agreement on several items, the most important for the moment is the handgun stashed behind the counter.

"Come out of there, Donald," I tell him. "And keep your hands where I can see them."

Grogan's hands are already over his head. Having been to prison twice, the man's well seasoned. By contrast, the eyes of the two women leaning on our side of the counter bug out of their heads. Prostitutes? Addicts? Ravaged is what they are, by harsh, self-destructive lives. When I tell them to get lost, they dash out of the building, feet barely touching the ground.

Vern's behind the registration desk before the door closes. A few seconds later, he comes up with a .44 caliber revolver. "Got it."

Baxter still hasn't surrendered to the free-carry fever. You need a permit to carry a handgun, open or concealed. The opposite prevails for personal protection inside a home or place of business. Almost any resident can walk into a gun store and come out with a weapon that'll fire as fast as you can pull the trigger. There is one exception, though. Ex-felons are not allowed to own firearms.

"You're under arrest," I announce. "Hook him up, Cade."

Grogan brings his right eyelid down, echoing the involuntary droop of his left. "That's not mine, Officer."

"Captain."

"Okay, Captain. But the gun belongs to my father. The bill of sale's in his name."

"How 'bout these?" Vern's holding up a clear plastic vial of pink and blue pills. "These belong to your father too?"

"I want a lawyer."

"Sure."

At the moment, I'm not especially interested in Grogan. My attention is focused on a CCTV camera located at the end of the registration desk closest to the outer wall. I've been inside the Prairie twice before, responding to a pair of overdoses, and been struck both times by the camera. Surely, the mutts who frequent the Prairie don't want their photos taken. But there it is, positioned to record anyone approaching one end of the desk, but leaving the other end uncovered. The arrangement lets Grogan conduct business without being recorded, but still have a record of anyone who enters or exits through the lobby.

With Grogan in custody, my three uniformed officers turn their attention to the entrance and the corridor across the way. They have a simple task. Keep the lobby clear. Don't let anyone inside and hustle anyone leaving through the door.

"Jerome, get Caitlin."

Jerome Meeks leaves without a word. He returns a few minutes later with Caitlin Capuano. Caitlin's cheeks are flushed. I think she's thrilled to be part of a real police operation, but her expression reverses as she takes in the lobby. I have to assume the wallpaper, a silvery gray speckled with doves in flight, was once vibrant. Now the wallpaper's thoroughly soiled in those portions of the wall it still covers. Much of it has been torn away, exposing stark white plaster and a sprinkling of cockroaches. Above our heads, a patch of black mold clings to the ceiling near the entrance to the main corridor. Its scent dominates the room.

Caitlin's a civilian employee. Along with a pair of assistants, she keeps our system up and running. Money in, money out, routine searches of relevant databases. She didn't sign on for this.

"Hey, Caitlin, you with us?" My voice is sharper than I would have liked, but I'm in a hurry.

"Yeah, Captain. What do you need?"

I point to the camera. "First, is that working?"

"The little red light's on?" Caitlin puts a question mark at the end of almost every sentence. If she was a cop under my command, I'd correct her. "That means it's getting juice?"

"Is it digital?"

"Yeah, like an early model. The new ones don't face straight ahead? They have more like a panoramic view?"

So far, so good. Now for the big question. "Does it record continually when it's turned on?"

"One way to find out."

Caitlin waves us out of the camera's view. A few seconds later, the little red light goes dark. The camera's motion-activated, a break. We won't have to review ten thousand hours of data.

Vern appears in the doorway leading to the office before I can take the next step. "Better come in here, Captain."

Vern leads me to a drawer with a false back. The drawer's been pulled out to reveal a metal canister with the lid off. There appears to be several hundred capsules inside. Perfect.

"Something else." He slides a pile of 8x11 photos out of a large manila envelope. The photo on top reveals one of our most prominent attorneys in bed with a heavily tattooed young woman.

"The others?"

"Different actors, same principle."

"Now we know why he had the cameras. Leave the molly in the drawer. We'll photograph it in place later on."

"And the photos?"

"Straight to the Chief, Vern."

"Not into evidence?"

I shake my head. Our warrant is specific. We can search anywhere in the lobby or office where ecstasy can be hidden. That does not include a flat manila envelope stuffed with photographs. Nor, concealed as they are, can we claim we found them in plain view. That bars their being presented in a courtroom, but not their appearance on some obscure website. Just as Joanna Young's home was ransacked after her overdose, I'm expecting the Prairie Hotel to be turned upside down once I take Grogan into custody. No way am I going to leave Baxter at the mercy of whoever finds the photos.

"Tuck 'em away, Vern. Let the Chief decide what to do. And we'll need to take the computer with us when we leave." I look out through the door and motion Caitlin inside. The office is in no better condition than the lobby, but she seems relieved. She points to a computer resting on a battered wooden desk.

"That for me?"

"Only if it's unlocked."

Caitlin reaches forward and taps a key, bringing up a ledger sheet on the monitor. "It was in sleep mode? Suspended animation? He was probably using it before we came in."

Caitlin and I have switched psychological positions. She appears to be in her element. I'm the one holding my breath. "I'm looking for data recorded by the lobby camera in early August. If it still exists."

"It should? The motion detector is designed to minimize the data in storage. There's no audio, by the way."

"Just find it Caitlin. The first two weeks in August."

I'm prepared for a long wait. Computers are foreign enemies to me. If you teach me how to accomplish some aim, I can memorize the sequence necessary to get the job done. But unlike Danny, whenever I try to muddle through on my own, I feel like I'm navigating a maze with no exit. In fact, it takes Caitlin only a few minutes before she announces, "Got it."

The monitor reveals the face of a man whose name eludes me. I recognize him though. A dealer not yet on my radar screen, he's hovering just over the horizon. The date stamp reads August 1.

"Show me how to fast-forward and pause." The demonstration is brief, the guide easy to follow. "I'll need you to wait outside, Caitlin. And thanks. You didn't have to do this."

The recognition calls forth a smile I read as genuine. Then she's gone and I go to work with Vern leaning over my shoulder. I'm looking for that out-of-place woman with the foreign accent. I won't hear her speak, but as I move forward, the females I encounter are all of a type. Junkie-prostitutes come in many shades of decline and these, some of them male, are hurtling toward the bottom end of the slide.

As I move forward through the month of August, I don't linger on any particular woman, or on the man who accompanies her. One glance and it's good-bye. But the work is tedious, as cop work often is. Endless telephone calls, knocking on door after door after door. But if there's to be a payoff, it's only through persistence, a belief that what you're looking for is under the stone you leave unturned.

A half hour later, accompanied by a noticeably younger man, she walks into the Prairie Hotel. The date stamp reads August 14. The time stamp reads 8:45 P.M. Behind me, I hear Vern draw a quick breath.

The contrast between the woman on the screen and the women who preceded her is stark. Her eyes look directly into what I assume to be Grogan's. They betray no fear, remarkable in itself because the average middle-class housewife wouldn't enter the Prairie unless someone put a gun to her head. Aside from the bravado, the woman is perfectly nondescript. Medium-length dark hair, the styling without style. Her makeup is also minimal. Pale lipstick, a touch of rouge on her cheeks, maybe a hint of eye shadow. The quality of the video leaves even that much in doubt. She's wearing a blouse over jeans, the blouse silvery, the jeans white, no jewelry, not even earrings.

"Gotta be," Vern mutters. Then he turns to me, his smile rueful. "Looks like Paolo was a step ahead. So, what's next"

I shift my attention to the man with her. Nearly a foot taller and at least ten years younger, he stands a couple steps in back so that his features are above the camera's field of view. Arms folded across a St. Louis Cardinals sweatshirt, he appears threatening and indifferent at the same time, a combination I've seen before.

This time Vern's tone is insistent. "What's next, Delia?"

Good question. I'll check the registry behind the desk, but I'm not expecting the woman's real name. And just knowing she was here? Normally, I'd show her photo to everyone in the building, and brace Grogan as well. But I can't be sure that somebody won't add two plus two and come up with Elizabeth Bradford. I can't take the chance.

"You with us, Delia?"

"Yeah, Vern. Just thinking."

"Thinking what?"

"That we need two things. We need to print this frame and we need to find a man named Quentin. In a hurry."

CHAPTER TWENTY-SIX

DELIA

The hurry part grinds to a halt when I receive a call from the Chief's assistant. The press conference will start at one-thirty. Be there.

We comply, arriving early enough to brief Chief Black in his office. His eyes widen as he slides the photos out of the manila envelope. I watch his mouth open, close, open again.

"Anybody else see these?"

"Donald Grogan, for sure," I reply.

"I mean does anyone else know you found them?"

"C'mon, Chief, you think we phoned Katie Burke?"

"No, no." He shoves the photos back inside the envelope, but continues to stare down at his desk. Finally, he says, "They never existed, right? The photos?"

"Fine with me, but you better take a close look inside his computer. Or somehow make it disappear. Because that's where they were before he printed them out."

◆

The press conference begins an hour late, then continues for more than an hour. On our part, the law enforcement end, we give up nothing. The FBI is investigating. The Baxter Police Department is investigating. We're on the hunt, but so sorry, we cannot supply you with a single detail. For obvious reasons.

Cynthia Bradford delivers the customary plea for her child's release. As she steps to the microphone, it's obvious that the days have taken their toll. The composed woman I first met has been replaced by a frightened mother having to face the possibility that she may never see her daughter again. She's dressed neatly, her makeup smoothly applied, the small pearls in her ears appropriate to the occasion. But her swollen eyelids, her bloodshot eyes, betray her. As do the slope of her shoulders and the odd way she pauses for breath, the words coming from her mouth obviously written out beforehand. On the advice, I assume, of her FBI handlers.

Christopher Bradford stands behind his wife, seeming bewildered and entirely out of place. I read his expression as intimidated, by the crowd of reporters that includes NBC and FOX, and by the situation itself. Sherman stands beside his father, so obviously distressed that I want to reach out, to draw him close, to hug him. That's not what he wants and I know it. Sherman wants his sister back. At one point, Paolo described the girl as her brother's spirit-guide.

I'm standing off to one side when I should be in the field, watching Cynthia respond to moronic questions she can't possibly answer. The reporters want her to provide details the FBI and the Baxter PD have already declared off limits. Katie Burke is especially persistent and I know we'll see her face on the local news tonight, appearing earnest.

Just when I decide the party will never end, it ends. I wait a few minutes, until Cynthia is off by herself, then approach her. I don't have much to say, but I need to say it.

"We're looking, Mrs. Bradford. I want you to know. We're looking."

"Thank you, Captain."

I skip out before Katie Burke's able to corner me. I know she'll ask me a dozen questions that I'll refuse to answer. I also know that my refusal will become part of the story. Vern's waiting for me in the parking lot behind the station house. The obvious first step in identifying Quentin and the role he's played in the kidnapping, if any, is a visit to Palacio. That won't happen right away. Palacio's manager, Zane Yarmouth, is an ex-con with a serious attitude when it comes to cops. Not only will he not cooperate, his employees, who fear him, won't cooperate. I have no leverage, either, because Palacio doesn't tolerate drug use, much less drug dealing.

Fortunately, Yarmouth has a boss, the bar's owner, an old man named Zack Butler. Butler's the source of many rumors. He was formerly a gangster who made so much money he was able to quit the game. Or he's still a gangster, but too slick and too high up to be caught. Or he was never a gangster, his fortune tied to the millions he inherited from an unknown forebear. All true, or none, it doesn't matter to me because the certainty is that Zack Butler's heavily invested in the new Baxter. Discreetly aiding my crusade is to his advantage and he's reached out to guide me on several occasions.

I'm not fool enough to show up at Zack's and find him with people who can't know about our relationship. I call him on the very private number he provided at our first meeting. Zack's seriously ill with emphysema. He rarely leaves his home and requires care around the clock. When he answers, his voice is very soft, almost a whisper.

"Detective . . ."

"Captain now, Zack."

"Congratulations. So, what can I do for you?"

"You ever hear of a man named Quentin, probably a local?"

"Never."

"Well, I need to find him and your man at Palacio can help."

Zack starts to laugh, chokes for a second, then takes the time to draw a pair of noisy breaths. "That man wouldn't be Zane Yarmouth, would it?"

"It would."

"Zane hates cops. He'd rather bite off his tongue than help you."

"Yarmouth isn't the boss, Zack. You are."

Vern and I are wearing street clothes when we stroll into Palacio forty minutes later. The elaborately decorated interior reflects a corn-belt designer's fantasy of an Italian palace. Murals on three walls alternately reveal gods in battle and elaborate feasts with bare-breasted women. The fourth wall, the wall in back, is given over to the Roman circus. Gladiators, snarling animals, racing chariots, cheering spectators, an emperor with his thumb turned down.

Zane Yarmouth stands behind a black faux-marble bar. He's what locals describe as country strong. As tall as Vern, he's wearing a black sleeveless T-shirt that exposes muscles that remind me of braided rope. Zane's not happy to see us and his slash of a mouth tightens until his lips vanish. We approach him nonetheless, relaxed, seeking eye contact he refuses to make.

"Got some questions for ya, Zane." Vern takes the lead, as he usually does with locals. "About somebody you know."

"Ask 'em."

"We're lookin' for a drug dealer named Quentin . . ."

Zane interrupts. "Now, see, that's bullshit right there. Quentin Durwood ain't no dealer. The asshole's a boy tryin' to be a man. All mouth."

"Talks big, does he?"

"Dumb, too. Talks big and dumb."

"So how do you know him?"

"He ain't a friend, if that's what you're getting to. The boy started comin' round about a year ago. He's a regular now."

"You see him recently?"

"No, come to think on it. Ain't seen him for two weeks."

"What about friends? Quentin have any friends?"

Zane takes a minute to think it over. Should he shut down at this point? Wait us out? Or send us off to annoy someone else?

"Quentin, he has a thing for older women. Older than him anyway."

"Anyone special?"

"Giselle Omansky. They were tight for a long time. Ain't seen her for a while, either, but I heard they broke up and she wasn't real happy with how it went down."

Off and running. Zane may not have been happy about cooperating, but he didn't set off my bullshit detector. Giselle Omansky isn't hard to find in any event. She lives at the address on her driver's license and opens her door a few seconds after I ring the bell. When I flash my badge, she smiles. When I ask her about Quentin, she laughs. Two minutes later, I'm in her tidy kitchen, sipping hot coffee. Vern's outside, my fear being that he'll inhibit a woman talking about her lover. We're better off with girl to girl. At the same time, our phones are connected and he's listening to every word.

"Lost my husband to Covid more than a year ago," she tells me. "Thought I'd die myself, at that point. That's how much I loved him. But I lived on, the way folk do, and you could say I've run a little wild since then. Not drugs, though. Seen too many relatives go down those tubes."

Giselle's honey-blond hair is augmented by extensions. She has a generous body that compliments a strong chin, and I'm reading self-sufficiency in her body and her attitude. A woman who can take care of herself.

"I guess you could say I got lucky with Quentin. Mostly I keep away from younger men. They expect some kind of bullshit gratitude for their attentions, not to mention outright gifts. Meanwhile, most of 'em can't hold out for ten minutes."

"Quentin was different?"

"Yeah, I was what Quentin wanted, not what he settled for after a few drinks. Then the bitch . . ." Giselle nibbles at her lower lip as she rethinks her response. "Look, I didn't have a hold on Quentin, so I can't complain. We were good for each other, yeah, but then he found that Russian bitch and moved on. Skinny little thing from what I heard."

"What about Quentin's address? Do you know where he lives?"

"Sure do, but you're not gonna find him there. Quentin ain't been around for more than a week."

"I still need to check it out. And I'd appreciate a list of his friends and acquaintances. And where he worked."

"Never worked, far as I know, but I can help you out with his friends. Believe me, the list ain't all that long. He mostly hung out with the regulars at Palacio."

That's enough for me, but as I get up to leave, Giselle lays a hand on my arm. "Saw how you carried that girl away from the fire," she tells me. "Never was prouder of this city, Captain, and I ain't forgettin'. Nor anyone else I know. You want to, you can run for mayor."

And wouldn't Mayor Venn be happy to hear that.

It's after five when I rejoin Vern out front. Ordinarily, we'd begin an intensive hunt for Quentin and his girlfriend by questioning his neighbors, maybe showing the photo taken at the Prairie Hotel. As it is, we settle for a drive past Quentin's obviously empty home. Giselle didn't ask why the cops wanted to find him, but others will, and the more civilians we interview, the more likely that rumors will spread. If they should reach Katie Burke or Basil Ulrich, the consequences are obvious enough.

"I think we should call it a night, Delia. Quentin and his older girlfriend? What does it prove?"

"Especially when the original tip came from a pathological liar trying to stay out of jail. But the bit about the 'Russian bitch' has my attention. And it doesn't want to let go."

"Like we're close—I can feel it—but close may be the worst place for Elizabeth Bradford. My instincts? Same as always. Go for the touchdown. But there's the kidnappers' established pattern. The victims are released . . ."

I jump in before he can finish the sentence. "Except for one."

"Maybe he was killed trying to escape. Or died of a heart attack or a stroke before the ransom was paid. The point is that releasing victims guarantees payment in the future. That's how they're playing the game."

The conversation is maddening. Calculate the odds? Place your bet? Elizabeth Bradford isn't a horse running a race. If we investigate and it goes wrong, it's not me and Vern who'll pay the price.

"Elizabeth told her mother about a delay," I finally decide. "One or two days. So, I'm thinking we have too much wiggle room to make a snap decision. Let's call it a night. I'll arrange to get Caitlin in the House early tomorrow, see if we can turn up something on Quentin before we take the next step. In fact, maybe the magic computer will show us what that next step should be."

I arrive home at six, bearing the promised pizza. I'm half expecting to find Zoe and Emmaline in residence. Instead, I'm greeted by Paolo Yoma. Paolo's leaning against a Mercedes SUV, the one I last saw in the Bradfords' driveway.

"I'm acting as Sherman's security this afternoon." He raises his hand, palms out, and smiles. "Sherman's inside."

"And what exactly is Sherman Bradford doing at my personal residence? Who authorized him to come to my home unannounced?"

"Wasn't me, Captain."

"Then who ordered you to drive him?"

"That would be his mother."

I have a lot more to say—like how did Cynthia Bradford discover my unlisted address—but I'll save that one for later. Paolo will only take me in a circle that comes back on itself. "Alright, Paolo. Let it go for now. Did you check out the people still in the house when Elizabeth snuck out?"

"I did. The staff's been with the family for decades, but the employment records of the security personnel are very incomplete. Remember, they're supplied by a private contractor. That would be Kentucky Security Services. If more extensive files exist, Kentucky Services has them."

The sun is setting behind Paolo, turning the heavy, advancing clouds a smoldering crimson. The weather's about to change, our late summer heat wave to finally break. "If the inside informant isn't one of the staff, it must be one of the security guards. Keep looking, Paolo. Find an angle."

At each of the many checkups that marked his first five years, my son, Danny, was at the top end of the height and weight charts. You might describe his build as sturdy or robust, and his dedication to athletics has only added to that effect. Sherman Bradford seems diminished in Danny's company, made even more fragile, his feigned arrogance vanquished. Has he ever had a friend who wasn't a peer? How about a friend with a lesbian cop for a mom? But he's sitting at the kitchen table where we take our meals, he and Danny. They're huddled shoulder to shoulder, staring at a tablet. I carry the pizza to the kitchen counter, lay out four plates, place a slice of mushroom pizza on the closest plate.

"Sherman, carry this out to Paolo."

"Should I ask him to come inside."

"No, you shouldn't. Come in by yourself."

I wait until Sherman passes through the door, then address my son. "What am I dealing with, Danny? Is the kid off the wall?"

"That's what I figured when he showed up." Danny grins. "I was gonna kick him out, but he's a Bradford, right, and his sister's been kidnapped. So I listened and what he's talking about makes sense. Some, anyway."

Sherman returns a couple of minutes later, still anxious. I fill three plates with pizza, two slices each, and carry them to the table, finally returning to the kitchen for a pitcher of limeade in the refrigerator. The pitcher's resting beside the salad I asked Danny to make, but my maternal instincts, meager to begin with, are exhausted for the moment. I bring the pitcher and three glasses to the table and fill them.

"Okay, Sherman, let's hear it. Why did you show up at my home unannounced?"

Sherman looks at me, head tilted. Am I criticizing him? Fooling around? He's not sure, and I can see why his sister protects him. The boy's incredibly vulnerable.

"It's the first call Elizabeth made. You know, where she says that if the ransom isn't paid, they'll dump her body next to some highway where it's sure to be found?"

Again, that puzzled look. I motion for him to continue and he draws a quick breath. "I didn't get it at first, but doesn't that part about where it's sure to be found seem odd? And don't think Elizabeth went with the first words that popped into her head. That's not her. But if the kidnappers did . . . you know . . . did kill her, wouldn't they bury her where she'd never be found? You can find lots of forensic evidence on bodies. Plus, it's really hard to get a conviction when there's no body."

Sherman grinds to a halt and I look at Danny. His expression is almost protective. "It does seem kind of weird," he says. "If she thought it through, I mean. Because Sherman's right. They wouldn't leave her body where it was sure to be found. It's just too stupid."

It's my turn—both kids are looking at me—and I lead with a scenario that must be considered. "First thing, it's possible the message was written by her kidnappers and she read it word for word. But let's assume you're right and Elizabeth wanted to send a message. What do you think . . ." It came to me then, and I almost spoke the name of the murdered Deputy aloud. Only the eager expressions on the two young faces at the table stayed me. "What was the message? What did she want us to know?"

"The Deputy?" Sherman's holding a forgotten slice of pizza in his left hand. "The one who was murdered on Sunday night?"

"He means Deputy Sheriff York, Mom. We've been looking through the online coverage in the *Bugle*. The Deputy was killed sometime after four o'clock in the morning. So, if Elizabeth was taken around three-thirty, she could have been in Maryville County after four."

Sherman gives his slice a little wave, then cuts in. "A kidnapping victim in your car? That's a motive, Captain." He pauses for a second before adding, "And the item that links it together? The Deputy's body was found alongside State Highway 14."

I finally take a look at the map on Sherman's tablet. It's of Maryville County with Highway 14 centered. I don't have to back off or zoom in because the area's a clone of every county surrounding Baxter. Farms and ranches, farms and ranches, farms and ranches.

Homes in Maryville County are widely separated, sometimes by miles. Worse yet, farms and ranches have been steadily growing larger for almost a century, the small farms disappearing. But not the homes that once sheltered the farm families who moved on, or the weathered barns and outbuildings. I'm not contemplating a needle in a haystack. I'm looking at a hundred haystacks surrounded by a million acres of corn.

"What you've put together is intriguing," I tell Sherman, "and you surely know your sister a lot better than we do. So tomorrow morning I'll call Sheriff Martin, see what's up with his investigation. Maybe he's already got a suspect. Maybe there are details I don't know about. For now, though, it's pizza time. So eat up, kids."

I head for the kitchen and the salad in the refrigerator, but decide to call Zoe as I lay it out. She answers on the second ring, her tone a lot fresher than I'm feeling at the moment.

"Hi, Delia. What's going on?"

I glance back at the two kids. "Just an evening at home, me, Danny, and the paperwork I didn't get to this afternoon. How's Emmaline?"

"Better, I think, though she's still suspicious. Most likely, she's expecting all this bounty to vanish. She's just waiting. But I'm at Vern and Lillian's. They want to adopt Emmaline."

"What about you?"

"What about me?"

"Didn't you want to foster Emmaline?"

"That really doesn't matter. I'm a professional, Delia. It's my job to do what's best for the child."

I carry the salad to the table where the two boys are chatting away, then excuse myself. Paolo Yoma's still outside and I want a short talk with him. He's standing beside the car when I come through the door, leaning on a fender. His empty plate's lying on the hood.

"Tell me something, Paolo. Did you set this up? Was bringing Sherman to my house your idea?"

"No way."

"But you could have refused."

Yoma flushes. I've finally gotten to the guy. "Sherman's interpretation makes a lot of sense to me. I thought you needed to hear it. So, yeah, I could have come to your office tomorrow morning, but the boy . . . Sherman loves his sister as much as he loves his mother. Maybe more. And he's terrified, Captain. I'm hoping that personally taking part will ease his fears, at least a bit."

"You could have brought him to my office tomorrow."

"Wouldn't that be one too many visits from the Bradford family? If you're trying to keep any investigation quiet?"

"What makes you think we're investigating? No, scratch that." I pause to wait for a car to pass, a Dodge Charger blaring hip-hop loud enough to loosen the wax in my ears. "What are you doing in Baxter, Paolo? Why are you here?"

"Simple, I'm here to estimate the site-security costs for the demolition phase of the project. If not for the kidnapping, I'd already be out of the country."

"Doing what?"

"The Bradford Group's landed a construction project on a remote island in Malaysia. We're building an airport from scratch. The final plans have been drawn up, which means I can start work on the security arrangements. For the site and for any foreign nationals working the site."

"It's that dangerous?"

"The threat is ongoing, Captain, but we've arranged military protection. A Malaysian special-forces platoon normally stationed at the other end of the country will handle perimeter security."

"What, no cameras?"

Yoma laughs. "Cameras won't protect you against armed guerillas, or even saboteurs. But, please, don't tell Henry Bradford."

As I pick up Yoma's plate, I realize that I like the guy. The end result of a determined charm offensive? Maybe so, but I've also realized that I can't trust him. That's because he's at least as manipulating as he is charming.

"At the risk of being a bore, I'm going to repeat myself. I appreciate what you've done, but I want you to stay away from the investigation. I don't need any more wildcards in play."

"Does that mean you're making progress?"

"Just the opposite. We struck out at the Prairie Hotel and the only new development is the theory Sherman brought with him tonight."

CHAPTER TWENTY-SEVEN

ELIZABETH

Fear breeds fear, a cliché that proved true at my first encounter with it, Tashya's concern wildly contrasting with her previous cool, the man in the front seat, the man I cannot see, equally anxious. Fear once more envelops me as I'm returned to my basement prison, there to deal with the obvious. A submissive attitude will not protect me, Tashya offering no word of reassurance even as she closes the basement door and climbs the stairs, there being no need, apparently, to cajole my compliance. Brute force now sufficient unto the day.

Or the night, which is already upon us.

I hear footsteps above, a chair dragged across the kitchen floor, muffled voices, male and female, too distant to recognize individual words but they must be nearly shouting to be heard at all. Leaving me to sit and wait, no escape possible while they remain in the house, or even possible if they do leave. I look around for a weapon, an insane girl replicating futile efforts in hope of a different outcome.

Tears are the obvious next stage, of frustration or despair, yet they do not come and I once again take refuge in a rage that flashes through my body, a head-to-toe blush that demands physical expression. I'm out of my chair, breath coming in short, sharp gasps, fingers curled tight against my palms. I want to destroy something, anything; if Tashya was before me now, I'd wrap these fingers around her throat and kill her without a second thought.

Not possible, of course, and not only because Tashya's armed. The woman's life experience precludes strangulation by a fifteen-year-old girl who's never been in a fight because her peers settle their differences through innuendo-inspired gossip. Who's in, who's out, shaming and shunning, no hierarchy more settled than big kid–little kid, and me younger than my peers yet actually defiant, projecting an arrogance honestly felt. It wasn't they who skipped two grades, and not me who believes that ignorance is an outcome to be embraced, that knowledge, in the last analysis, is somehow demeaning.

I wish for Tashya and her companion to leave. Instead, she joins me in the basement, her footsteps on the stairs slower and seeming assured. A conflict resolved? A long-sought resolution suddenly uncovered? Orders from home: kill the bitch? The door opens with a squeal and Tashya comes through, alone, thankfully alone, her companion still unseen, the possibility of my release not yet foreclosed.

"Here, for you. A treat."

Tashya proffers a brown paper bag which I accept, though it does exactly nothing to assuage my anger, not even when I peer inside to find a container of raspberry-chocolate ice cream and a metal spoon. I imagine jamming the spoon into Tashya's eye as I dutifully shovel ice cream into my mouth.

"Have you heard from . . . your home base? Did you resolve your problem?"

"Not yet, but they are working hard. We have no more wish to remain in this country than you to remain in this basement."

"Then let me go and catch the next flight out."

"We cannot leave until the ransom is paid."

"No matter how long that takes?"

Tashya leans back, eyes suddenly withdrawn as she contemplates the question, perhaps considering an unknown set of contingencies, perhaps speculating on my sharp tone, the underlying dismissal, even contempt. What's up with this girl? Shouldn't she be grateful? It could be so much worse for her.

I dig my spoon into the softened ice cream, guide the spoon between my lips. I want to appear indifferent, not unaware, just unconcerned with her speculations, and I am, truly, because I know I can't be left in Quentin's basement for long. The danger of discovery is too great.

"You are very unlucky girl," Tashya announces.

"Thanks for sharing."

"The snotty tone does you no good. No harm, either. It is not relevant, but if it makes your stay easier, then go ahead.

I have suffered too many degradations to fear the contempt of a pampered child."

We're going there again? I can't bear it and change the subject. "So, how have I been unlucky?"

"In Lexington, your security defeated us. Six months and never an opportunity that doesn't carry risks unacceptable. Give up. This is what my family concludes. Return home, prepare for next project. But we are still monitoring public communications and we read that Christopher Bradford and family will move to the little city of Baxter. At first, my family resists. What do we know of this place? And what of the preparations we made in Kentucky? Are we now to improvise? To accept risks undetermined? But I explain that my relocation to Baxter is only to explore. Perhaps we'll be as lucky in Baxter as we have been unlucky in Louisville, and this is how it happens, yes? Everything falls in place, click, click, click. I find Quentin, he has cottage, you have adventure with boyfriend at an hour when there is no one to witness."

Tashya breaks off for a moment, eyes flicking to the side as she marshals her grievances. "If there was no delay, all would be finished tomorrow morning. Demand made, ransom paid, you released. But delay comes. This is not my fault, but I am not allowed to protest. They are too big to be wrong. They are too big and I am former prostitute who should be forever grateful."

Okay, I've got it, finally, the purpose for this visitation. My captor wants to vent, to demand justice, her guarantees genuine, their ineptitude manifest. And who am I to correct her?

"They call it a pecking order, Tashya. Chickens in the barnyard don't criticize the rooster."

Tashya ignores the observation. "This is what I have to tell you now. My associate and I cannot remain here. We must go a short distance away. But we have eyes in place and you cannot escape. So, you must handle the time as best you can. You must resign yourself. I will protect you, Elizabeth. This I promise."

I don't voice my doubts, but I can't bring myself to thank her, the lie far too obvious, and there's no need as she climbs the stairs, as she locks the door behind her.

Tashya's taken the spoon, leaving me to use my fingers or allow the ice cream to melt and drink the sludge. I choose my fingers, the tips growing numb as I finish and hear a door close, then very faintly an engine starting. I tell myself that I have to wait, to be sure, but I can't be sure. Can't be sure this isn't a test, that there's not someone sitting quietly upstairs, waiting for me to make a very fatal mistake.

As the quiet settles around me, a profound silence that leaves me to the blood pounding my ears, I take the time to review our situation, theirs and mine. Tashya and her companion haven't deserted the ship because they want a decent night's sleep on clean sheets in a heated bedroom. They're acknowledging the real possibility that investigators will uncover the Quentin connection and show up at this very cottage. And I am alive only because there remains the possibility that I'll be needed to contact my family one more time.

That last part is hardly an imperative and Tashya will sooner or later choose the wiser course. Put me in the ground and the FBI's investigation doesn't matter, they can search my dungeon on their hands and knees, find absolute proof that I was, once upon a time, held in this room.

So what?

With neither a live girl or a dead body, the ransom will have to be paid. And surely, for Tashya and her companion both, the prospect of spending the remainder of their lives in a cage looms large. So will Tashya's handlers in Georgia resolve their Bitcoin problem before Tashya decides to guarantee her continued freedom?

CHAPTER TWENTY-EIGHT

ELIZABETH

Measure twice, cut once, the carpenter's cliché but a rule of thumb in the Bradford Group, where overlapping divisions do the measuring and Uncle Henry or Father determine the value of their recommendations. For now, I'm content to measure.

Three narrow windows mark the wall farthest from the door, the windows almost at ceiling height and covered with plywood panels. First, I move the table to the wall below the closest window, position the chair before the table, creating what has to serve as a ladder. Then I step onto the chair's seat, eyes fixed on nothing, my body adjusting to the balance, testing the strength of its sturdy legs. The chair's rock solid and I crawl onto the table, straightening slowly, fixing again on my balance. The table, with its longer legs, is more unstable than the chair, no surprise, and I'll have to be very careful.

I slowly rise to my full height, my head now almost centered on the panel covering the window, and I know immediately that my situation could have been a lot worse. Plywood comes in three thicknesses, three-quarter-, half-, and quarter-inch. The first two are quite stiff, with little give. But this pine sheet is quarter-inch and it bows in the center when I wrap my fingers around the top and pull toward me. Not that it's loose, or about to give way with a tug of my fingers, but the sheet is nailed only at the corners and yanking back will place maximum pressure on the nails as the corners try to follow. And the window frame is aged, the dry pine split in several places by seasonal expansions and contractions. Properly seasoned wood grabs onto a nail, as if trying to restore itself, but the same nail, driven into wood this dry will make a simple hole, the wood pushed aside and unable to spring back.

I'm feeling calmer now as I move the table to the second window, as I climb up and test the panel, as I move on to the third. I feel the urgency, true, but time, I tell myself, is not of the essence. Tashya will not return until she must, her reasons for keeping her distance the same as her reasons for leaving, a risk-avoidance strategy that carries risks of its own.

I decide on the middle panel after examining all three, then position the table and climb aboard, thinking I'd be willing to give up a fair piece of my inheritance for a pry bar. Then it's right to work, pulling, releasing, pulling, releasing, initially finding no change at all in the panel, no movement. But then a loud screech erupts, reminding me of a door opening on a long-unoiled hinge, as a nail at the top left of the panel moves a fraction of an inch. I'm sweating now, and remembering a side trip to one of our worksites in Egypt. We were touring Spain, visiting one gilded cathedral after another, Sherman predictably obsessed with the gargoyles, when Father escorted us to a small plane. No questions asked or answered.

Though shaded by a canopy, we couldn't escape the midsummer Egyptian heat. Neither could a long column of laborers carrying hundred-pound bags of cement along a wooden ramp stretching from the ground to the second floor. They wore pants cut off at the knees, no shirts, feet jammed into sandals, torsos glistening, sweat falling from hair to shoulders, faces revealing no expression beyond the patience of broken animals.

I'm trying to emulate that patience, encouraged whenever I feel the panel give, refusing to acknowledge a growing fatigue, failure not on the menu tonight, do or die more than a cliché. I'm succeeding, or so I tell myself, though only the one nail moves and that only by millimeters.

Minutes later (ten, twenty, or thirty, time without meaning here), I call a halt, stymied because I can't put my weight into each pull, my balance too precarious and nothing to brace myself against.

I climb down, open a bottle of warm water and drain it, as sweaty as any of those Egyptian laborers, hair clinging to my neck, the insoles of my tennis shoes little more than soaked sponges. I can stop here, of course, move table and chair to their proper place, have a candy bar or a bag of stale popcorn soaked in a greasy substance designed to simulate butter. Because the only alternative I can see would, in the event of failure, be a confession of guilt.

It was a Greek named Archimedes who claimed that he could move the Earth if provided with a big enough lever and a fulcrum. At least according to Ms. Delroy, who taught Physics, a class I completed at age thirteen when other girls my age were discussing their training bras. I recall this now as I cool down, as I focus my front brain on the problem at hand. How much time do I have? Enough to manually loosen the panel? Maybe, maybe not, but the only alternative, the only levers, are spoken for. At present, they're parts of the chair I've been using to climb up on the table.

Almost every part of the chair, I now realize, can be used as a lever. The top rail, the stiles, the legs, the seat, the apron, even the backrest, the splat. Disassembled, the heavy chair is a collection of levers that can be jammed behind the panel and worked against the nails. One problem, though, a big one. The chair can never be reassembled, rendering my escape attempt painfully obvious the next time Tashya descends the stairs. And after she told me she would be leaving the cottage, after she advised me to stay calm and right where I was.

There's another problem as well. There don't appear to be hinges on the inside of the windows covered by the panels. Do they open outward? Or are they fixed in place, meant never to open? That would leave me to break the glass and very likely cut myself on the way out.

I open a second bottle of water, suddenly imagining Tashya and her companion following my blood trail through the forest, perhaps assisted by a pack of beagles.

I've calmed by the time I finish the water and start on a bag of M&M's. I'm now my father, and not my brash uncle who bullies his way through life. There's a problem and problems call for solutions. My first thought is for the obvious, the chair's legs, but they're too thick to jam behind the panel covering the window. Something else, then, something I might have noticed sooner. The top rail on the chair is narrow and projects a good six inches beyond the side rails. If I can slide a projecting edge of the top rail behind the panel, I can test my leverage without destroying the chair in the process.

Probably.

I put it together as I go, step by step. I will climb onto the table, pull the chair up behind me, lift it upside down, insert the protruding top rail behind the panel until it's jammed tight. Then I'll take hold of the two closest legs and pull toward me, a force multiplier that should yank those nails out of the frame, assuming the top rail doesn't snap, a lever turned back on itself, the tool insufficient, the chair now torn apart. And little Elizabeth? My brain shifts gear without notice, the obvious arriving in bits and pieces: ripping off the top rail will allow me access to the rest of the chair, all those mini-levers.

I surprise myself by hesitating, Quentin suddenly rising into my consciousness, shovel in hand, his ugly smirk abruptly banished. Real, real, real. This is not an exercise, a test of my coping skills, my superior intellect, with only my ego at stake. This is not finishing second in a cross-country race, passed in the final fifty yards, the medal awarded to a prancing competitor.

I climb up on the table, kneel and reach for the chair below, some part of my brain solely concerned with balance, the chair heavier than expected, and all I have to do is stand, lift it above my head and force one edge of the top rail behind the plywood sheet.

My legs shake, the table shakes, my brain shakes when I slowly rise to my feet, and no improvement when I try to raise the chair, slipping twice before I lift it high enough to slide the rail behind the panel.

I manage to catch my breath as I carefully work my hands from the seat to the chair's legs, reaching up as high as I can to maximize leverage. I'm thinking I should pray, but I don't, my fate utterly dependent on physical calculations I don't have the data to make. Then I yank hard, expecting hours of work, but something gives and I fall to the table top, then slide over the edge and crash to the floor, the chair landing on my shins before rolling off.

Dazed for a moment, I finally collect myself and take inventory, finding my body sore but not disabled, nothing broken, no limb that will not move. Only then do I look up to find the panel jutting out, the nail free of the window frame. That leaves three nails still in the frame, but not for long, my escape now assured even if I have to break the glass in the window and crawl over the shards.

I roll onto my knees. The chair next to me has split along the top rail. No big deal. I work the rail off, then the backrest, then a leg, even more frenzied, the prospect of freedom, of standing outside the cottage, as intoxicating as the wine Sherman and I sneak at family gatherings.

I stack my levers on the table, heavy legs on top, then climb aboard, forcing myself to rise slowly, forcing myself to ignore a sharp pain in my lower back. Erect, I jam one of the legs behind the remaining top nail, yank more carefully this time. The nail screeches as it slides back a few centimeters at a time, the progress inexorable, my work relentless. It will come free and it does, only the bottom nails holding the panel in place now. I go to work on the one to my right, sliding the chair leg closer and closer to the bottom of the panel until the nail suddenly pops free and the panel swivels downward on its remaining nail.

I'm looking through a dirty window at a tangle of deep grass rising from pebbled soil. Better still, less than a foot away, a simple hook-and-eye latch holds the window closed and what's held closed can be opened. I flip the hook to the side and push gently on the window. It's stuck after years shut tight, but I know what to do. I punch the heel of my hand onto the frame, working around the edge, excitement rising, every calculation essentially correct, freedom denied me only by a pane of glass, that impediment suddenly gone when the window slides up and away, turning on its outer hinges.

The cool air that sweeps across my sweat-soaked face and clothing sobers me. The wind's up, the temperature dropping, and I can't know what I'll face once I'm outside. Yet the urge to crawl through the opening is overwhelming, as if the transition will produce absolute safety, an illusion I finally acknowledge by retrieving one of my blankets, climbing back onto the table and pushing it through the window. I follow a second later.

Still agitated, I rise to my feet, then abruptly shut down, the new world I've entered somehow unfamiliar, a dream I've just awakened from or fallen into. I'm on one side of the house, facing a stretch of weedy, knee-high lawn bordered by a dense grove of young conifers. A rising wind whistles in the trees' long needles as it drives ragged clouds past a crescent moon, and for a long moment I can't make sense of where I am. But then I begin to shiver, the cooling wind on my damp clothes and body insistent and vital, a reminder of a conclusion I reached earlier. Do or die.

I wrap the blanket around me and circle the house, the view no longer unfamiliar, the house on its oval lot forming the center of a tennis racket, the road before me a handle extending for a hundred yards before curving off to the right. I find myself wishing I'd taken a greater interest in my nature class in junior high, that I'd memorized the position of the moon in its phases, the location of the North Star or the sweep of the Milky Way. As it is, I don't even know the time, can't measure the hours until daylight, much less chart a path through the forest.

Still, the deep shadows beneath the trees lure me with a promise of absolute safety from Tashya. Given a head start, there's no way she can find me, or even establish a starting point, if I walk into the forest and keep walking, the danger then turning from my abductors to nature itself. The terrain is flat throughout the forest and certain to be swampy in every modest depression, with me already soaked, already cold. And there's the real possibility of endlessly walking the same circle through the woods, no landmarks, no convenient cliffs or running rivers to mark the way.

I walk slowly to the edge of the forest, tell myself I'm not a child to be afraid of wolves, bears, or coyotes, of trolls, zombies, or the cottage of the wicked witch, but the dark patches beneath the tallest trees take on the appearance of black holes in the only universe that matters.

My fear is primeval, as elemental as my genes, a tangled line of RNA too essential to be removed. The road beckons now, seeming safe, the eerie glow of a crescent moon enough to light my way. How far to the main road? A half mile? A bit more? I have to decide, indecision my enemy, and where do Tashya and her companion lurk, what refuge have they sought? And there's Tashya's parting comment, about having eyes on the house, as necessary to avoid a trap as to prevent my escape. Yet the graveled road continues to beckon.

I don't get far, only about halfway to the first turn, before the van sweeps into view, coming fast, headlights off, and I'm revealed at the edge of the forest, bathed in moonlight. Then a slight shift and the van's driving straight at me, the sudden flash of its headlights motivating my feet, Tashya's threat banishing any fear of ghost or goblin, of wolf or bear. I turn and push my way through the brush at the edge of the forest, ignoring branches that tear at my legs.

Running for my life.

CHAPTER TWENTY-NINE

ELIZABETH

They won't shoot. That's what I tell myself as I run. The noise, the flash? They can't take a risk, can't afford to attract attention of any kind, every hope of success depending on stealth. And even when the first gunshot rings out, my brain won't stop repeating this lie.

My feet catch on roots, or maybe vines, I can't stop to check, or take care, even knowing the next step might bring me to the ground. The blanket makes it worse, clinging stubbornly to every tiny branch, dragging at my feet. If I want to survive, I have to let it go, cold be damned.

"Elizabeth, please." Tashya's voice reaches me somehow. "Do not play the fool. There is nowhere safe for you in this forest."

Or with her and her partner. I'd rather die alone, my body left to the Earth, than allow myself to be summarily executed by these bastards. Let them never be sure that I won't turn up, let them explain my escape and disappearance to whoever's running the show back in wherever Tashya really came from. And there's every chance, with a cold, insistent breeze slithering across my body, impossible to ignore despite the building sweat, that I will die out here, the process to begin whenever I stop running.

No more shots now, the gunfire replaced by a pair of light beams that flicker between the branches, the pattern random, yet relentless, and why not as my feet crunch down on brittle leaves and dead branches that seem as loud as gunshots when they snap beneath my feet. By instinct, I lurch from deep shadow to deeper, avoiding the pools of moonlight where my dilated eyes can see clearly and where I can be easily seen. Each shadow hiding its own set of obstacles, a vine catches my foot and I stumble forward into a branch that scrapes the side of my face. And now I'm cut, leaving a blood trail in lieu of the breadcrumbs I forgot to pack.

Tashya and her partner were forty yards behind me when they entered the forest, but they're closer now, guided by their flashlights, avoiding the vines and branches, unafraid of the little clearings, of the moonlight. They advance relentlessly, monsters I can't escape in a nightmare with no just-in-time awakening. I'm not going to surrender, to kneel and beg, please, please, please, but there's nowhere to hide, my pursuers too close, demonstrated when a flashlight beam flashes over my body and a shot rings out, near enough for me to hear it rip through the leaves of a tree only yards from my head. I dodge to one side, put a tree, then another, between me and the gun, buying time only, the gap closing, yard by yard, no surrender possible on either side.

Luck again, as Mother insisted, steps in to alter reality as I stumble onto a trail, the track firm and free of vines and branches. I turn left and pick up speed, a cross-country runner with no talent beyond stamina to keep me competitive.

"Elizabeth, you must listen." Tashya again. "You will not survive in this forest. You have nothing to keep you warm."

I glance over my shoulder. I can't see Tashya, hidden by the trees, but I glimpse the blanket she's holding, rolling in the wind like a flag on a pole. I'm supposed to think that she's right, but I'm lost in my own fear, an antelope fleeing a predator, only one escape for my species: run, run, run. Two hundred yards, three, four? My brain won't keep track, but nature reaches in because this trail wasn't created by Park Rangers anxious to guide human beings through the forest. This trail was made by animals over years upon years, coming from somewhere and going to somewhere that has nothing to with human endeavors. First the track dwindles, then it vanishes near a low point in the terrain, a marsh that grabs an ankle when I stupidly dash into it. I pull my foot free, then finally stop, sitting on the ground while I swipe at the mud on my shoe.

Tashya hasn't found the track, can't know where I am, the flashlight only a dim glow in the branches of trees far away. I've escaped. Escaped to nowhere. My brain tosses up a single observation as my pulse slows and the immediate fear recedes. You're lost, you jerk, as you knew you would be, lost in a forest covering thousands of acres, with the wind rising and the temperature . . .

Shut up. That's what I tell my brain as I stand. Then a shadow whips across my face, another over my head, and I see them for the first time: bats, thousands of bats, crisscrossing the marsh, making impossible turns, impossible dives, somehow evading each other as they pursue the tiniest of prey. This is not my world, not a human world. My understanding will not prevail here, my very existence of concern only to the large and small creatures prepared to feast on my body.

I back away from the marsh and the bats, their understanding far too basic, eat, sleep, reproduce, my own flesh beyond clumsy, my world full of irrelevancies. I look behind, over the space I crossed, no hint of pursuit to be found, any immediate danger vanquished by a stroke of luck. But the cold already penetrates and I have no idea where I am, every difference the same, the marsh, a grove of pine trees, birch at the edge of the forest, hardwoods deeper inside and low-growth brush in every clearing. All different, all the same.

I'm left to wander and I know it, still dependent on luck, the hope of stumbling on a trail, hiking or horse, while I put off hypothermia, while I wait for the warming sun to finally rise high enough to find me. Not so my pursuers. I imagine Tashya firing up her cell phone, calling up a map of the park, marking my likely place and hers, the hiking trails, the horse trails, my distance from a visitors' center and the lake I discovered when I explored the park online.

Nothing I can do, no countermove, my only hope to continue on at a sustainable pace that will keep my body reasonably warm without reducing me to utter exhaustion. I find another trail, but I'm not fooled this time, the track too narrow and meandering to have been made by humans, and this time I have company, a dim shadow that resolves itself into a porcupine. It must be aware of my presence but doesn't stop or even slow down, its waddling gait projecting a clear message: get out of my way, which is exactly what I do, stepping into the shadows, waiting patiently for my turn.

The night passes, the time unmeasured, and me only sure that my thighs and calves ache, that a pause will be followed by a cooling that seems at first refreshing but will soon sap the little strength I have left. Uncle Henry has always insisted that surrender isn't a possibility, not for a Bradford, as it wasn't for Ulysses Grant. One can be beaten finally, all resistance crushed, consciousness lost or consigned to a ragged edge of a barely sustained awareness. That's okay, being carried off the field of battle, with your shield or on it, but not surrender.

Dawn finally arrives, so slowly I want to protest, to cajole, to beg, hurry up, for Christ's sake, but here again the revolving world is unconcerned with the needs of adolescent humans. I backtrack to the edge of a treeless marsh, work around its perimeter until the marsh is between me and the rising sun, then dance in place to keep warm, considering what I might give up for a match, Richard's kingdom, my own fortune.

The sun takes its sweet time, until it finally rises above the trees and finds my body. I have survived.

I like the way that sounds and repeat it to myself, knowing it's bullshit, a momentary consolation, because I have no idea where I am, sure only that the sun rises in the east, which means I'm on the western end of a marsh, and why should this matter, the marsh surrounded on all sides by forest and me without food or clean water. There's no rescue party out there, no swarm of anxious adults calling my name, no rescue dogs following invisible scent trails, no helicopter crisscrossing the dense canopy. Yet I know, driven by a necessity that rivals my own, that Tashya hasn't given up, hasn't retreated, that she awaits me, her and her partner, and I know, as wipe my hand across the side of my face and come up with blood on my knuckles, that luck is the ultimate controller now. Pure luck.

CHAPTER THIRTY

DELIA

Zoe called from Vern's last night, asking if she could, perhaps, drop by. I think every part of me wanted to say yes, but I couldn't do it. It's not that Danny wouldn't approve or understand. He would and I knew it. I was the one embarrassed, the proposition just too bold. I searched my brain for an excuse, but Zoe beat me to the punch.

"I know it's late. Why don't we let it go? For now."

That wasn't quite right, either, so I invited her and Emmaline for breakfast, and now Danny and I are at work in the kitchen. Danny's grating a block of cheddar while I whisk a half-dozen eggs. We have a laptop on the counter, the text of Elizabeth's second call on the monitor. I've become more and more obsessed with the girl's words. More and more convinced that her words were carefully chosen. And I can sense the answers, just out of reach, an apparition that refuses to solidify.

You need to stop being an asshole, Uncle Henry, for the first time in your fucking, battle-scarred life. This is not a war, it's a kidnapping. A transaction. This for that, me for money. So, keep a civil tongue in your head. These people are professionals and once they get started, they never stop coming. Christ, it's no wonder a judge granted your wife a divorce and all that money. They should have given her a medal for putting up with you.

"Okay, Danny, let me play devil's advocate. Cops are good at devil's advocate. The pair of us, we read Elizabeth's message over and over again. Like the words are hieroglyphics chiseled into some ancient ruin. But what if it's just what it appears to be? A frightened girl delivering a message to an uncle with a bad temper?"

"What about the Deputy?"

"We're linking Elizabeth to Deputy York with a single word: highway. But there's nothing specific in either message. Plus, even if Sherman's right, even if the kidnappers shot him, it really doesn't help us. Let me show you something." I work the touch screen for a minute, until I find what I want, an overhead view of farm country just north of the city. "Okay, take a look."

Danny and I switch places and I give him a minute to study the simple image on the monitor. The view covers two or three square miles of farm fields, with a cluster of buildings at the center. An overgrown driveway runs fifty yards, from the main house to a county road.

"Now zoom in, slowly."

It becomes clear, as the margins shrink, that the farm has been long abandoned. The roof on the largest building, probably a barn, has collapsed.

"You getting this picture?"

Danny's laugh is short, but seemingly sincere. "She could be in this building right now. There's no house within miles of this place."

"That's the point. Over the last hundred years, farms have been growing larger, with the big farms swallowing up the small ones. In most cases, rather than tear down the farm buildings, they just planted around them. That's why the buildings you're looking at are enclosed by fields, almost up to the doors. The corn's been harvested . . ."

"It's just stubble, Mom. You can see for miles in any direction." Danny stops for a moment, his mouth tightening, then says, "Does that mean you're giving up?"

"C'mon, son of mine, you know me better than that."

The remark earns me a grin. "Yeah, sorry, but what are you gonna do, Mom?"

"Run down Quentin Durwood. I got a list of his friends, a very short list, from his ex-girlfriend. Let's see where that goes. On the other hand," I take a second to return the original message to the screen, "if you can translate those runes, give me a call. Only one thing, Danny, you can't show the message to your buddies. Right?"

The doorbell cuts off Danny's reply, but I'm sure he gets it. This is ground we've covered before. I wipe my hands and head for the door. Zoe's standing there when I pull it open, Emmaline beside her. The girl's smile runs from ear to ear and she raises her hands. When I pick her up, she drapes her arms around my neck and lays her head on my shoulder.

"Mommy," she says.

"No, Emmaline, I'm not your mommy. I'm your Aunt Delia."

Emmaline doesn't respond, and I reach around her to give Zoe a little hug, the child squeezed between us.

Zoe's dressed for the job, slate-gray slacks, a white blouse, a blue blazer. As I back away from the door to let her inside, I'm reminded of the advice my mother gave me when I was about to be interviewed for my first job. You don't have to be confident to project confidence.

Emmaline still in my arms, I step back to let Zoe into my very simple home. Three rooms basically, two bedrooms with the living room and kitchen a single space. On those home-rehab cable shows, they call this an open floor plan. Here, it was all about saving money on the original construction costs. But the place is clean and relatively neat, the couch and chairs obviously used, but not shabby. I've got posters on the wall, crime movie posters chosen by Danny. *This Gun for Hire* and *The Tattooed Stranger*. I'm planning to replace them when Danny gets a bit older. With exactly what depends on my financial situation at the time.

I put Emmaline down and she runs over to Danny. I'm distracted for a second and Zoe, as she walks past, takes the opportunity to brush against me. I'm tempted to yank her off her feet and carry her into my bedroom. Unrealistic, yes, because she outweighs me and I'd have to employ a fireman's carry.

"Coffee?"

Zoe takes a seat at the kitchen table. "Please."

I close the cover on the laptop as I set out a mug and fill it. "Milk and sugar?"

"Just milk."

I pour the coffee for Zoe, add a glass of orange juice for Emmaline, then leave Danny to prepare and serve the strawberries in the refrigerator. Somehow, scattered among the enormous farms and ranches that dominate the area, a few truck farmers survive by marketing a wide range of produce to the city's restaurants and Saturday farmers' market. I'm not sure how they manage to grow strawberries in September, but these are fresh and luscious. I watch Danny add a dollop of heavy cream and a sprinkling of sugar before carrying them to the table. Then he fetches a stuffed cushion from our couch and sets it on one of the chairs around the table.

"You sit here, Emmaline." He waits for her to take her place, then nods toward her spoon. "Not with your fingers, right?"

"Right," Emmaline returns.

I pick up the whisk, trying not to roll my eyes. This, I tell myself, is not Delia Mariola, this homey, heartwarming family scene. Then my phone rings and I glance at the screen: Baxter Police Department. Our civilian dispatcher, Kathryn Abbatello, is on the other end.

"Good morning, Captain," she chirps, her tone so cheery I want to spit. "We have a . . . maybe a homicide? In Oakland Gardens."

"What does 'maybe a homicide' mean?"

"Well, maybe suicide or an overdose, but a body definitely."

"Who's over there?"

"Bert Granderson. He's, like, alone."

Patrolman Granderson isn't expected to handle this. A body calls for a detective. I look over at Danny and my guests. Danny's unsurprised. He's been through this before.

"What about Maya?" We always have at least one detective working the late tour. Last night, it was Maya Kinsley's turn.

"She's at Baxter Medical. A domestic assault."

I glance at the table again. Emmaline's happily shoveling strawberries into her mouth. Zoe's looking at me, her expression somewhere between concerned and resigned. But she needn't worry. I'm not going anywhere. Not today.

"Give me Bert Granderson's cell number."

Bert answers on the second ring, half whispering into the phone. "Granderson here, Captain."

"What have we got, Bert?"

"Overdose or suicide. There's heroin and a used syringe by the bed. This is his parents' house, by the way. They're just about destroyed. His mother found him."

"How old is he?"

"Seventeen." Bert hesitates for just a second. "Boss, it's a fucking war out here. New dealers set up as fast as we arrest the old ones, which makes for new casualties. There's no end to it."

It comes to me as I hang up, the war part. Elizabeth's message contains several war references. Battle-scarred, that was one, and her declaring that her kidnapping is not a war, and something about a medal.

I glance at the closed laptop. I'll have time to consider the exact phrasing later on. There's work to do just now. I consult my contacts for a moment, then tap in the phone number of Detective Jerome Meeks. I discovered Jerome when he first joined the Baxter Police Department. He's thorough and competent, if not terribly imaginative. He's also thrilled when I put him in charge of the response. Thus far, he's been another detective's assistant.

"You'll want to take it slow here, Jerome. The kid's only seventeen and he's living with his parents."

"I hear ya, Captain."

"Then go to work."

The breakfast passes smoothly, with the possible exception of Zoe reaching beneath the table to stroke my shin with her foot. Emmaline and Danny chatter away, mostly about the picture books they've read, with Danny playing the part of a big brother explaining the rules to a kid sister. The atmosphere attracts and repels me at the same time, my thoughts wandering between Elizabeth Bradford and the parents of an addicted boy who now lies dead. Norman Rockwell's vision of the family isn't a possibility for cops. The claim that you can somehow leave the nightmares you witness behind you at work is a bad joke.

I'm impatient as well. I want another look at Elizabeth's message, a chance to discuss it with Vern, to conduct interviews with Quentin Durwood's few buddies. Still, our breakfast passes quickly, the school day putting a limit on the time we can spend together. I work up the courage to give Zoe a little kiss as we part. Then I squat before Emmaline.

"Are you gonna be a good girl today, Emmaline?"

"Yes, Aunt Delia."

Now I want to cry.

CHAPTER THIRTY-ONE

DELIA

After dropping Danny at school, I head back to my house and the laptop. The little something that won't stop nagging at me wants a closer look at a map of Maryville County. A map that includes the entire county instead of a few buildings in a cornfield. I'm not an outdoor type, unlike Vern, who takes his family camping whenever he has a chance. No backpacks for this woman, no mosquitoes, no blistered heels, no tents, no sleeping bags. Too bad, because if I'd spent more time communing with nature, I would certainly have visited Ulysses S. Grant State Park.

The park's tucked into the northeast corner of Maryville County. It's quite small relative to the entire county, but when I jump to the park's website, I find it covers ten thousand acres, or fifteen square miles.

I return to Elizabeth's message and print it out.

You need to stop being an asshole, Uncle Henry, for the first time in your fucking, battle-scarred life. This is not a war, it's a kidnapping. A transaction. This for that, me for money. So, keep a civil tongue in your head. These people are professionals and once they get started, they never stop coming. Christ, it's no wonder a judge granted your wife a divorce and all that money. They should have given her a medal for putting up with you.

Battle-scarred, war, grant, a civil tongue, give her a medal. It adds up, including Ulysses Grant's signature approach to war, remembered from high school. Grant never stopped attacking, even after losing a battle. "Lick 'em tomorrow, though," he was supposed to have said after a disastrous day at the Battle of Shiloh.

Returning to the park's website, I explore for a few minutes, until the obvious finally becomes obvious. A file of twenty photos reveals, first, a small "village" that includes a Park Center, the inevitable gift shop, a few "settlers' cabins," a horse stable, and a petting zoo. All clustered on the southern end of the park, close to State Road 88. Beyond the village, except for a few horse and hiking trails, the park is heavily forested.

I call Chief Black at home, tell him I've made some progress on the kidnapping, and he invites me to come by. Or commands me, depending how you categorize invitations you can't refuse. Fifteen minutes later, he leads me into a home office that he shares with Orianna, his wife. Orianna's been a real estate broker for decades, limping along on the opportunities offered by a city everyone's leaving. But times have obviously changed. A lot-by-lot street map of Baxter, with numerous locations circled in red, dominates the wall behind her desk.

Orianna greets me, smiling as always, a trim woman dressed in a jet-black pantsuit. "Cup of coffee, Delia?"

"No thanks, Orianna, I'm already floating."

"Then let me head out. I've been hired by a developer who's incorporated in Delaware. I'm her agent." Orianna's smile has always been engaging, the one she now flashes no exception. "The whole city's up for sale," she adds, "and I'm the girl to do the buying."

The Chief waits for his wife to close the door to the office before motioning me to a chair. I don't know Orianna very well. Maybe she has a big mouth. But Chief Black waits a few more seconds before speaking.

"I haven't heard from the FBI, so I can't say for sure, but I assume it's still about waiting on that end. Their advice hasn't changed either. Pay the ransom, hope for the best." He shrugs. "And you?"

"I've got a name, Quentin Durwood. And a photo of a conservatively dressed woman with a 'Polish' accent booking a room at the Prairie Hotel. . . ."

"The hotel you raided yesterday?" The Chief's smile is genuine. "It's a dump."

"Right, but it's anonymous. The Prairie takes cash and they don't check anyone's ID. Look, Chief, it's adding up. The FBI's description of the gang's operations, specifically their use of a woman with a foreign accent to shepherd the victim through the ordeal. Vern and I interviewed Quentin Durwood's ex-girlfriend yesterday. She claimed their relationship was tight until he took up with an older woman. 'That Russian bitch,' was how she put it."

I've always known Chief Black to face problems squarely and he doesn't disappoint this time out. He rubs at the healing wound on his scalp, then nods. "It's good work, Delia. No, make that great work. Tell me what you have in mind. The next step."

"Quentin's girlfriend gave me a list of his friends, a short list, all male." I hesitate for a moment. "I'm not forgetting the part about Elizabeth's kidnappers spotting me as I get closer, but if we decide to move, I'll contact the men on the list. Maybe he confided in someone. And there's something else."

"Let's hear it."

I go over Elizabeth's first message, the part about her body being found alongside a highway and the murdered Deputy Sheriff. "Highway seems a strange choice, especially for a half-panicked child. You'd expect something like in a shallow grave, or maybe at the bottom or a lake. Or even that her body would never be found, or found by the side of a road."

"That's pretty tenuous, Delia."

"I checked it out, Chief. Deputy York's body was found alongside State Highway 14. But leave that aside for a moment. Elizabeth's second message is also revealing." I hand over the text of the second contact. "It's the martial aspect that finally caught my eye. Battle-scarred, war, grant, a civil tongue, give her a medal. Ulysses S. Grant State Park is forty miles from the murder scene, in Maryville County where Deputy York was killed. And the timing works, Chief. The approximate time of Elizabeth's kidnapping and the approximate time when Deputy York made that traffic stop."

I'm just getting started and I have to force myself to shut down. My job right now is to lay it out there, not convince. The stakes are too high. Almost high enough to make me wish I'd played it safe, that I'd conducted a quick, fruitless investigation. That would put the focus back on the FBI, leaving the Chief to claim that we didn't just sit on our hands.

"This park, Delia, it's how big?"

"Ten thousand acres, boss. Fifteen square miles."

"And you intend to do what? Organize a search team? Because you could put up a tent in the middle of those woods and hold someone indefinitely."

I don't argue the point, though I can't picture Elizabeth held in a tent. Too much risk bringing her in and out. And we know from the location of the cell towers that she was many miles away from the park each time she called her parents.

The Chief's voice cuts into my chain of thought. "Delia, take a look at that map. You see Pendleton Street."

"Yeah." Three blocks long, Pendleton Street runs east from Baxter Boulevard at the northern edge of the city.

"A month ago, with a few exceptions, every house on Pendleton Street had either been abandoned or condemned. No more. The outfit Orianna represents has purchased each of those properties, save one. And they're negotiating with the holdout. They plan to build thirty three-family attached homes. . . ." He threw up his hands. "Money's pouring into Baxter. Not just from Nissan, but from a dozen directions.

Five years from now, our population's expected to increase by fifty percent."

I'm nodding, and I intend to keep nodding until my commander makes a command decision. He sputters on for a moment, then stops and lowers his chin. "Tell me what you recommend?"

"That's easy enough. I'm meeting with Caitlin Capuano a few moments from now. We're going to do a little computer research, check out Quentin Durwood, and any other Durwoods living in the area. After that, if you're on board, I'll work the names on the list of Quentin's friends. See if that takes us anywhere."

"I can't say I like this. Heads I lose, tails I lose. But we can't walk away either. So do what you need to do, but for Christ's sake, be careful."

Caitlin Capuano's standing outside my office when I arrive, a bag from Lena's Luncheonette in her hands. I'm hoping the bag contains two cups of Lena's coffee, with cream and sugar on the side, and it does. I accept gratefully, then put Caitlin, who's as upbeat as ever, right to work.

Quentin Durwood has a driver's license and a registration for a 2013 Ford F150 pickup, his current home address listed on each. A check of other state agencies, including rehab and training programs, produces zero results. Caitlin then segues to the FBI's criminal database. I'm hoping that Quentin's on parole or probation, but he's never been convicted of a crime. Undiscouraged, Caitlin shifts to a Baxter County database and discovers a DUI charge that's still pending. Better yet,

Quentin failed to show up for a preliminary hearing ten days ago. Though a warrant for his arrest has yet to be issued—delay is the norm in Baxter's understaffed courts—I now have a good reason to ask after his whereabouts.

We continue with a general search for Durwoods living in and around the city, turning up a dozen possibilities. Are they members of an extended clan? Unrelated? For the next ten minutes, I watch Caitlin search various databases, property, marriages, divorces, even births, growing more and more impatient. Until I call a halt.

But Caitlin's not quite finished. It seems she's applied for a full-time position with Mayor Venn's about-to-be-formed City Planning Office. And used me for a reference.

"I should have asked first," she explains, her tone far from apologetic. Then she adds, "This town is going places, Delia, if we can just get past this kidnapping bullshit."

Ten minutes later, I'm on the road, driving the oldest car in the Baxter PD fleet, a 2015 Chevrolet Malibu. Cade Barrow's sitting beside me and we're casually dressed. Cade's in jeans and a Fort Bragg sweatshirt. I'm wearing black slacks and a faded denim shirt. Both of us wear jackets, the weather a good fifteen degrees cooler than yesterday. Cade's jacket is leather and a shade of blue just a bit this side of navy.

I want to keep things low-key, but I'm having my doubts because I can't disguise my rank. A DUI violation, warrant or not, doesn't merit the involvement of a captain.

But you do the best you can and I'm keeping Cade in the dark for the time being, only showing him the photo on

Quentin's license, a predictably low-resolution likeness that reveals a perfectly nondescript man in his early twenties. Quentin's ears stick out a bit. His eyes, probably light brown, are a bit small, his mouth a bit tight, his chin a bit weak. If I passed him on a sidewalk, there's a good chance I wouldn't recognize him.

"You expecting trouble, Captain?" Cade stares straight ahead as he asks the question.

"Not expecting, really, and I hope everyone on the list's a good-citizen type."

"But probably not?" Cade turns toward me. The guy's impossibly good-looking. That won't hurt either. "I don't question orders, Captain, but I'm not sure why I'm here."

"To keep things friendly, Cade."

"Whether they like it or not?"

"Exactly, Cade, whether they like it or not."

Our first stop is Alex Cooper's home in Oakland Gardens, a couple blocks from the Yards. I'm not really expecting cooperation, because Giselle Omansky described Quentin's friends as "lowlifes, one and all." Her characterization is confirmed when I step onto a tiny porch and the unmistakable odor of marijuana greets me. For the most part, Baxter cops don't pursue marijuana busts, not for its use or even the sale of small amounts. That's because the State legislature's already drafting a bill to legalize and tax its use. But exceptions can always be made.

I stand off to one side before knocking on the door. Cade's a bit behind me and standing on the other side. Just in case.

But no shots are fired from inside and the door opens a few seconds later. The woman filling the doorway is middle-aged and severely overweight. She's wearing a blue apron over a housedress, the apron dusted with flour. There's flour in her short hair as well, and flour on her hands.

"You're the one who saved that little girl," she says.

I ignore the remark. "I'm looking for Alex Cooper."

"What's he done now?"

"Nothing, ma'am, just want to speak with him for a moment. And you are?"

"Bethesda Cooper, if you must know. I'm Alex's momma." She put her hands on her hips and stares at me for a moment, then turns toward the house. "Hey, Alex, come on out here."

Alex shows his face a moment later. He's a very large man, larger than Vern, wearing a Harley Davidson sweatshirt with the sleeves cut away. A tangled beard reaches the top of his chest, just about matching the length of his thinning hair. I glance at Cade, find his expression merely curious, and recall his claim to being special forces in the military. Now I'm thinking Navy Seal or Delta Force.

"Wha'chu want?" Alex says, his voice raspy, his eyes red and swollen.

"We're trying to locate Quentin Durwood. We understand you're a friend of his."

Alex looks at me, then at Cade, then finally at his mother. I can measure a degree of relief—this isn't about him—along with an effort at calculation. What will it take to be rid of us?

"Ain't laid eyes on Quentin in . . . gotta be about three weeks. Not since he took up with that woman. The Russian."

"Any idea where they might have gone?"

Mom cuts off whatever lie Alex was about to tell. "Whyn't you go ask his old man?"

"His father?"

"Stepfather." She ignores her son's frown. "That'd be Ezekiel Frazier. Lives nearby. I ain't sure exactly where." She stares at me for a moment as a slow smile lights her face. "Piece of advice, though. Bring your Bible."

CHAPTER THIRTY-TWO

DELIA

I'm not enthusiastic and neither is Cade. We're both thinking that Quentin is more likely to confide in a friend than a stepparent. Especially a Bible-toter. But when a quick visit to a second friend produces little more than shakes of the head, I decide to go forward. Ezekiel Frazier's listed address in Dunning is empty when we arrive, but a neighbor, a woman hanging laundry on a backyard clothesline, tells us that Frazier's probably at his church. The First Apocalyptic Church of Gethsemane.

"Do you know where the church is located?"

"Not sure, Captain. In Oakland Gardens is what I heard." She takes a clothespin out of her mouth, then nods once. "What you did, saving that girl? You wanna run for Mayor, you got my vote."

Two votes now. A couple more and it'll be a landslide.

◆

I call in to the House and request a search for the address of the Apocalyptic Church of Gethsemane. The search is unproductive and I'm disappointed, but not surprised. Baxter sits almost dead-center in the Midwestern Bible Belt. Men and women who feel the call regularly lease storefronts and open churches. Overwhelmingly, these churches fail, in large part because the call to service is heeded only by the reality-challenged.

"Why don't we try Carroll Street?" Cade suggests. "I think it's the only commercial street in Oakland Gardens."

Carroll Street offers no surprises. The entire neighborhood was once a solid, working-class community, but many of the stores that lined both sides of the street are boarded up. A few remain: a check cashing operation advertising payday loans, a nail salon, a tiny convenience store, a barber shop with no customers. The barber's sitting in the store's only chair.

"Let's stop here," Cade suggests. "Barbers usually know everybody in the neighborhood."

The barber looks up when the door opens. He's in his fifties, wearing a green smock over a T-shirt. His eyes are shot with red lines and the dark patches beneath his eyes are big enough to be carpet bags. Both Cade and I have our badges clipped to our jackets, but the barber hardly reacts.

"Good morning," I say, always polite.

"Yeah, good morning. What could I do for ya?"

"We're looking for a man named Ezekiel Frazier, or maybe his church, the Church of Gethsemane."

"That nut?" The barber shakes his head. "Don't know what you want him for, but the man's a walking insanity defense. You comment on the weather, he quotes Leviticus."

"We only want to talk to him."

"Yeah, I heard that one before."

Cade jumps in. "If you're not gonna tell us where the church is located, say so. Enough with the bullshit."

"C'mon now. You're my first company in two days. Leastways you could be sociable." The barber's smiling, apparently unintimidated. "Okay, Zeke's so-called church, which far as I can tell has a congregation of two, Zeke and his . . . his companion? It's right around the corner, on Whalen Street.

The sign above the storefront window is hand-painted: Apocalyptic Church of Gethsemane. The window itself is covered by a steel shutter, but the door's open and I step inside. A handmade cross dominates the back wall, with a lectern in front. Several rows of folding chairs face the lectern, their gray paint chipped, their faux-leather seats torn. The floor's linoleum is also torn, though spotless. In fact, the whole church appears recently washed, even the faded paint on the walls.

A man and a woman sit together in a middle row, the man bent over a spiral notebook. He stands as I approach, turning to me. His eyes are a startling blue, almost electric. They project a mix of confusion and anger that I can't quite read. His companion stands alongside him. Probably in her sixties, she eyes Cade and me with obvious suspicion.

"Can I help you?" she asks.

"I'm looking for Reverend Frazier."

"That would be me." Frazier rubs the side of his face. "What can I do for ya?"

"You're Quentin Durwood's father?"

"Stepfather. And I don't know where he is. And don't wanna know. And don't care what he did or didn't do. The boy left my concern when he abandoned his God."

Frazier delivers the message with considerable force, but I'm pretty much unmoved. "And you, ma'am, please tell me your name?"

"She'll do no such thing. And you have no right to bring weapons into my church. 'He makes wars cease to the end of the earth. He breaks the bow and cuts the spear in two. He burns the chariots with fire.' "

Far from inspired, I want to punch him in the mouth. I can't, of course, and I'm grateful when the woman gently nods to me, then leads us out of the church. She closes the door behind her and takes a deep breath.

"It's gettin' harder," she tells Cade, apparently assuming he's the top cop here.

Cade glances at me, notes the smile on my face, and jumps in, his tone a good deal milder than I would have predicted. "I didn't get your name, ma'am?"

"Milly Durwood."

"You're Quentin's mother?"

"His aunt. Quentin's mom passed more'n six years ago." She looks at me for a moment, then returns to Cade. "Before she passed, on her last day, she asked me to care for Ezekiel. Man of God aside, and I ain't doubtin' his piety, the man never could take care of himself. Now, with the dementia . . . if I didn't keep watch on him, he'd be in the nut house for sure. Close call, as is. Couple nights ago, I fell asleep and he got out. Walked the streets round here preachin' at the top of his lungs. The cops was nice enough to bring him home. This time."

"I see, Ms. Durwood. It must be awful hard. And the way you're keepin' the promise you made to your sister? That's admirable." Cade pauses long enough for Mildred's sudden blush to fade. "I suppose you know Quentin?"

"Course I do."

"Do you know where he's currently staying?"

"Heard he's rentin' a place in town, but I can't say exactly where. And before you get goin', me and Zeke ain't laid eyes on Quentin since we left the cottage."

"The cottage?"

"Uh-huh, in Grant Park."

Better to be lucky than good? Or did we simply turn over the relevant rock, persistence finally rewarded? Either way, I step in at this point, mainly because Cade still doesn't know why I'm looking for Quentin Durwood.

"Is that where you all lived? In Ulysses Grant Park?"

"That's right, till they threw us out. Quentin couldn't handle it, bein' as he had no place to go at the time."

"And his stepfather? It was okay with him?"

Mildred looks down at her feet as she gathers her thoughts. I have a feeling that her life with Zeke and his dementia is a lonely one. That she needs company, even a pair of cops looking for her nephew. "Okay, the forest out there, it only became a state park seven years ago. Fore that, you go back a hundred years, it belonged to Aaron Struther. He founded Struther and Son Lumber. Made millions and the forest was his private hunting preserve. Then like eighty years later, when the family got tired of payin' taxes, they converted the hunting preserve into a public nature preserve. The change didn't amount to more than lettin' visitors hike through it. So . . ."

I cut her off right there. "And what was the Durwood family's role in all this?"

"The Durwoods, running back three generations, were the preserve's caretakers. Our duties weren't much. We created and maintained the horse and hunting trails, markin' them out and the like. And we shooed off trespassers, or called in the Sheriff when things got rough. But that was pretty much it. The horses were stabled outside the preserve and we hired locals when we needed extra hands."

"You said something about a cottage. Did I hear that right?"

"You did. The family wasn't paid much in wages, but they lived rent-free in a cottage Struther and Son built on the property. Living room, kitchen, and three tiny bedrooms, but sturdy enough to be home to four generations of Durwoods."

"I assume that came to end?"

"Four years ago, when the State took charge, the Struther Nature Preserve was transformed into Ulysses S. Grant State Park. What they call 'a village' got built next, with its own maintenance center. That took three years, after which there wasn't no more need for the Durwood family and they sent us an official notice that we was to vacate within sixty days."

There's nothing left to be said, but I allow her to go on for a few moments. Quentin, she tells me, wanted to hire a lawyer. He was convinced the right to live in the cottage was hereditary. That was nonsense, but it wasn't the reason they left. Zeke, as it turns out, is big on predestination. God's will prevails in God's creation. The Durwoods, meaning Quentin and his aunt, were out of the picture by then. Any right to live in the cottage had passed to Zeke when his wife died and Zeke decided that God wanted them to vacate. The State was prepared to evict in any event.

CHAPTER THIRTY-THREE

DELIA

I leave it there, thank her for her cooperation, and wish her luck with Zeke Frazier. Cade still hasn't asked any questions and he maintains a collected silence all the way back to the House. I thank him, too, then tell him to stand by while I consult Chief Black. He nods, but still asks no questions as he heads off to our coffee room.

By now, I've almost convinced myself that Elizabeth Bradford's being kept in a cottage in Grant State Park. What I need, though, is a little push. I need to find the cottage on a map, which I do, in a small clearing well away from the park's village. I stare at the house for several minutes, as though expecting someone to walk out the door. It's taken me a little time to locate the dwelling, even knowing it's there, because the surrounding trees overhang much of the clearing. But I do find it. I find it and carry it on a tablet into Chief Black's office. He alternates his gaze between the cottage and the text of Elizabeth's second messages while I describe the interviews and lines of reasoning that leads me to suspect that Elizabeth's being held in the house.

Chief Black finally responds by turning the tablet on its face. "The words you've plucked from Elizabeth's message: battle-scarred, war, grant, a civil tongue, give her a medal? What about kidnapping, transaction, professionals, divorce, me for money? Delia, if we put our heads to it, we can manufacture a dozen plausible scenarios. But it doesn't matter. I just got off the phone with Special Agent Eli Carson. They're expecting a final request for the ransom money to come at any time. Please terminate any line of investigation already opened."

I find myself growing impatient. "So, that's it? Shut it down? Look, Chief, even if Elizabeth's message is ambiguous, you still have to deal with the interviews. The FBI first described a woman with an Eastern-European accent and I've found her. Along with the location of an isolated dwelling where Elizabeth could be held with minimal risk to the kidnappers." I maintain a level gaze, until the Chief drops his eyes. "I think we both know that if the FBI wasn't involved, I'd already be on the road. We're talking about eighty miles. Even on state roads, it won't take longer than ninety minutes to get up there."

I point to a faint, curving line on the tablet. "This has gotta be the driveway. It's hard to see because it's narrow and overhung by tree limbs, but it runs more than a half mile from the cottage to a public road. I can use the road to guide me and still come up through the woods. If the house is locked up, if there's nobody around, then great. We tried. But if there's activity in the house—remember, it's slated for demolition—I can back off and call for reinforcements."

"You're serious? You want to go alone?"

"Me and Cade Barrow. With body armor under our jackets and fully automatic M16s in the trunk."

Chief Black rolls his chair back a few inches. "Barrow? Odd choice." He hesitates, but I have nothing to add. "Have you briefed Detective Barrow, Delia?"

"Not yet, but the man's not stupid and I'll have to brief him anyway. I can do it on the way to the park."

"You did all this on your own? Turned up Quentin Durwood, his stepfather, the cottage."

"Lotta luck involved, Cade. And help, too, from a security executive named Paolo Yoma and from a kid named Sherman. Elizabeth's brother."

"Well, for what it's worth, that second message the girl left, it's too bizarre to be off the cuff."

"My take, exactly. It troubled me from the first time I read it. Interpreting it, on the other hand, took a lot longer."

We've left Baxter and its incessant noise behind. Fields line both sides of State Highway 14, relieved only by an occasional meadow where cattle graze peacefully, or an isolated farmhouse shielded by a row of windbreaking pines. The morning chill has burned off and the mostly harvested fields glisten beneath an autumn sun. I'd planned to ride with lights and siren going full out, but there's no traffic and we're making good time.

"What we're doing this morning," I tell Cade, "it's more of a scouting expedition. I'm not planning an assault unless we have backup in place."

"You're telling me that we stowed away body armor and AR15s in case we run into an early Halloween party?"

"That's a joke, right?"

"A pitifully poor joke." Cade's behind the wheel, following a GPS along roads that run straight for mile after mile. "But I'm trying."

"Trying for what?"

"Good question." He taps the wheel with a forefinger. "My childhood was pretty chaotic. Back and forth between relatives who really didn't want me. I couldn't wait to get off on my own, so I joined the Army right out of high school. Not even eighteen. Captain, the army felt more like home than any home I lived in as a kid. Maybe it was the structure. You generally knew where you stood. And the reward system too. I was Airborne first, then moved up to the Rangers, and finally to Delta Force."

I'm impressed. Only the best of the best . . . No, make that only the most lethal of the lethal make their way to Delta Force. The training regimen is equivalent to that for the Navy Seals. Still, I drop the subject and don't take it up again until we come to a dead stop behind a long line of cars.

Five minutes later, I'm considering a shift into oncoming traffic. I'm only seeing an occasional oncoming car or truck. Between my lights and siren, I'm pretty sure I can squeeze by. Then I spot a State Police cruiser inching its way between the cars behind me and a drainage ditch just off the road. I jump out of our car and hold up my badge.

The news is reasonably encouraging. The Trooper inside, a woman riding solo, tells me that a farm truck rolled over about a mile ahead, blocking both sides of the road.

"We've got it upright, Captain, so it's just a matter of towing it out of there and cleaning up the debris."

"Which is?"

"Hay bales. Piled on each other way too high. You try talking to these farmers, they'll yes you to death. Next harvest, it's the same damn thing. Figure a half hour to forty-five minutes until you're out of here. Is this some kind of emergency?"

I find her cheerful tone annoying, but keep my annoyance to myself. "I'm trying to reach Grant Park."

"Straight ahead."

"No way to go around?"

"If there is, I don't know it. The farms around here are mostly corporate, so the farm roads are cut off."

Cade and I stand outside the car, a gray Impala. No coffee, though, or donuts from Lena's Luncheonette. Just the pair of us staring off at two horses in a distant corral. The horses stand close to a split-rail fence, facing a pasture on the far side of the road.

"Think they want out?" Cade asks.

"Can't say. I've never been on a horse, or around horses." We stand for moment in silence before I ask the obvious question. "If the military was home to you, why'd you leave?"

The question's unnecessarily personal, but Cade merely nods. "I trained as a sniper with the Rangers. Not a role I really wanted, but I was the best marksman in my training unit and the brass made it clear. I could be a sniper or I could wash out. The Rangers are big on gung ho. You do what you're told. You follow orders."

Cade bent to pick up a small rock and scale it into a field of stubble. He watched for a minute, then looked back at me. "Eventually, I became very good at my job, killing the enemy on the field of battle. And why not, since they were trying their best to kill me? That's what war is all about, kill or be killed. Delta changed that."

"How so?"

"No battles, Delia. What we did—what I did—was assassinate targeted individuals living far from any battlefield. I'm not trying to make our targets innocent victims. They were often the worst of the worst. Militia leaders who organized suicide attacks in civilian neighborhoods. Bomb makers from Saudi Arabia. Arms dealers from Pakistan."

He pauses and I feel the need to fill the silence. "There are times," I tell him, "when I wish we could assassinate a few of the worst ourselves. It's frustrating when you know someone's a bad actor, even a killer, and you can't find the evidence to make an arrest."

"But are you sure they're guilty? Without a trial? So, yeah, some agency, usually the CIA, labeled our targets as terrorists, or whatever. But what did they base that identification on? Some POW telling tales, maybe to avoid Guantanamo?" Cade pauses, his gaze more intense now, but I find myself with nothing to add. "I usually killed these men in front of their homes, sometimes with family members standing alongside. When you're eight hundred yards away, it's easy to make a mistake. I never did but . . ." Again, he paused, this time shaking his head. "No sense dragging this out. I couldn't handle it and I went to my commanding officer and told her so. She didn't give me any grief, didn't make any threats, but I became instantly unreliable. In a matter of weeks, I was honorably discharged."

Several hundred yards away, the vehicles at the head of the line start to move. Cade circles the Impala to take his place behind the wheel. "So," he asks as I slide onto the seat beside him, "did I pass the audition?"

"You passed a long time ago, Cade. But I'm curious about one more thing. You're not local, so how in the world did you end up in Baxter?"

Cade puts the Impala in gear, though we're a long way from the moving cars ahead. "That's an easy one. My fiancée was raised on a farm about ten miles south of the city. We both needed a quiet place to regain our bearings and, what with the Nissan factory on the way, Baxter seemed like a decent bet. Lotta hope in Baxter."

"Is she a vet too? Your fiancée?"

"Yeah, we met in a field hospital."

"Were you wounded?"

"No, some kind of amebic dysentery. Annie, though, she lost her left hand."

"I'm sorry to hear that."

"Hey, not to worry. Annie's not big on self-pity. She's pregnant, Captain. We're gonna be married in June."

CHAPTER THIRTY-FOUR

ELIZABETH

I did not keep my wits about me this morning, didn't calculate my best hope, didn't formulate a strategy, even if that strategy amounted only to rambling through the forest and hoping for the best. The sun warmed my body as it dulled my wits and I fell asleep, dropping back onto the weeds and the grasses, rage, fear, thirst, and hunger banished, not even the mosquitoes enough to call me back. I awoke an immeasurable time later to find a deer and a pair of yearling fawns nibbling on the grass at the edge of the marsh, heads rising and falling, ears turning like radar dishes. Tails aloft, they fled when I sat up, darting into the safety of the dark forest.

I stood then, my first instinct to follow, but a steady breeze caught me off guard, prickling the exposed skin on my arms. The threatening cold of last night had diminished, but not disappeared, and I became suddenly aware of a gnawing hunger quickly overwhelmed by thirst. I raised my head, drawn by an unfamiliar smell, sharp and sour, that radiated from my own body. With no mirror handy, I couldn't inspect myself, not fully, but I knew my hair was in a tangle, as my clothing was a mass of sweat stains and wrinkles, and again I sensed that I was being slowly transformed by forces beyond my control.

I laughed then, at the irrelevance, at the idea that maybe I was about to become dead, at the obvious truth. And I couldn't sit still, a fawn in the grass. With no search party scouring the forest, every step I took enhanced the probability that I'd stumble on a trail made by actual humans, a trail that led to a road or a Ranger Station, a safe path through the forest its only purpose.

I couldn't measure time, didn't know how long I'd slept, or how many hours until sunset, or how far the temperature would drop. I was only sure that I couldn't spend another night on the run, my calves and thighs already producing a dull, persistent pain. And so I finally moved, constantly shifting to bypass obstacles, a tangle of immature pines, knotted brambles, bone-gray branches rising from tangled vines, fallen trees coated with green moss. And everything the same, always the same, an illusion or cold reality, I couldn't know. Is this tall, isolated conifer the same one I passed fifteen minutes ago? Are the tiny blue flowers clustered near a damp hollow the same flowers that earlier attracted my eye? Or the mushrooms sprouting from the trunk of a rotting tree? Or the blue jay on that branch? Or the gray squirrels frantically gathering fallen acorns beneath every oak?

I continued on, no choice in the matter, until an overwhelming thirst drove away useless speculation. One foot in front of the other, step after step, I placed my fate in the hands of a luck god I'd never acknowledged, embracing meritocracy though I could make no claim to choosing the womb that bore me.

I kept at it until I stumbled upon a little brook, still running when it should be dry in mid-September. Drawn as if by pheromones, I walked against the current for five or six minutes, emerging finally in a small glade with a pool of clear water in the center. I could see past a lone tadpole right to the bottom and my eyes focused on the tiny bubbles rising from somewhere below the pool's bottom. This was a spring, not muddy runoff from a stagnant pond. I looked at my filthy hands for a moment before dropping to my knees, then to my elbows, finally pushing my face into the water, exactly as I'd seen all those animals drink at all those waterholes in all those nature documentaries.

Far from demeaned, my body screamed with joy, its central intelligence operating on a single principle: keep this moron alive despite herself. And I kept looking up, turning my head from side to side, as if expecting that pack of hungry coyotes to appear any moment. Followed by the wolves and the bears.

As I finally stood, I realized that I'd never find my way back to this spring, that remaining close by was no option at all, that I had no vessel to carry water, no handy gourd. Nor could I know what pathogens might be hidden in water clear enough to be invisible. Surely animals drank here, animals less than fastidious, and it might only be a matter of time until I became sick. Me already weakened by hunger.

And so I continued, admitting that nothing had changed, to wander and hope the order of the day, or wander and don't hope, only keep on moving. Sooner or later, you'll stumble onto a hiking trail or a horse trail or even discover the edge of the forest, even burst into overwhelming sunlight and harvested cornfields stretching to the horizon. With, of course, a picturesque farmhouse in the center.

Instead, a time later, I found a blackberry patch, enough berries still on the vines to make a meal, squirrels, small birds, and insects already at work. I told myself that I should move on, the risk of contamination too great, but the Elizabeth I knew didn't have a say in the matter and I endured the protests of the squirrels, drove the birds to nearby branches, filled my mouth even as a hatred beyond emotion, beyond anger, beyond even rage, grew inside me.

If ever given the chance, I would, I knew, give birth to it.

Now fed, however poorly, I took up my wandering. I still had no sense of direction beyond the nagging fear that I was walking in circles. Above, the clouds darkened as the temperature sank a few degrees, as the breeze sharpened. Irrelevant, all irrelevant, and I ignored the conditions, pushing forward until I finally stumbled on what was left of a trail. Little more than a slight depression, overgrown in places, I might have seen it for what it was, a cut through the forest made decades before, probably when the forest was still being logged. I didn't. Instead, my heart nearly exploded and my brain simply wouldn't entertain the possibility that I'd happened on another dead end.

Yet, dead end it was, leading from a marsh on one end to a pond on the other. I stopped at the edge of the pond, needing to drink again but afraid, the water here streaked with tiny green plants that didn't concern the geese flying over the pond, two adults and three fledglings. I watched them come down into the water, landing heavily, honking at the top of their lungs. They rested for only a moment before they began a clumsy ascent, running over the surface until they gathered enough momentum to lift their heavy bodies from the water.

I sat and watched for a few minutes, until I finally got the point. They were preparing their young for the migration, perhaps to the bayous of Louisiana, or even into Mexico, a do-or-die journey of at least a thousand miles that some would not complete.

I have a cousin, an addicted gambler who refuses to acknowledge fixed odds. Everybody knows that you can't beat a roulette wheel, or overcome the fixed advantage of a house slot machine, but in his cups at family gatherings, this cousin inevitably tells whoever's willing to listen that luck always turns. Unless you give up.

CHAPTER THIRTY-FIVE

ELIZABETH

A line from a poem read last year hops into my mind, something about the poet's end being his actual beginning. I can't remember the author's name, but the words take on a new meaning as I squat behind a fallen tree, shielded by the dried leaves of its lower branches. Having traced a full circle, I'm looking at the driveway connecting Tashya's little cottage with the main road. The cottage is fifty yards to my right and there's a white van parked in front with the rear doors open. I didn't anticipate this development, simply assuming that Tashya would now be somewhere over the Atlantic, bound for home and safety, a self-serving excuse for the operation's utter failure already composed.

An explanation appears only a moment later, a man coming through the front door, a black trash bag in each hand. His name is Pierce Donato and he's been a part of the family's security detail for several years, a quiet type and very professional though always distant. I can't remember his ever calling me anything but Miss. Not Miss Elizabeth, only Miss.

Donato's cleaning up because he has no home in a faraway country, no mountain family to protect him, and it's certain, should I find my way to safety, that the cottage will be scoured by an FBI forensics team.

I watch him toss the bags through the van's rear doors, then take a quick look around, his eyes sweeping past me, before returning to the cottage. It's late afternoon, my sense of time now restored by the shadows creeping across the driveway, and I know what I should do next. I should make my way to the main road, staying back in the trees, using the driveway as a guide. If there's no farmhouse in sight, I can flag down the first vehicle to come by.

Directly across the drive, half-hidden by tall grass, a small metal box painted black almost assuredly contains a motion-activated security camera. I know there'll be others, especially at the main road. Tashya will not be taken by surprise.

Again, I tell myself to move, no point in waiting, nothing I can do without weapons or the skills to use them, but my body aches with the hatred that rushes through my flesh and I stay where I am. I'm still there, kneeling on the piled loam, when Tashya and Pierce Donato come through the front door. They walk a few feet into the yard, both focused on the drive. I can hear them talking, and though I can't make out the words, their tight expressions are intense.

Donato nods agreement to some unknown request, the gesture decisive, before they retreat to the interior of the cottage. I listen to the wind moving through the trees for a moment before I see them, a woman and a man just rounding the curve closest to the house. They're on the far side of the drive but a few yards from the edge, half-concealed, but maybe not trying all that hard. The woman carries a handgun, barrel down by her hip. The man carries an assault rifle with a long magazine, holding it across his chest with the barrel resting on his shoulder.

I don't recognize either, but as both wear badges on their chests, they're surely cops, most likely Baxter cops, come to check out the cottage. I want to call to them, to warn them, but I can't bring myself to utter a sound. I know their appearance will occupy my kidnappers' full attention, that I can slip away unnoticed. And besides, I tell myself, I'm not in the cottage. So Tashya can allow the two cops inside, can encourage them to look around.

Hey, see, no spoiled rich girls in residence, your errand that of a fool.

My pitiful rationalizations are cut short by Tashya, who walks into the yard, apparently unarmed, her hands by her side. When the two cops step out of the woods thirty feet away, her expression doesn't change.

"I'm Captain Mariola," the woman announces. "And this is Detective Barrow. Who would you be?"

Tashya ignores the question. "What are you wanting here?"

"We're investigating a disappearance."

"And this has what to do with me?"

"It might not have anything to do with you, but we have reason to believe the person who disappeared is inside the house."

"There is nobody inside."

"You live here, then? By yourself?"

"Yes."

This is completely untrue and the cop probably knows it, though her expression barely changes. Most likely, she's weighing the odds. Retreat? Force the issue?

"And the house is empty?"

"I have already said this."

"Then you wouldn't mind if we have a look around?"

Tashya finally smiles and a certainty slams into my brain. They're going to kill the cops, the decision already made, the electronics planted at the main road assuring Tashya that she's not dealing with a SWAT Team, only a pair of cops pursuing an unlikely hunch. I tell myself to stand up, to warn the cops, to embody my father's definition of family obligation and honor. I tell my legs to straighten, tell the long muscles in my thighs to contract, but nothing moves. When I open my mouth, the emerging sound is little more than a hiss.

It's too late anyway.

A figure appears in the window behind Tashya, bearing a rifle that instantly flashes, shattering the glass. Detective Barrow drops a fraction of a second before I hear the shot, an explosion seeming louder than summer lightning. I cringe, pulling my shoulders in, covering my ears, but the second cop, Mariola, raises the barrel of her gun, firing twice at the window, the sequence too quick for me to measure.

Pierce Donato falls forward, onto the shards of glass remaining in the window, while Tashya dashes into the house. I watch Mariola train her gun on Tashya's back, but she doesn't pull the trigger. Family honor? I can only wish it was my finger on that trigger. But Mariola doesn't hesitate once Tashya disappears. She moves to the side of the cottage, away from any window, and pulls a cell phone from her jacket. Head swiveling from side to side, she lays her phone on the ground where she can operate it with one hand, her left. Her right hand, the one holding her weapon, moves with her head, side to side.

I watch Mariola speak into the phone, very briefly, then continue along the side of the cottage, ducking beneath a window, until she disappears behind the house. Seconds later, the same window rises and Tashya climbs through. She's also carrying a handgun and she follows Mariola without hesitation, guided no doubt by the cameras around the house. She looks neither right nor left, simply following.

Alone now, I find my legs, crossing to the fallen cop. He's been hit somewhere in the head, but he's definitely alive. He's moaning softly and his eyes are open, though unfocused. He's breathing, too, despite a steady flow of blood from his wound. Some part of me demands that I do something, but I'm not a doctor and I can't help him.

Then I hear a shot fired at the back of the house. A second shot follows.

I hesitate for only a second before I grab the dropped rifle and trace the route taken by Tashya and the cop, jogging along the side of the house, peering around the corner, only my head exposed. Tashya stands with her back to me, perhaps ten feet distant. The cop, Mariola, lies facedown in the grass, her gun off to one side. She turns over, very slowly, and stares up at Tashya, who can't resist a final speech.

"You have come on a fool's errand. This girl, Elizabeth? She is not here. She has escaped and I have failed. Only a few hours now until her discovery, if she has not already found refuge. You will die for nothing."

I raise the rifle, press the butt against my shoulder, no mercy now. Mariola has to see me, but I can't find a hint of recognition in her expression as she sits up, in obvious pain, then comes to her knees, looking to me like a beggar. I press my finger against the trigger and pull, then pull harder. The trigger only moves a fraction of an inch before freezing. There's a safety catch, obviously, but I have no idea where it is, or even what it looks like.

I can't back off though, my rage overwhelming now, and the cop's life on the line. I raise the rifle above my head and cross the ten feet in three steps, my intention to bring the weapon down on Tashya's skull. At the last moment, Tashya hears my approach and turns, moving slightly, and the barrel lands on the point of her shoulder hard enough to send her own gun flying. I step back, stupidly, the brutal violence almost paralyzing me.

Not Tashya, though, who dashes toward the dark shadows of the surrounding forest even as Mariola retrieves her gun. Once again, she points it at Tashya's back. Once again, she holds fire, unwilling, apparently, to shoot the woman who intended to kill her. Tashya's unarmed, her own weapon still lying on the ground, and she's retreating.

A blizzard of thoughts runs through my brain. Tashya's no longer a threat to anyone. Alone in the forest, it's unlikely she'll avoid the search parties sure to form. Even if she does, if she initially escapes the forest and the cops, the odds against her making it back to her family in Georgia are incredibly steep.

Let her go then?

I can't do it. I'm remembering the eyes of that Deputy, and the dirt I shoveled onto Quentin's face. Quentin, the ultimate sucker, a pawn to be sacrificed when the time was right. And nothing in Tashya's manner to indicate that killing either was more than a chore, like emptying the garbage or cleaning the toilet. I wouldn't bother if there was someone else to do it, but there isn't, so bang-you're-dead.

Savagery won't help her, not this time, because she can't outrun me, not with her right shoulder hanging lower than her left, not in obvious pain, not with the noise she's making, the crackle of dried leaves beneath her feet betraying her every step. I follow behind at a steady lope, gaining ground, relentless, my mind slowing until thought becomes irrelevant, until I'm consumed with the hunt, Tashya to finally pay up, no sob stories allowed.

The chase continues for perhaps thirty yards, until Tashya turns and puts her hands up. Or attempts to put her hands up. Her injured right shoulder leaves her heeled over, her right hand barely above her waist, and I'm amazed that something inside me recognizes her vulnerability. I charge at her, accelerating with every step, and drive the butt of the gun into the right side of her face. She drops, unconscious, a dead weight, a sack of flour. And I'm still not satisfied. I raise the rifle above my head, holding it by the barrel, barely aware of its weight. I won't be satisfied until . . .

"Elizabeth, stop. I know you saved my life, but for right now I don't give a damn. You hit her again, I'll arrest you."

Her words flitter through my awareness, a flock of birds changing position with every swoop and turn. What is she talking about? And why? Then I realize that she's in pain, that she's wearing a bulletproof vest beneath her jacket, that the vest saved her life.

"She killed Quentin and that Deputy last . . ." But I can't remember how long I've been a prisoner. I'm trying, but I can't.

"She's going to pay for it by spending the rest of her life in cage. And it may be a short life if she's handed a death sentence." Mariola squats and removes a pair of handcuffs. She winces several times, but cuffs Tashya's hand to a nearby sapling. Tashya's moving now, rolling from side to side. Her eyes are still closed and the lower part of her smashed face is covered with blood. Apparently unconcerned, Mariola rises and lays a gentle hand on my shoulder.

"It's over now and you're free, but I have to tend to my partner and you can't stay here. It's time to begin putting your life back together."

CHAPTER THIRTY-SIX

DELIA

So, I'm a hero. Again. And through no fault of my own. The circumstances surrounding Elizabeth's kidnapping and escape haven't been made public and may never be. That's how the Bradford family wants it, and Elizabeth's youth provides the necessary justification. Still, two facts are undeniable. I was present when she was finally rescued and I was wounded. Me and Cade Barrow.

As for Tashya, her fate is unknown. That's because our esteemed District Attorney, Tommy Atkinson, after consulting with Henry Bradford, Mayor Venn, and the Maryville County Prosecutor, handed Tashya Didiani to the Feds. The kidnapping and the murders will be prosecuted in Federal Court. If it ever gets that far.

The FBI is an international organization. It cooperates with Interpol and police agencies on every continent save Antarctica. All are in agreement. The Didiani crime family is an international cartel with branches in many countries. It needs to be stopped and Tashya has decided to cooperate.

The prevailing attitude here in Baxter can be communicated in a pair of sentences, which Katy Burke has already written. Let's put the whole affair behind us. There's a Nissan plant to build.

Which leaves Delia Mariola the last girl standing. I was at the scene with Elizabeth, present when the Maryville Deputies pulled up. And I killed Pierce Donato, and was wounded in the process. Mayor Venn himself authorized the release of these few details. And with nothing else to go on, and me turning down all requests for an interview, our fearless journalists at the *Bugle* and WBAX have drawn their own conclusions and decided to anoint me.

I don't know how I feel about any of it. Especially about Cade Barrow. He and I were taken to a local hospital. The pair of bullets meant for my back had failed to penetrate my vest. That was the good news, but I was in terrific pain. The doctor who examined me in the emergency room diagnosed a pair of "deep" bruises. I know it hurts, he told me, but there's no treatment outside of an icepack. Go home.

According to the same physician, Cade was lucky as well. A bullet meant to kill had only "grazed" him. The doctor who delivered this diagnosis probably considered it upbeat. But Cade was "grazed" hard enough to fracture his skull. Hard enough to force a surgeon to relieve internal pressure by installing a shunt through a hole drilled in his head. Cade was in the hospital for ten days and I visited him several times.

"Captain," he told me on my first visit, "early in my service, I obsessed over why a bullet fired at random hit a man standing a few feet away instead of me. There was no maneuver I made that he didn't. No skill we hadn't both mastered. So, was it pure luck? God's will? After a while I stopped asking and faced the obvious. You can only avoid risk by avoiding combat."

"Which you didn't do. You didn't quit."

"No, I didn't. And I won't."

On my second visit, I met Annie Versalle, Cade's fiancée. Cade had been right about Annie. I didn't find a trace of self-pity in her attitude, or a reluctance to share her journey. Annie had piloted rescue helicopters in Afghanistan and Iraq until a stray bullet fired from the ground passed through the palm of her left hand. Unfazed, she landed the copter one-handed, saving the doctor and paramedics on board. In recognition, the Army awarded her a Silver Star, a Purple Heart, and a prosthesis.

A small woman, her pregnancy beginning to show, Annie projected a hurricane of can-do energy. When I first saw her in the room, I was afraid she'd blame me for endangering Cade's life. Cade hadn't resisted when I suggested we check out the house. He hadn't complained afterward either. But I've known family members who were desperate to hold somebody responsible for whatever misfortune befell the family. There had to be bad guy.

Not Annie.

"He always had a hard head," she told me. "Now that there's a hole in it, maybe he'll develop a little common sense. Maybe he'll get himself assigned to a traffic detail. I can imagine him now, standing at a school crossing, blowing his little whistle, waving the kids across the street."

Later on, she invited me to their wedding in June.

Cade didn't blame me, Annie either, but I couldn't stop blaming myself. We'd pulled up to find a thick chain padlocked to steel posts blocking the gravel drive leading to the cottage. A metal sign hung from the chain's center: NO TRESPASSING.

I had a number of choices at that point. I could have contacted the nearest Sheriff's station, or even the State Police, and convinced them to provide backup. Or I could have contacted the FBI and sought help from that direction. And I probably would have gotten it because the FBI had done more than sit on their hands. They'd touched base with Martin Leland, Maryville County Sheriff, in an effort to link the murder of Deputy York to the kidnapping. But there was nothing to learn. York hadn't radioed in to report a traffic stop, or any other suspicious activity. A car chase to the south of Baxter had further distracted the FBI. The vehicle being chased had escaped on back roads, Bonnie and Clyde style, and there were as yet no suspects. Another dead end.

The FBI had kept both efforts to itself and I assumed there'd be a long delay if I asked for help. Plus, I had no solid proof that Elizabeth was being held in the cottage when I decided on a limited set of goals. I'd reconnoiter, staying well back in the trees as I approached, then withdraw to evaluate my observations. Meanwhile, the entrance to the drive was thoroughly covered by solar-powered, motion-activated cameras. I might have spotted them if I was more careful. Cade too. Instead, we walked into a trap that would have left the both of us dead were it not for Elizabeth Bradford.

It's early October and the weather still warm enough for a backyard barbecue. I'm at Vern and Lillian's, watching Danny and Mike play catch. Mike's tossing the ball on the ground while Danny scoops it up and throws it back. Danny explained the purpose of the drill a few nights ago. You can't just grab the ball and heave it. You have to grip the ball across the seams in order to throw it straight. More to the point, you have to find the grip while the ball is still in the glove. Without looking.

Danny hasn't questioned me about what happened at the cottage, but my injuries were obvious enough and there's no escaping the fact that I could have been killed. At some point I'll have to tell him the truth, including the errors in judgment that led to me and Cade being shot. Not yet.

"Emmaline got into a fight yesterday," Lillian announces. "On the playground."

I'm standing with Lillian and Zoe by a charcoal grill. Lillian's preparing to load the grill with chicken skewers and ears of corn. Potatoes spiked with butter and wrapped in aluminum foil rest on the coals and a large salad's already out on a picnic table. Vern's thirty feet away, pushing Emmaline on a swing. The girl wears a red dress, blue sneakers, and yellow socks. Her delighted laugh echoing in the small yard, she swings her legs up each time Vern give her a gentle push.

"Tell me," Zoe replies. "Was the other girl hurt?"

"It was a boy, actually, and he grabbed Emmaline's toy unicorn." Lillian begins to arrange the skewers on the grill. "She lit into him, Zoe, fists flying. I had to pull her off."

Emmaline's now living with the Taneys. They're fostering her until the adoption goes through, a process that will run at least four months.

"Did you speak to her about it afterward?" Zoe asks.

"Yeah, she looked confused."

"That's most likely because she really is confused. In the world she came from, flying fists are the appropriate response when someone takes something from you."

"Do you think she can adjust?"

As she works on her response, Zoe watches Lillian arrange the last of the skewers on the grill. I understand Zoe well enough by now to recognize the effort she's making to choose her words carefully. "Imagine it from Emmaline's point of view. The life she knows, the only life, is one of chaos and neglect. Then she's rescued, in the course of a gun battle, from a fire that would have killed her. She's rescued and her life instantly changes for the better. Regular meals, pretty clothes, a clean bed, and abundant affection. Affection more than all the rest."

Lillian begins to lay the ears of corn on the grill. "She comes to me every night, Zoe. To sit on my lap and be held until she falls asleep."

"Call it paradise. That's the way it must have seemed to her, a perfect world in which she'd live happily ever after. Now she's discovering that paradise comes with rules she doesn't yet understand. Rules she needs to master. Time will tell, but I've had her examined by a therapist who works with abused children. He's confident that she'll eventually figure it out. All she needs is time and affection. To know that she's loved and valued."

I should be paying attention, but I keep drifting away. Zoe was right there when I came home. There for me and for Danny. I was in terrific pain, the ibuprofen I took marginally effective, and Danny was totally shaken. Zoe cooked, cleaned, and sat with Danny for hours on end. She rubbed my back with drugstore creams, held me through a long night when I couldn't stop shaking. And she understood when I explained that killing Pierce Donato might be the worst part of the whole experience. Donato had fallen onto a shard of window glass that tore his throat open. According to Arshan Rishnavata, who performed the autopsy, he bled to death.

I had visitors every day. Paolo Yoma came first, on his way to Malaysia. We congratulated each other on our detecting skills, and our dogged approach to investigations. Then all my detectives, one by one, and Chief Black, who assured me that he'd soon retire and I'd be appointed Chief. Though I haven't told him, not yet, I don't want the job. I don't want to spend the rest of my cop life behind a desk, working on next year's budget. Or giving speeches to civic groups at rubber-chicken dinners. I need the streets. More than ever.

◆

Everything stops for a moment when Sherman Bradford walks into the backyard. Sherman's called several times, each time thanking me for rescuing his sister. Was he told that Elizabeth rescued herself? I'm thinking no, but I wasn't foolish enough to ask, or to supply the details his sister wouldn't.

Mike and Danny walk over to greet him, but Sherman hasn't come for the party. Elizabeth spoke to me last night. She and her brother will leave Baxter tomorrow, headed for the family home in Louisville, and she wants a final meeting, just the two of us this time. There'd always been someone else in the room as she told her story, FBI agents, Baxter cops, our prosecutors, an Assistant US Attorney, one of her parents, Uncle Henry.

I come around the house to find an enormous SUV parked at the curb. Two large men stand beside the SUV. They wear dark suits, black ties, and aviator sunglasses. Maybe they've watched too many Hollywood movies, but they're intimidating nevertheless.

The bodyguard closest to me opens the back door without speaking and I slip inside. The door closes behind me and I'm sitting across from Elizabeth Bradford. She's wearing black jeans and a lavender blouse that leaves her shoulders bare. Her makeup has been perfectly applied and every hair is in place, a far cry from the disheveled girl I met at the cottage. We stare at each other for a moment, then Elizabeth reaches for my hands. A second later, we're holding each other.

"You saved my life," I tell her. "You could have escaped without notice, but you didn't."

She pulls away and leans back against the seat, dropping her hands to her lap. "Was it to save you? Or because I wanted to kill Tashya? Because I did want to kill her and I can't get past that. Law, reason, my superior breeding? Jokes, Captain, and bad jokes at that."

"Well, I succeeded where you only tried. I killed Pierce Donato."

"You had no choice. You acted in self-defense."

"You're right. If I hadn't killed Donato, he would have shot me next and my body armor wouldn't have protected me. Not from a rifle. So, yes, I had to neutralize Pierce Donato. But it's no small thing to kill another human being, even in self-defense."

"Do you feel guilty?"

"No, I feel something else. Something I can't name."

Neither of us speaks for a moment, until Elizabeth says, "I would have beaten Tashya to death if you hadn't pulled me off. That's certain, the fact of it. Only I can't stop justifying my rage, Captain. I need excuses and I've got plenty. My confinement itself? Quentin and the Deputy killed in blood so cold it must've been frozen? I can't get Quentin's last look out of my mind. I dream it almost every night, Quentin climbing out of his own grave. First disbelief, then shock, then him knowing that he's been a sucker from day one. Can I be blamed if I thought I'd be next? How could I not? And Tashya did shoot at me." The girl looks up, her gaze seeming quizzical, as if she expected me to supply her next sentence. "Tashya changed me. I can't go back to who I was before I was taken. And I liked the pompous brat that I was. I'd settled into the role and it felt comfortable. Now that's gone and I don't know how to replace it."

There's a moment in combat, according to Cade Barrow, when the civilized part of the brain shuts off and the lizard brain takes control. That's part of how you survive, which is fine for a soldier trained in combat, but a lot more problematic for a privileged teenage girl.

"Tashya told me that one day my kidnapping would be an anecdote I blabbed at cocktail parties after a few drinks. Do you think that day will come?"

"You're strong, Elizabeth, a strong, intelligent young woman. What happened will become part of you, something you'll never completely shed. But the intensity will fade over time. You'll create an accommodation with yourself. You'll cut a deal." I reach out to take her hands again. "Look, it's a beautiful day and there's food on the grill. Why not take the afternoon off? Why not hang out for a while? Maybe we can even sneak you a beer."

Elizabeth raises her eyes to the SUV's roof for a moment. "You mean it, right? You want me at your barbeque?"

"Yeah, I can use the company of somebody who understands."

"Alright, then, let's go. I can use the company too." She smiles for the first time, a mischievous smile I wouldn't have expected. "And, besides, this'll give me a chance to practice relating my anecdote. Tastefully edited, of course."

Read on for a preview of **BOOMTOWN**, the next novel in the Delia Mariola series, in stores now

CHAPTER ONE

CHARLIE

You're a psychopath. That's what my father said when he kicked me out of the house for the last time. I was nineteen, still a kid, but I'd always been trouble. Like from birth. No, make that from conception. My mother, according to him, was sick the entire time she was pregnant.

I wasn't ready for independence, I admit that, and I ran from home to the office, where I pleaded my case to Mom. She wasn't impressed. "If it was up to me," she said, "I'd have thrown you out when you turned eighteen."

"But I'm your oldest son." Though my parents insisted that I'd never spoken a truthful word in my life, this much was undoubtedly true.

"First thing, I have three other children, normal children. Second thing, what's wrong with you can't be fixed." She rubbed her hands together. "Good money after bad? I don't play that game."

◆

My parents owned and operated Starstone Imports. The firm imported finished gemstones. We buy the rough material at mine sites all over the world, then ship it to Mumbai where Indian jewelers cut the gems before dispatching them to our offices in New York. They go from there to high-end jewelers throughout the country.

I'd failed at just about everything by then, having already flunked out of the college my parents spent a fortune getting me into, but I appreciated gemstones. Their beauty didn't particularly interest me, only their value, which is why I helped myself on the way out. And I wasn't about to settle for a few citrines and an amethyst with a window in the middle. I needed a decent start in this life I had to live on my own. So, along with a handful of smaller stones, I snatched a forty-carat, trillion-cut tanzanite. The blue stone came with a cert from the Gemological Institute of America declaring it to be vivid, the highest classification for a tanzanite. Vivid referred not only to its perfect saturation, but to patches of violet that flashed whenever the stone was moved. Looking into this stone was like staring into an indigo sky as the last daylight fades. It was the kind of stone that designers sell to their superrich clients for upward of eighty large.

As it turned out, I made a big mistake. I figured my parents would never call the cops on their eldest son. Beep, wrong. If I was more experienced, or even if I'd given it a little thought at the time, I would have known what was coming. That's because unless a theft is reported to the police, no insurance company will accept a claim.

Two days later I was arrested in a Bronx pawn shop where an old man offered me a hundred bucks for what he claimed was an "over-saturated topaz."

I got eighteen months in a minimum-security prison. Partly because my parents wouldn't pay for a decent lawyer and I had to go with a public defender. Partly because I'd been arrested many times for petty offenses like shoplifting or selling small amounts of coke to my classmates. And partly because I refused a plea bargain that would have put me back on the street in five or six months.

I was furious on sentencing day, not that it did me any good. For the first time in my life, I was out of options. But life can fool you. Prison was just what I needed. Call it a great awakening, but my time at the Beacon Corrections Facility led directly to where I am at this moment, driving through a rinky-dink city named Baxter with a dead whore in the trunk and a guinea head-breaker named Dominick Costa sitting alongside me.

◆

The whore wasn't murdered. Overdose, probably, or suicide. Which doesn't matter. What matters is what I found on my plate when I got to the double-wide trailer where she and the girls live (or in her case, lived). The other girls were freaked, but not me. Everybody dies and it's no big deal unless you die in a whorehouse. Then somebody has to get rid of your body. A headache, yeah, but that's what I'm here for. To solve problems. To keep the operation up and running. To maximize the return on my employer's investment.

"So, you think Corey offed herself?" Dominick half whispers. "I mean, why the fuck would she do something like that?"

Dominick Costa has committed murder. How many times I don't know, but he's pure muscle, which is why Ricky sent him to Baxter. *We'll need an enforcer,* he said, and I couldn't disagree. Only Dominick Costa has the IQ of a frog and he's only manageable because he's scared of Ricky Ricci, who's a thousand miles away in New York.

I normally stay in Boomtown, away from the city, but it rained last night and half the dirt-and-gravel roads are knee-deep mud. I can't risk getting stuck, not with the whore in the trunk. So, I'm driving through Baxter in a three-year-old Honda sedan, keeping my speed down. There's a cop in Baxter, a dyke captain named Delia Mariola. She's a real crusader, gonna make her city safe, and I don't doubt her commitment. But she's got exactly zero say in Boomtown, which is in Sprague County.

"Maybe she OD'd," I finally say.

"On a coupla bags a day?"

"And whatever she might have bought on the outside. Or the johns put up her nose."

Technically, our girls aren't trafficked. These women are older, the youngest past thirty, and they've more or less adjusted to the life and the working-class johns they service. They get a piece of every trick they turn, less room and board, and they can leave anytime they want, no hard feelings. As long as they've paid off debts, including the loans they took prior to working for us. Loans we retired before we transported them to Boomtown. And there's the drugs, too, which we are happy to supply.

I have a hard rule. No shooting up. I don't need the johns walkin' away because some bitch's tracks are oozing. Other than that, it's whatever you want, as long as you work your shift and pay for your highs out of your earnings. No earnings, of course, no drugs. One hand washing the other.

◆

Ricky did the original research and set the goalposts on the day he called me in. I assumed that he'd sniffed out my side deals, which could've gone very bad for me. But Ricky had something else in mind. Somethin' much bigger. First, he showed me a map of this little city. You wouldn't give it a second glance, your eyes passed it on a map, but that was about to change.

"Nissan's building a factory there. Gigantic, right? Like three million square feet, I kid you not. Like fifteen hundred acres. So, who's gonna build it? The locals? There ain't enough workers in the whole city to build that plant, even if they had the skills, which they mainly don't." Ricky was talking with his hands, which he does when he gets excited. "They're gonna come runnin', Charlie, construction workers from all over the country, and they're gonna leave their families behind. So, whatta ya figure they'll want after work?"

I responded without hesitation. "Broads, drugs, gambling . . . and loans when they burn up their paychecks and can't send money home."

"How 'bout truckers haulin' the iron, the concrete, the wiring, the rebar? How 'bout them?"

"Same thing."

"I want every cent, Charlie, and soon. The construction won't last that long, and when it's over, most of those workers are gonna head home. We gotta get it while we can."